A CLEAN KILL

AN IAN BRAGG THRILLER BOOK 2

CRAIG MARTELLE

Version 1.0

Cover by Stuart Bache
Editing by Lynne Stiegler
Formatting by Drew A. Avera

CRAIG MARTELLE

Website & Newsletter:
https://craigmartelle.com

Facebook:
https://www.facebook.com/AuthorCraigMartelle/

Ian Bragg 1—The Operator
Ian Bragg 2—A Clean Kill
Ian Bragg 3—Replacement
Ian Bragg 4—A Fatal Bragg

CHAPTER ONE

"To be, or not to be, that is the question:
Whether 'tis nobler in the mind to suffer
The slings and arrows of outrageous fortune,
Or to take Arms against a sea of troubles..." William
Shakespeare

We are what we must be, the whole greater than the sum of the
parts.

"Come on! Throw that iron. Dominate it." I laughed
with demonic glee. Jenny had gone beyond high
repetitions for endurance before deciding she needed
more strength. She did a few power sets three times a week
to build a maximum lift. We'd been at it for a month.

Jenny grunted and groaned. I held my hands under the
bar, not touching it. With a final surge, she drove it
upward. I grabbed the hundred-and-fifty-pound setup at
the top and guided it onto the rack. She let her arms drop,
chest heaving from the effort.

I kneeled and kissed her upside-down.

Jenny and I found each other during my previous gig in

Seattle. In days, we were inseparable. Within weeks, we had survived more than most couples go through their whole lives.

I had gone to Seattle to eliminate the future mayor, but that was a misguided contract because the future mayor was a good guy. I became an operator to kill bad people. After I reconfigured the contract, my employer, the Peace Archive, had issues with me that resulted in a bit of back and forth on people trying to kill each other. Jenny had been there for the spectacular closing of that contract.

One week with Jenny Lawless had solidified our lifetime companionship.

We still worked for the Peace Archive but in Las Vegas. We had a different job now. I called it contract assessment. We needed three hits a year to make our quota. I'd received three contracts to evaluate in the first week. That was a month ago. I had not yet approved any.

Good hitmen kill bad guys. Period. If I wasn't sure, there would be no hit.

Welcome to what kept me awake at night.

"Next week, we'll add five more pounds." Jenny smiled as she stood and stretched, loosening her shoulders. I kept the two forty-five-pound plates and removed the small donuts leaving only the two plates on the forty-five pound bar to give me one hundred thirty-five pounds. I nudged her out of the way and started my last set, a single run of as many repetitions as I could manage. Ten, twenty, thirty, forty. I started to slow down. Fifty. They started to get hard. I finished number fifty-five, took the bar back to my chest, and started to push. It wouldn't move. I chuckled as my face turned red.

"A little help," I managed to say.

Jenny pulled, but it still wouldn't move. She braced

herself and lifted the bar almost completely for me to finish the last rep.

"Epic fail." She laughed and gave me a sweaty hug before we changed places. Jenny made it to seven before I had to help while watching her muscles ripple with spasms.

"And that's another day in the Ian and Jenny Bragg gym show."

"I was never a gym rat," she admitted. "But I like this because I don't have to do it alone."

"Necessity dictates that we learn what we need to know before we have to put it into action. What do you think, a shower, light lunch, and then the dojo?"

She lifted her shirt enough to expose a bruise across her rib cage. "How about we let this heal for another day before going back to sparring?"

I had caught her chest-high with a reverse spin kick after she overextended a jab and attempted to grab my arm. Jenny got the worst of it. I felt terrible, but she would get angry if I took it easy. I didn't go full speed on her because she had much to learn, but the tae kwon do dojo had plenty of willing sparring partners. I usually only fought people who were bigger and faster. I wanted my opponents to be better than me.

It was the only way to improve.

My opponents never knew why they couldn't beat me.

It was because they'd never had to kill someone. It gave me the edge. I was still in the game, staying honed to a fine edge, sharpening Jenny with each new day as my partner. The bruises earned in combat made her better.

"We'll run through routines at home, but no sparring. Tonight, we have to work."

She nodded and winked. *Work.* Out on the town to

observe a target. Living the high life while watching, taking mental notes, and preparing a dossier.

A good dossier would be turned into a lucrative bid package. Many operators on the Peace Archive's site were good, and I wanted those bidding on my packages to be the best. I would never meet with them, which meant the dossier was the way I could influence the hit and set it up to be clean.

I wrestled with the decision. It would be easier to make the hit myself, but that wasn't my job.

It made me edgy. I didn't trust that the operators came to me fully trained. I expected the opposite. A good dossier minimized the risk that the operator would be less than thorough.

But I wanted to give them training. It was my region. I could run it as I saw fit. However, the Archive maintained the operators. If I could get access and teach them what I knew, the organization would be better. I was convinced of it.

Better hits meant better contracts.

That was my plan. Time to get to work. That kind of planning didn't happen overnight.

"Dr. Julian Guanore." I let the name roll off my tongue. I searched once again through the dark web for more information, but there was nothing new. Sexual assault allegations by numerous patients, buried. It was enough for me to give this request the most serious look.

Julian was a plastic surgeon who catered to a wealthy clientele. Even when getting paid a premium, he didn't think that was enough. The allegations had been buried by husbands who didn't want their eye-candy wives to make it known they were the products of surgery and not clean lifestyles. The price was a grab, a feel, and more. The wives complained. The husbands shouted them down and had everything deleted.

No one ever filed charges. The politicians were recipients of his largesse. He was good at his job, and that brought the A-Listers.

Until he crossed the wrong families: powerful couples in love, but not power couples. Nothing was worth the extras the doctor attempted to extract. They were willing to go public but found out there was another way. They found the Peace Archive.

Guanore lived and worked in Bel Air, but he spent almost as much time in Vegas as he did in California. In the high rent district of Los Angeles, he was protected by other rich and powerful people. In Vegas, he stayed in the best suites.

"A predator," I mumbled.

Jenny watched over my shoulder. "He makes my toe hair curl."

I had to look at Jenny's toes. I didn't see any hair. She slapped my shoulder.

"It's just an expression. I don't allow toe hair to survive beyond the verification of its presence. Just like spiders."

"How did I not know you were so diabolically intolerant?"

"You were in a hurry to get married so you took shortcuts, and you're stuck with me. We have a piece of paper signed by Elvis. So there. Next time, you should make up a survey or something. I shall forever remain intolerant of aberrant hairs and spiders, which are also hairy."

"I'm hairy."

"Furry, like a puppy. Completely different."

We kissed slowly while behind us, the image of Dr. Julian Guanore loomed. When we came up for a breath, we both looked at the screen.

"Completely different," I told the image.

"I'd off him myself. That guy needs to die."

"And that's why I'm taking so long with these packages." I looked for Jenny's understanding. "We have to investigate, and then we have to rule the death sentence is appropriate. If we get it wrong, innocent people die, and justice isn't served."

"I know, sweetie. Take your time. When we met, you were struggling over Jimmy Tripplethorn because it felt wrong. And then you thought it was his wife, but you dug deeper. When you found the real perp, that's when you acted. And then that evil woman tried to do us in. *We* killed them. I've come to grips with that. Life is better when bad people aren't in it." She shrugged. I couldn't have loved her more for how she rationalized our lives together. "I'm going to catch a shower. Join me?"

She didn't wait for an answer. She tossed clothes aside as she walked. I watched her go before returning to the computer.

Julian Guanore. I decided to call him Guano because I liked to dehumanize my targets. I had made my decision. This guy's days were numbered.

The dark web showed me a couple of his email accounts with their hacked passwords. I tried one, but it didn't work. I tried the other, and I was in. The first thing I went to was his schedule. He was in Vegas. I logged off and redirected my VPN to Vegas, then logged back in to his account.

An email confirmation for reservations at LAGO for tonight at eight. I searched for it, and it popped up as the first sponsored ad. I clicked the sponsored ad to make sure that Google made a little money from the MGM Grand Resorts' advertising budget.

LAGO. High-priced, small-plate designer Italian. It wasn't a place I would have casually walked into, not when there was a first-class steakhouse nearby. We liked Italian food, and the price meant nothing. The Archive had given me the magical gold credit card that I used to pay for nearly everything. I shouldn't have worried about the price, but I did.

It came down to value. Was my client getting their money's worth? Even if my client was not yet a paying client. Was I doing right by my employer? I generally would never know because they were as easy to get a hold of as smoke on a windy day.

"Yes" to all the questions. I could still hear the shower running. I closed my computer and ran for the bathroom, not wanting to miss an opportunity. We were still newlyweds, which I intended to use as an excuse for as long as humanly possible.

The Bellagio catered to high-end gamblers. From check-in to the rooms to the tables, everything was first class. We strolled through like we owned the place. Jenny wore a slinky black dress with low heels. I wore a dark suit with a red satin shirt and no tie. We stood out to the staff while looking normal to everyone else. It was Las Vegas. Dressed-up people were a dime a dozen, but we were heading to an expensive restaurant.

I expected that we'd be pampered.

At LAGO, I handed the maître d' a fifty-dollar bill to get the table next to the one where I expected Guano would want to sit. His reservations were for two. She probably wasn't someone he wanted to parade around. His public profile showed pictures of him alone. It made him look more available. *Lonely man seeks the right woman for a short-term relationship.*

I bit my tongue. We'd get to see him soon enough. We took our time ordering because I felt he'd be late. I was confident that he would always be late as a way of exercising control over the rest of the world, a way for the world to bend the knee to him.

I never planned for how late he would be. Reservations usually canceled after fifteen minutes, but it wasn't a busy night. We dithered, ordered a couple of samples. Ate them, then ordered another one. Drank casually. At nine, an hour late, the bad doctor rolled in with a young blonde woman.

Jenny leaned close. "What's with guys and their fascination with fair-haired maidens?"

"I have no clue, my chestnut-haired beauty."

"I could color it just for fun." Jenny took my hand, her nose nearly touching mine. Watching with my peripheral vision, Guano and his date walked by on their way to the table behind us. I kissed Jenny to hide our faces before leaning back.

Jenny called the server over. "Can we get the menu, please? I think we'd like to order another entrée to sample. Your food is so good!"

"Anything for the signora," the server replied before rushing away to retrieve menus for us.

I listened closely but couldn't hear anything. I didn't want to turn. Jenny was facing them, and I wanted to see what she saw. I casually scratched my face, pointed at my ear, and shook my head. Jenny smiled and shrugged.

"Silence is the beauty of love," she replied, eyes flicking from me to over my shoulder and back to me.

"Anything for the beautiful signora," I repeated. "You make that dress come to life."

Jenny pointed with her eyes. We held hands as I tried to listen. The conversation was at the edge of what I could hear. I closed my eyes to focus.

"You are a gorgeous babe, better than I expected, better than I deserve. You know, I could touch up your chin, make it more Marilyn Monroe if you'd like."

"You want to change me?" the "starlet" replied. "How much will it cost my husband?"

"Don't worry your pretty little head about that. He'll pay it." His voice lowered; he must have leaned closer to his woman du jour. "I can't wait to get you back to my luxury suite."

She giggled, but it sounded forced. "How about we eat first?"

"I want to skip straight to dessert, but you're right. I need to keep up my strength if I'm to satisfy a woman like you."

She shushed him before the server brushed past to deliver two glasses and a bottle of prosecco. He stopped by our table to take our order. I hadn't looked at the menu, and there was no need.

Life had grown better and far more interesting since I stopped trying to do everything myself.

Jenny ordered without hesitation. "Lobster gnocchi and lasagna Bolognese. Can you bring a couple glasses of prosecco as well, please?"

"Or the whole bottle, signora?"

"Just two glasses, please." Jenny smiled and tipped her head to the server. He happily carried our order to the kitchen, not having written anything down.

I listened behind me, but they had stopped talking again. I slid my chair out and bent over to tie my shoe, watching them out of the corner of my eye. He leered at her like a bald eagle watching a fish flopping on the surface of a lake. She looked anywhere but at him while she fiddled with her hair and checked the plunging neckline of her dress.

The body language shouted loud and clear. The only thing he wanted was sex, and she knew it. Why was she going along?

I finished with my shoe and returned to facing our table. Jenny looked concerned at my troubled expression.

The server returned with an appetizer. Dr. Julian Guanore was loud enough that I could hear without trying.

"My good man, box it all. We are going to dine in our luxury suite right here in this fine hotel. As a matter of fact, can you have it sent to my room? I won't take no for an answer."

"We can eat here. This place is charming," the woman countered. She wanted to be wined and dined first. For him, eating was a means to an end. The server was torn between the two.

"Fine. We'll eat here," he conceded before sniping at the server, "Take it away. We don't want that."

The server gave his apologies and promised that the entrees would be right out.

"Why are you being such a dick?" the woman asked. I wanted to cheer for her. Jenny bit her lip.

"Am I? You'd have to tell me what one tastes like." I wanted to see the look on his face but didn't dare glance at him. I held up my spoon, trying to see his upside-down image in it, but it wasn't big enough. Jenny reached across the table to pull down my spoon. It was killing me not to watch. So much better than reality television. Jenny gave me her best judging look.

"I'd say you are what you eat. Maybe we can order a bag

of them for you?" the woman shot back. Something fell over on his table. I had to turn around at the noise. He had stood and was grabbing at her arm.

"Come on," he snarled. "We're leaving."

"I'm not going anywhere with you!" She threw her glass of water at his face. He balled up a fist. I shot to my feet. He glared at me while he lowered his arm.

I shook my head. "Maybe it's time for you to go," I told him, voice low so as not to attract attention.

"I paid for this, *everything* you see," he emphasized.

"I'll pay for your meals." I moved closer to him, putting the woman behind me. He backed up. Dr. Julian Guanore was a coward *and* a bully. People like that needed to be put in their place.

That shouldn't have been a death sentence, but in his case, it was. He had just sealed his own fate. The hit would go out for bid first thing in the morning.

Guano made a show of using his napkin to wipe himself off and dropped it on the floor at my feet before casually strolling away, head turning back and forth as he checked out the women at every table as he passed. He never looked back.

"My apologies for interfering, ma'am." I sat back down.

"I have the worst taste in men," she muttered. "I think I'll just go home to LA." She reached into her purse and pulled out a bill and a business card. "Thank you for saving me from making a terrible mistake, one I won't repeat. You are very kind, a champion in the new world." She dropped both card and cash on our table and strode elegantly toward the entrance.

After she had gone, I turned back to our table. Jenny was holding a hundred-dollar bill and flipping the business card from front to back.

"I love how you care about people," Jenny said softly

before handing over the business card. She slipped the c-note into her clutch and winked. "My champion of the new world. I didn't know Hollywood starlets talked like that."

The name on the business card told me all I needed to know. *Leonid Silverstein—Producer.*

I pulled out my phone, but Jenny was ahead of me. She turned her screen around to show the Hollywood Reporter's article on the biggest name in the industry. She slid the screen to show him with his wife on the red carpet. "Look familiar?"

"Why can't they keep it in their pants?" I asked, throwing my hands up in mock surrender. We both chuckled softly.

The server for the next table returned, confused by the sudden departure. I tapped him on the shoulder. "They were late for an appointment with their divorce lawyer. We'll take it, and just add their bill to ours." He put the boxes on the side of our table.

"I wish that was the first time I heard that," the man quipped. "Alas, Vegas can bring out the worst in people."

"It can bring out the good in people, too. This is a place of wonder, a magical oasis in the desert where it's okay to be in love if you only let it," I remarked.

"We need more people like you. Thank you for picking up their check. I would have had to eat it otherwise."

"This is fine dining. Eating it couldn't be that bad." The expression on his face suggested otherwise.

"I see how the food is prepared." He tapped our boxes. "Enjoy your dinner." He took one step away before returning. "I kid. You have made my evening. Thank you."

When we were alone, Jenny beamed at me.

I frowned. "Don't tell me. They ordered something I don't like."

"Mushroom parmesan and tomatoes and capers, so

yeah. They ordered *everything* you don't like, but that's not it." She looked around and leaned close to whisper conspiratorially. "You're supposed to keep a low profile."

"I keep telling myself that, too. I have no idea why I don't listen to my own *excellent* advice."

Our last main course arrived, and I did my best to eat it, but I wasn't that hungry. Jenny watched me pick. She was full too, done in by the roasted garlic bread.

I looked at the doorway where my future target had gone through to find his next mark. He needed to go away, and the sooner, the better. My dossier presupposed a hit in Vegas, but now that we'd been seen together, nose to nose, Los Angeles was looking better and better. I'd adjust the dossier to give the operator the choice but slant it toward Bel Air.

The police in Los Angeles county were underfunded and overworked. More and more murders were going unresolved. More criminals were going free because the police couldn't properly collect evidence. There weren't enough of them to gather witness statements. It was becoming a crime-infested wasteland. Bel Air had hired private security, a small army to protect the rich and famous.

Whoever won the bid would have to find a vulnerability between the security of his Bel Air existence and the full-time coverage of the expensive Vegas casinos.

There would be a blind spot, and that's when the operator would make Dr. Guanore wish he'd been a better man.

CHAPTER TWO

"No one saves us but ourselves. No one can and no one may. We ourselves must walk the path." Buddha

My finger hovered over the enter key. It would upload the file for bid. Jenny watched me. She had already read it twice and agreed. It was a good package.

"It's not going to change while you wrestle with your concerns. Time to get it done." She stared at my finger as if that would make it move.

"Fine." I tapped it and immediately closed the computer. "My first contract."

"Seventh. Eighth, if you include the couple who tried to take us out."

"That's not what I mean." I stood up and stretched. We were in our prime. Mid-thirties. Fit. Mentally sharp. "Makes me feel old, being on this side of the game."

"For Pete's sake, is that what's getting you down? You feel old, my stud-muffin of a man. Let's do some ATVing in the desert. That'll perk you up."

I had to contemplate what she was thinking. "Why do you think that'll make me feel better?"

"Because there's no reason for you to feel bad, so let's do something you've never done before to take your mind off it. When you get back, there will be bids, and it'll be out of your hands. Nothing left after that except to watch the news for a report of the bad doctor's untimely demise. Talk to me, Ian. Why are you so bummed about this? You looked the man in the eyes. What did you see?"

"I saw his very soul. He's one step above pure evil, one who will continue to make people's lives hell."

"The stars and power players will have to find someone else for their tummy tucks and facelifts."

Jenny straddled my lap and faced me, touching her nose to mine.

"It's so much easier being on the other end, relieved of the responsibility of determining the fate of another human life."

"And that's why you took the job. It's not for the timid. You risked everything to fix it. Now you are giving everything to make sure it stays fixed."

"What would I do without you?"

Jenny answered readily, "Wallow in the misery of a rudderless existence, clearly."

"Clearly. It's hard to argue with that, but first…"

Jenny bit my lip.

"Hey!"

"I knew there was a *but*!" Jenny's green eyes sparkled like gems in the bright daylight. Brown flecks twinkled like gold stars.

"Let me put together the first draft of a training proposal for the head shed, and then I'll be ready to get down and dirty."

"That isn't a way to take your mind off things. ATVs. In

the desert. Followed by ice cream and the passion of life." She kissed me lightly. "Work on the training plan tomorrow. And then look at those other two packages. Don't second guess yourself, my love."

It was hard to argue. Jenny's newfound confidence was enticing.

I let my hands roam freely over my wife's body, glad that it still gave us both thrills.

"And thank you for not punching that asshole last night. He'll get his when the time is right." Jenny squirmed when I pinched her backside and jumped up. "Are you ready to go?"

"Now you're starting to sound like me." I headed for the door to put on my shoes, realized I was wearing shorts, and returned to the bedroom for my blue jeans. All the while, I was thinking, *How can I train operators to recognize when a target doesn't need to die?*

I doubted I could teach them the foundation of a moral compass. I started to laugh. Jenny appeared behind me when I only had one leg in. She tipped me onto the bed and jumped on top of me.

"What is making my husband laugh?"

I didn't waste time with all the steps in between. I jumped to the punchline. "How does one teach a trained killer to embrace a moral compass?"

She shrugged. "You'll figure it out." Jenny climbed off me and headed for the door. She was ready to go.

I was still figuring out the relationship thing because I thought there was something else on her mind. Alas, I was wrong. As I watched her, it came to me like a lightning strike: Jenny wanted to ride ATVs in the desert. That made me laugh even harder. I needed to play the game better. And she was right. It *was* time for a break. Even though we didn't have normal jobs, we worked every single day.

Tomorrow, I'd get back to it, evaluating bids and contemplating a training program that could never leave the Peace Archive, never be seen by the public or law enforcement. I had a plan to make a plan.

And it was good. I jumped up and rushed my wife before she could escape. I pinned her to the front door, and passion ignited as I hugged her tightly. She responded, grinding her hips against mine. I breathed deeply of her before stepping back and keeping my expression neutral. "Time to go?" I asked.

"Well, now I'm thinking there might be something else that we should do first." She reached for me, but I held her off.

"Next time, if you want to go ATVing, just say so."

She assumed her angry stance, fists on her hips, and tried to glare, but she couldn't hold it. "Checkmate. I shall try harder next time to be less transparent."

Now it was my turn to reach for her. "It's not about that at all. It's about seeing everything from different angles. I can't see what an operator sees. I can only *guess* what he or she will see. Perspective was all I needed. I have to give up control. That's hard for someone in my former line of work. Now I know how the skipper must have felt while we were deployed to the combat zone. He had to carry that burden that the front-line Marines would do the right thing, but he didn't have the shield of anonymity like we do. He had everyone watching him, from the public to the media to Congress. And that makes the training program even more critical. In the Marines, we trained every day. Every. Single. Day. We should demand no less from our operators. I'm good now. Let's hit the desert. We'll make up for lost time when we get back."

I wiggled my eyebrows at her. She licked her lips

slowly, with just the tip of her tongue. I blinked quickly, and my eye started to twitch.

She raised her chin, grabbed the car keys, opened the door, and walked out.

Her opening move on the reset gameboard put me on my heels. "Dammit!" But in our game, even when I lose, I win.

I slept in, which meant that I didn't get up until five in the morning. Jenny wasn't a fan of anything before seven, so I went through my usual routine of checking out the windows for something out of the ordinary, seeing what there was to see and then looking high and low, too. I started a cup of coffee and opened my laptop, sending the VPN through Malta for a change of pace.

I dug through multiple layers of Archive security to finally get on the backside of the bid process, a place that had been blocked from me as an operator. The resources behind the final wall were not great, but they helped me manage from my end. They also had a communication process that might have seemed cumbersome, but if anyone managed to hack this far into the system, they would not find any addresses or emails.

There was one way to contact the Archive, and it would cost me. I'd have to make two five-figure transfers into their bank account, then they'd call me on my burner at a time of their choosing.

The two deposits would be the number for a burner phone with no call history. I'd be able to talk to Chaz or Vince one time, and then I would destroy the phone.

It was an expensive but necessary policy. Nothing the Peace Archive ever did could give someone access to all the secrets in one place. There was no single source to find all the operators as long as the Caymans never divulged their banking information. And they wouldn't because far too many powerful people hid their wealth in those banks. Too many politicians who got rich in public service taking money when they shouldn't have, doing things they shouldn't be doing.

That was my speculation, and the Archive took advantage of the safe haven.

After a quick perusal of the basics, I reviewed the bids.

I knew the angered husband had paid one and three-quarter million for the job, which gave me a good margin since I had posted a minimum bid of half a million.

The two bids that had come in so far were wildly different in format from the six successful ones I had submitted. One bid came from a middle-aged man and the other from a woman my age.

The man's bid looked similar to the ones I had made, detailing costs in addition to the hit, but his went more in-depth and even included speculation on how he was going to make the hit. I had never included that since I didn't want to presuppose where I would find an exploitable vulnerability.

Contract SV1744

Transportation - $15,000

Lodging - $10,000

Meals - $1000

Support systems - $20,000

Implementation - $650,000

Total - $696,000

Observation period—one month.

A mugging gone bad.

I had to look through it twice. Metadata contained

within the bid showed that he was a confirmed bidder with two previous successful contracts.

The woman's bid was minimalist but impossible to discount.

Contract SV1744

One million. One week.

She had fifteen successful hits. Fifteen. She was supremely confident. She had her price, and it was well within the range of what I could approve.

As soon as I accepted a bid, the package and dossier would be pulled offline. I wanted to accept the woman's bid on my expectation that she knew what she was doing. I preferred her experience for my first project because I wanted it to be successful.

Guano would see a woman as less of a threat. She could get as close as she needed. A man would always be held at arm's length. There was one flaw in the man's plan; muggers didn't ply Bel Air with impunity.

I left that part of the net and logged into my transfer bank account. I rolled a hundred and twenty-five thousand dollars into it, followed by an immediate transfer of seventy thousand, two-hundred and fifty-five dollars into an account that I had memorized. Later in the day, I'd transfer another fifty-some thousand to complete the telephone number of my burner phone.

The Archive didn't want anyone calling them. One had to have a good reason, good enough to justify spending a lot of money to make contact.

I closed the laptop and strapped on my running shoes. I finished my coffee and headed out, locking the door and carrying my keys in my hand, a small knife attached to my keychain and a mini can of mace in the other. I didn't want anyone or anything to get too close to me, and they wouldn't since it was six in the morning. Few were up at that hour, and those who were were going to work. I had the sidewalks to myself.

The desert morning was crisp and clear, perfect for running hard, head up, looking everywhere, exercising my peripheral vision, staying alert. When Jenny ran, she wore headphones and listened to music. I never did, not because I didn't want to, but because I had to be vigilant at all times.

I was still in the game, and it was unforgiving when it came to letting one's guard down. I wondered if I would ever reach the point where I felt safe enough to ignore the world around me.

Probably not. I would watch out whenever I was with Jenny. Keeping her safe was my responsibility, even though she said it wasn't. I had dragged her into my world, and I didn't want to see anything happen to her. There was a fine line between protecting her and hiding her behind an impenetrable barrier. She was good with the former and not the latter.

I was good with it too, even though I couldn't convince her to run without headphones. I continued down the block to the main road, then turned onto a bike path where I was the only one. The streetlights winked out, catching my attention. I slowed to look for an ambush.

The dawn was brightening. Streetlights in the shadows were still on.

Why so jumpy? I stepped to the side of the path to watch and listen. Cars drove by. A semi used its jake brakes in the distance. Birds flew high overhead. I listened to my instincts and turned back toward the subdivision where we rented the Air Force sergeant's house. I glanced over my shoulder and caught sight of a shadow emerging from the brush beyond where I'd stopped. The shadow moved away from me.

I sprinted across the high-speed four-lane road. On the other side, I ran up the sidewalk parallel to the bike path. The shadow kept glancing over its shoulder, watching the bike path I had vacated.

I ran past, staying as low as I could behind decorative greenery and welcoming signs. The shadow saw something and slipped back into the bushes that lined the community's wall. A biker was riding down the path. I bolted across the street, making a beeline for where the shadow had tucked itself into the bushes. I figured I would arrive at the same time as the person on the bike.

I couldn't tell what the shadow was doing in the bushes. I figured it was a mugger, and I didn't want one of those in my neighborhood. Just like those who lived in Bel Air wouldn't allow one in theirs. I accelerated the last ten yards to cross the ditch beside the road and come up well in front of the bicycle. I plunged into the bushes and caught the hands as they came up.

"What the hell are you doing?" I shouted into the man's face. I guessed he was older than me, but not by much. He was wiry and strong, but I kept him off balance. The biker stood on the pedals and raced away. As I dragged the man into the open, I repeated my request. "What do you think you're doing?"

He looked afraid. Wrinkles from a hard life. Seeing him in the light, he might not have been as old as I first guessed; the wear and tear on his body had aged him far beyond his chronological years. He started to shake, but not with fear.

The man was having a seizure. I checked his pockets. He had an older phone that opened without a password.

I tapped 9-1-1 on the buttons and waited. When the emergency operator answered, I gave her the basics: seizure, on the sidewalk, size, approximate age, and his location, then wiped off the phone before tucking it into his pocket while it was still connected. I took off in the direction the bike had gone, rounding the corner and running down the back side of the subdivision. I took the road in before I heard the sirens. I finally slowed, running at an easy pace. My chest heaved with my efforts to outrun the emergency services.

I went straight back to the house. Once inside, I opened my laptop and navigated my way to the back end of the bid screen. No new bids. I clicked accept on the female operator's bid and powered down my computer.

Another cup of coffee and Rush sounded perfect right about now. I checked the time, started a new pot brewing, dialed up *Dreamline*, and let it roll.

CHAPTER THREE

"Avoid the crowd. Do your own thinking independently. Be the chess player, not the chess piece." Ralph Charell

"I picked the woman."

Jenny stood there, naked, having just gotten up. She yawned. She took my half-empty cup and sipped it. "I'm missing something, like what is this related to?"

"Two bidders on the job, a man for seven hundred thousand and a woman for a million. Her profile showed fifteen successful hits. I'm sorry, but I cut into our bonus."

"Sounds like there's nothing to be sorry about. A year ago, I would have never imagined that I'd be in the position to judge whether people should live or die. I taught middle school. I try to act cool for my husband, but being the arbiter of someone else's life is something we can't ever take for granted. I'm glad that it bothers you. I hope it always bothers you, just until you get out of the game."

"Just until *we* get out of the game. I thought it poetic

24

justice that a woman take him down. I also liked her experience. We can't have our first package go awry."

"I agree. How much more money do we need?" It was a loaded question.

Even after spending over a hundred thousand dollars to have a phone call with the Archive, we were still worth more than four and a half million dollars, growing at a rate of five percent plus half a million in salary each year that we didn't have to touch. "A druggie wanted to roll me this morning."

That got her attention. Money talk bored her. "And?"

"I *felt* he was there. Maybe I saw a shadow and it registered on the subconscious level, but I didn't *know*. Something felt off. I bailed, and a bike rode by. Then I saw him. I confronted him before he was able to assault the biker. And then he had a seizure, so I used his phone to call 9-1-1. I took off before the ambulance arrived."

"So, you probably saved someone's life this morning, maybe two." She slid behind me to wrap her arms around my chest.

I shook my head. "That's not what I was looking for, but I always appreciate a good hug from my wife. It was the sensation of knowing he was there. I'm happy that I'm not losing my edge."

She drained my cup and took it with her to refill mine and get a fresh one for herself. "What about your training program?"

"I've sent a message for them to call me. I need to find a burner phone with a two-oh-one area code. This seven-oh-two is a bit spendy. I feel like I'm throwing money away."

"It's an investment, but yeah. No sense tossing away a hundred grand when thirty will do."

"Or a hundred twenty."

"It took me two and a half years to make that much money." Jenny breathed deeply of her Colombian blend before taking a sip. She wasn't judging, simply acknowledging the new world in which she lived.

"I need to get my training plan put together since I'm going to make the pitch. I need to have my ducks in a row before I drop the second deposit."

Jenny meandered toward the bedroom. "Then we better get started."

She returned shortly wearing her workout gear but went straight to the kitchen and started breakfast.

I was confused by the inconsistency. "Are you going to the gym?"

"Later." She swept her hands in front of her body. "This makes me feel like I'm burning more calories."

"That's one way to look at it. Actually burning the calories…" She held up a finger that suggested I shouldn't continue my line of thought. Her smile told me I was safe. "What do you say we take a ride into the desert, see if there is a remote ranch we can rent."

"You already have something in mind, don't you?" She flipped the bacon.

"I might. I set the VPN to New York City and browsed dude ranches for rent, but they were all hotels with restaurants. Even if we bought them out, they would have staff. That's not what I was looking for. We need complete anonymity.

"Then I searched for shooting ranges outside Vegas. I could rent one and have it all to ourselves, but the usual guests could show up and see us. I then did a map search looking for roads that trailed into the hills overlaid with properties for sale. Some improved, most unimproved. I want a house with at least three bedrooms, preferably five or six.

"There is a great deal of property for sale at high prices. Even fifty miles from Vegas, sellers are asking one hundred to two hundred thousand per acre. What would it cost me to have them pull it from the market for a week or simply make it unavailable for viewing during that time?" It was a rhetorical question, just like my entire train of thought.

I continued, "Where would we stay? Where would we meet? I need electricity and internet to show them the intricacies of the dark web if they aren't familiar. Or VPN.

"I expect most would know how to eliminate a digital footprint, but if they don't, this will be critical for their long-term health. Nothing can be traced back to them or the Archive, ever."

Many questions needed answers. I needed to collect my thoughts, and bouncing them off Jenny helped. I was getting closer with each passing idea. I listened to the bacon sizzle as I closed my eyes and ran through an operator setup in the safe confines of my mind.

After breakfast, I looked for a pad of paper but didn't have any. I wasn't used to writing things down. I sure as hell wasn't going to use any online programs where my data was not stored locally or where it could be shared in any way. I didn't want to use the secure area behind the Archive's board. Not yet.

"We have to go to the store," I said, picking up the car keys to our Nissan Maxima, a vehicle we had bought for cash. We had not yet registered it and wouldn't, either selling it or giving it away before buying another.

The Maxima didn't stand out in a city filled with high-performance sports cars and limousines, so we drove in anonymity.

Jenny looked down at herself.

"It's Walmart."

"If I must assault the world's eyes, then so be it." She

threw her hand to her head and sauntered toward me. I held the door for her, then waited for her to go back to get her sunglasses. It usually took her two steps out the door to remember them. I suggested she buy a second pair to put in the car, but she didn't want to waste the money since her pair had cost a couple hundred dollars. We had paid with the gold card, so it didn't cost her anything. She was funny that way.

She kissed me when she returned, and we walked out together.

"We can pull this off," I said more to myself than Jenny.

"Of course, *you* can." I hurried past her to open the car door, closing it once she was inside. After I climbed in, she continued. "I will act as a runner to the training, bring lunches, get stuff, clean up afterward. I can't teach an operator anything to help keep them alive. That's all you, honey. But I can take some of the burden off of you."

"I could not have asked for a better partner in life. Operators. It'll probably be a lot like teaching grade school, so you'll have to clue me in on how to keep them in their seats between recess." She smirked at me. "I'm thinking a digital part of the course and a physical part, but in surveillance techniques, how to spoof cameras without looking like you are, movements, and things like that. I won't go over how to kill people. They wouldn't be operators if they didn't know how to do that. This isn't a recruiting class. But then I need to work on the morality. How to know when you've got a bad target. We need a safety switch."

"You mean like a leather collar, whips, and chains safe word?"

"A what?" I glanced at her when we reached a stoplight. She made a spanking gesture. "I see, but no."

The rest of the trip consisted of verbal foreplay that led

us to rush through the store to throw a few things in a handbasket and race to the register and back to the car. We were suddenly in a hurry to get home.

I made sure my burner phone was charged and on when I transferred the last sum into the Cayman account. I needed to buy one with a better number if I was going to call them again. It would be cheaper to drive to Los Angeles and buy a phone than call from a seven zero two area code again. I had more money than sense.

When I decided on something, I wanted it right then. I wasn't willing to wait a week, and my impatience came at a steep price.

"What a waste," I mumbled as I pressed the send button to deliver the second deposit into the Archive's transfer account. "Now we wait."

I spun up *Hold Your Fire* and let it play while I looked out the window, my pen and pad of paper forgotten in my hand. I spent a great deal of time thinking and not enough time doing. The experience of thinking it through helped my mind see the possibilities of future actions. They were necessary to avoid repeating mistakes *if* mistakes had been made.

I almost jumped out of my skin when my burner phone rang. I didn't bother looking at the number before answering. "I want to make a proposal." There was no reason for small talk.

"Propose," the voice replied. I couldn't tell if it was Chaz or Vince. It could have been someone else entirely. Whoever it was had their fingers in the company bank account.

"A training session for operators to help them do their jobs better."

"We only hire people who can do the job."

"I'm not talking about that. We'll call it professional development. I'm talking about not leaving a digital fingerprint. Surveillance without being caught. Movement without being tracked. Making sure the operators have a minimal understanding of anything that will keep them from exposing the company, and I believe it's worth the risk. We are smarter together, even with the challenge of bringing the operators to one place at one time."

"We have looked at this, and last time, we considered the risk to be one step too far."

"Making the operators better at what they do through sharing their knowledge and wisdom. One time. We can't let anyone know that we had been together. One compromised person would expose us all. High risk, high reward. Better for the company in the long run."

"We added a layer of protection between us and the operators through regional directors like you. That cushion is important, but if the regions want to bring their people together, we might get behind that."

"That's all I'm asking. I'll run it for those who bid on my stuff. I don't want any problems, especially ones that could have been avoided with a simple conversation."

"We'll talk about it and get back with you. On a different topic, we saw this morning's contract come through. You chose wisely. We were pleased to see, not unexpectedly, that you aren't greedy. That's good. You'll go far in this company."

The line went dead.

Jenny turned the music back up, but only halfway. I hadn't realized she turned it down. As usual, she was looking out for me.

"We need a distraction," she said.

"You heard?"

She nodded. I wished I could hear as well as she could. Her hearing was so good that I was convinced she could hear things that I thought and never said aloud. "You have to wait for them to make a decision."

"I think we had a pretty good diversion earlier today. I still have a handprint on my butt cheek."

"No doubt, you do. It probably looks like mine." She smiled fully with a small laugh, her tongue darting in front of her teeth. "I would have been a little more festive, but my ribs still hurt." She rubbed the spot where I had kicked her.

"Protect yourself better next time." I forced a shrug, trying to act nonchalant because she knew it bothered me. I was obligated to act like it didn't. "A distraction. What did you have in mind?"

"A quick trip out east. We've never gone on a flight together. I'd like to do a little tourist stuff."

"Aren't your brother and sister out there somewhere?" I was onto her.

She frowned. "I'd like to see my nieces and nephews. They will love you."

I walked to the window and looked out at the desertscape. Jenny came up behind me to rest her chin on my shoulder. She knew my opinion of family. It took me a while before I reiterated what I had said before.

"We don't get to live a normal life," I said. "And your family doesn't get to know me."

I could feel her chest heaving against my back. I turned to see tears streaming down her face. Waterworks to manipulate me would have made me angry, but that was not what these were. She had gained hope from our sense of normalcy over the past few months.

"I would have thought your run-in with an operator would have convinced you."

She nodded but didn't say anything. I tried to hug her, but she pulled away. My chest grew heavy, and my insides screamed in anguish.

"If we go, we need a story that they'll accept. I'm okay with lying, but I don't want to make it so complex that they get suspicious."

She pulled a tissue from a box on the coffee table. "They're already suspicious because I left my job," she muttered, still crying.

Jenny had called them both once a week religiously. She tried to ask more questions than she answered, but every week seemed like a new grilling. They hadn't accepted me because I was the mystery man who had uprooted their sister from all she had known.

I took Jenny by the arms. She resisted weakly as I pulled her close and hugged her. I whispered into her ear, "We'll go see them. I'll win them over and put their minds at ease. But we'll tell them the truth. By truth, I mean a convincing lie. I'm in witness protection, and if they tell anyone, I'm as good as dead, and so are you."

She sniffled one last time, blew her nose, and looked up at me with her puffy red eyes. "Okay," was all she managed to say before laying her head on my chest. I held her until the call from too much coffee became overwhelming.

"Let's buy a couple tickets and then pack." I pointed at my computer as I raced for the bathroom.

CHAPTER FOUR

"It's far easier to lie convincingly to someone than to convince someone that they were lied to." Elim Garak, *Star Trek—Deep Space Nine*

I looked forward to the opportunity to buy a couple of burner phones from a two-oh-one area code. I dreaded everything else related to the trip.

We checked one bag, filled mostly with gifts for Jenny's family.

Of course, we purchased first-class tickets. The Archive was paying for our luxury, and we had all the benefits of a rapid security check without the intrusion of a background check. I wore slip-ons, and we didn't carry a computer. We weren't trying to hide anything, and we didn't look suspicious.

Far from it. Jenny acted like she had won a slot machine's biggest jackpot. That disarmed everyone. We were through security quickly, finding ourselves on the other side of the checkpoint with a great deal of time to spare. Inside a gift shop, I perused the books, but the selection was limited to the biggest-named authors. I looked for a hit-man title and found one called *The Cleaner*. I picked it up in hardback, the only version available, although I preferred paperbacks. I'd leave it somewhere common when I finished in order to give someone else a free read.

I fancied myself a library of one.

Jenny looked at halter tops with a Vegas theme. She caught me making a face and stuck her tongue out in reply. I headed to the counter, trying not to laugh.

"Newlyweds?" the female clerk asked in an accent I couldn't identify.

"That obvious? I expect you get quite a few through here. We only met last week but hit it off."

The clerk scowled while she rang up my book. Jenny tossed two tops on the counter.

"I'm kidding. I've been in love with this woman my entire life. I finally wore her down. Persistence is my key to success."

The clerk perked up, glancing from me to Jenny and back. She added the two tops of questionable quality and aesthetics to the bag.

"He's not kidding. A man chases a woman just until she catches him," Jenny added with a wink.

"Don't I know it, sister," the clerk replied, her accent making Jenny's quip even more mind-bending.

After we left, I tried to get my book without touching the clothing, but they were wrapped up together.

"Give me that." I gave her the bag. She dug out my book and handed it over. She pulled out the shirt and held it in front of her—pink with sequins around a picture of the Welcome to Las Vegas sign.

I stood with my mouth open before delivering the

ultimatum. "I won't be seen with you while you're wearing that."

"This is something we do between my sister, sister-in-law, and me. We get the tackiest shirt we can find at the airport on the way to visit. The others have to wear it as penance for not being the ones who traveled."

"I think you'll win this round."

"If I wore this, you wouldn't be seen with me?" She gave me her best puppy-dog eyes.

I tried to look at the shirt dispassionately but couldn't manage. "It's not the hill I'll die on, but it's in the foothills leading to it."

"Are you distracted yet?" Jenny asked.

"Making your best moves when I'm not paying attention? Well-played, Miss Jenny." I hugged her in the middle of the terminal. People walked around us. "I am. This has the potential to be fun, and I love seeing you happy." I looked around to make sure no one was close. I rested my nose on hers to keep people from seeing my words. "But they can never know what we do. Not ever."

"I know, Ian. To keep them safe. To keep us safe."

"I don't ever want to fly anything but first class ever again. That made the flight not just tolerable but enjoyable. Why, yes, I *would* like another mimosa, and the lobster spread was fabulous with those designer crackers!"

"I spoil my baby," I replied. Reagan National Airport had few customers milling about. It was late afternoon, and the sun in the western sky backlit the terminal. We walked casually over the sky bridge toward the rental car side of the terminal. I'd conceded to visiting Jenny's siblings, but I refused to stay at their houses or be trapped without wheels. Jenny was so happy to be going that she didn't argue too long or hard. We reserved lodgings not far away, a boutique hotel, not a chain. That was my way to minimize the opportunity of our travel beyond the airport becoming common knowledge. The flight and rental car were bad enough.

But the feds weren't my enemies. Not yet. And now that I wasn't active in the game, maybe I could stay below their radar for the rest of my career. There was also the little thing about not paying taxes on my income. That was the only thing that stuck on Al Capone.

I added that to my mental to-do list. This would be my first year where I had no income from regular sources. I had to come up with something and throw a few nickels to Uncle Sam.

To stay under the radar, of course.

We went with a compact rental car since Jenny's brother lived in Alexandria and her sister lived in Woodbridge. Traffic would be heavy, and parking spaces hard to come by. I went with the most pragmatic car I could think of.

We walked up to the counter hand-in-hand, dragging Jenny's old roller duffel.

"Ian Bragg. I have a reservation." I gave the college-aged agent behind the counter my most winning smile. Jenny rested her chin on my shoulder. I kissed the side of her forehead.

The agent put her hand over her heart and sighed before returning to the system and hammering the keys while looking at my shiny new Nevada driver's license.

"Your reservation is for a three-door sub-compact." She made a face. "That can't be right." I started to interrupt, but Jenny tugged on my arm. "There! How about a Mustang GT convertible? Please sign the screen."

The screen before me showed a place for initials regarding insurance and liabilities. I checked the box for maximum coverage from the rental company and signed. The agent ran the gold card and handed it and my license back. She folded the contract and slid it across the counter to us.

"Enjoy your stay in our great nation's capital."

"Go Steelers!" I blurted. The woman started to laugh and shook her head. She stepped back and showed her colors. The local team. "That's what I meant. Go them!"

We meandered to the garage next door to get our car, the one parked in the spot designated on our paperwork. I walked around the vehicle to check for damage before chucking the duffel into the trunk, along with the small backpacks we used for carry-ons.

We unhooked the roof and powered it down. "It's a little cool here," Jenny observed without saying directly that she wasn't sure going topless was best.

"We'll max the heater. It'll be great." I dialed the temperature into the red for the driver and passenger, turned on the heated seat, and cranked up the fan speed while I connected my music. Jenny gave me the hard side-eye. "Can't race off before we're ready. Bad things could happen."

I tried to sound solemn, but I wanted to jam Rush to relax because I was nervous. I turned on *The Enemy Within* from *Grace Under Pressure* and let the album play. Depending on traffic, we could get there in ten minutes or two hours. The car's GPS showed we were less than two miles away.

"Onward, trusty metal steed!" I declared, and finally pulled out and angled toward the exit. The throaty growl of the beast was invigorating. I'd have to resign myself to enjoying the low-speed growl. There was no chance of getting any performance from the car. DC traffic was legendary for being among the worst in the world.

We hit the highway and instantly slowed to a crawl. "Look at their faces."

Jenny tried to peek into the other vehicles. "They look miserable."

I laughed and turned the music up. "Yes, they are. Better them than me."

I propped my elbow out the window, and Jenny did the same thing. I didn't need the GPS because Jenny knew the way. "This turn." She pointed to make sure I didn't miss it. I tipped on the blinker, which pegged me as an out-of-towner with the local, non-blinking crowd. We took a couple of turns and pulled past a thin house squeezed between other thin houses, each with its own unique brickwork. Like condos, but individual. There was no space between the buildings. It made my chest tight, just seeing it.

"That's it." Jenny nodded toward it without pointing.

We were able to park on the next block. We put the top up and locked it into place. Jenny pulled her backpack out of the trunk. The entire time, I watched the area to see if anyone was looking at us, seeing that we had luggage, but I saw no prying eyes. We walked back to her brother's place, taking in the history of it all.

"About two-hundred-years old," she said. I held her hand, which was warm. The heater had done the trick. I slowed to a stop. Jenny faced me and leaned close, resting her forehead on mine. "It's my brother, his wife, and their three kids. There's nothing to worry about."

I snorted. "I'd rather be on a contract, but this is important to you, so it's important to me. I'll put on a good show for your family. But one thing that isn't a show is how much I love you. They'll realize that when they see how happy we are."

We kissed while I stroked her hair.

"People get arrested for doing that kind of stuff in Alexandria," a husky voice said from nearby.

Jenny let me go and faced her brother. The family resemblance was undeniable. She reached upward before delivering a finger strike to his solar plexus. He grunted and staggered backward. When he righted himself, she wrapped him in a hug.

He rubbed his stomach. "You caught me off-guard. That won't happen again!" He moved his sister to the side and sized me up.

I offered my hand. "My name is Ian, and I'm the luckiest man in the world."

"Jack, Jack Lawless. I'd say we're lucky. We were worried we'd have to take care of my sister in her old age."

"You bastard!" Jenny squared off to punch him, but he dodged out of the way.

"You'll want to steer clear. We've been doing a lot of lifting and sparring. I served in the Marines and never stopped training. Now I have a convenient workout partner."

"I'll say. I'm not sure I've ever seen her so fit. A man looks good on you." He dodged out of arm's reach before his sister could pummel him once more, rubbing his abs. She had hit him a lot harder than he had been prepared for.

I tried to look as innocent as possible by wrapping an arm around Jenny's waist and pulling her close.

"There is no doubt that he's your older brother." We followed Jack into his home. On the street corner at the end of the block, a couple of young men dressed in loose black pants and black hoodies watched us. I didn't try to stare the punks down. I wasn't armed and they probably were. If I needed a gun, I knew where I could probably get one. Jenny glanced at the young men.

"No," she said, tightening her grip on me. She knew exactly what I was thinking. "You can't fix all the world's ills. Under the radar doesn't seem to work with you. How about under the blankets? That's where I'll be."

I saw the wisdom in changing the visual. I refused to look back one last time before we went through the door, where confusion gripped me tightly. There were no children, but young people who looked like college kids. They stood around the living room, watching me, not playing with toys as I had expected. I sought solace in Jenny's face.

She chuckled as she took my face in her hands. "My brother is quite a bit older than me."

"Did you expect little kids? Way to go, Sis!"

There wasn't anything I could do except admit that I hadn't dug too deeply into Jenny's family. "I've been punked by my wife."

Jack turned to face his spouse. "You should see your face. Looks like she got you, too."

"I'm new to the club, ma'am. Is this an ongoing thing that I should expect more of?"

She hugged me. "Kate, please. You'll learn to tolerate them."

Jack pulled his sister aside for rapid-fire whispering. I ignored them while Kate introduced me to their children, Jack Junior, Brooke, and the youngest, the high-school senior, Patrick.

"Your aunt punked me. She didn't mention the part about you guys being adults. Call me Ian." I shook their hands.

"Are you really married?" Brooke asked.

"I'm afraid so. We got married in Vegas by Elvis, and not that one. The fat one."

Kate snorted. "It's going to take a while for us to get used to the fact that she not only has a boyfriend but that she's married."

"I'm the cat's meow," I replied with a straight face.

"You're something. Jury's out on what." Kate matched my expression. I guessed that she was about ten years older than me but had led a respectable life. Wrinkles around her eyes suggested she didn't wear a lot of warpaint, just enough. She looked fit, probably wearing the same size since she had the first of the three children.

"Are you a lawyer?"

"We both are. I went to school after the kids were a little older, but here we are, living the glamorous life." She gave me the impression that she meant the exact opposite. A thin condo-style home on a street where your parking spot was not guaranteed.

The two oldest kids waved and walked past to hug their aunt goodbye.

"Where are you going?" Jenny demanded.

"We have tests. Georgetown is unforgiving if you blow them off," Jack Junior replied matter-of-factly. They strolled out the front door. Jack locked it after they'd gone.

The glamorous life.

We retired to the dining room to chat. Kate and I made faces while Jenny and Jack poked each other endlessly. Jack was constantly on his heels, but he countered with a certain grace that only a lawyer could manage.

Patrick helped himself to something from the fridge after having enough adult talk for the evening. He said, "Call me when dinner's ready."

When the creaking stairs signaled that he had made it to the second floor, Jenny turned serious and looked to me.

41

I leaned on the table. "I know you two are wondering who the hell I am. You may have even checked the net to do a background check on me. I know what you found. Nothing. This guy is a ghost." I leaned close and spoke barely above a whisper. "You can never tell anyone this. Never. But we feel like you should know. I'm in witness protection. Ask me no questions about it. Stop searching my name. Don't do picture searches of me on the net. Just don't. You'll put me and Jenny at risk."

"But, but..." Jack leaned back and crossed his arms. "That sounds like a load of bull." He turned on Jenny, his face turning red. "What kind of scumbag did you get mixed up with?"

Jenny's hand came up from her lap, the fist already formed. She started the swing. I caught her fist in my hand, and she almost pulled me out of my seat. She was furious. I wrapped my other arm around her to give her a hug and kissed her neck.

She calmed and looked at me.

"I'm the opposite of a scumbag, and that's why we stay secretive. You're a lawyer. You have to know that there are some really bad people out there. I've had the pleasure and honor of taking a few of them down, but that came at a cost." I lifted my shirt to show the scars on my rib cage. "Jack, why don't you tell me about some bad guys you put away?"

Jenny's brother retreated from his aggressive stance.

"Go ahead, tell him," Kate pushed.

"My firm works on the details regarding selling surplus military hardware overseas."

"The sound of an AK-47 firing is unmistakable, as is the sound of an M-4, or a nine-millimeter Beretta or a Dragunov seven-point-six-two by fifty-four millimeter. It would have been a safer trip overseas if we didn't have to face our own surplus gear, but I don't blame you."

Jenny squeezed my hand.

"I work family law, adoptions mostly," Kate said into the uncomfortable silence.

The irony wasn't lost on me. The two had probably been at odds for the entirety of their individual legal careers.

"That is most excellent. We don't know if we'll have kids, but adoption is a good alternative if we ever get the green light to live like normal people." I held out my hand to Jack. He looked at it for a long time before he shook it.

"I almost forgot," Jenny said. She got up to retrieve her bag. I knew what was coming, but I was still shocked when I saw it—the pink halter with sequins around the Welcome to Las Vegas sign.

Her brother took it from her. "I think this will look perfect on you," he told his wife, his features relaxing with the normalcy of the jibe. Kate took it with two fingers and carried it at arm's length while heading toward the bathroom.

Jack's gaze drilled into his sister. "Is that why you are in shape and hit so hard? You might be running from mobsters?"

"Let's just call them bad guys. And yes. We don't need to work since Ian is quite wealthy. We live in Las Vegas, hiding among all the others like us, just two more faces in a crowd of faces that don't want to be seen. In the movies, you might see witness protection people sent to a small town. I don't know how that can work because people are nosy. Vegas is perfect for us for the moment." Jenny was smooth once she got past the initial outrage. I squeezed her hand back, and she let go and ran her fingers up my leg.

I coughed to hide my surprise, but I didn't stop her.

"You aren't living off Jenny?" Jack demanded of me.

She laughed. "Oh, heavens, no. I haven't spent a penny of my money since we met, which leads me to the house. I have Lois checking our home a couple days a week, and I hired a yard service to keep it looking neat and trim. But we won't be able to move back there no matter what. I'll talk to Jasmine and see what she wants to do. If we need to put it on the market, then one of you will have to go back there to get it ready if we're willing to sell it."

Kate returned. Jenny clapped. I had to look away. Jack glanced at his wife before glaring at his sister. "That is the worst shirt ever."

"You should visit me sometime," Jenny suggested, knowing she would wear whatever they brought if they came.

Jack shook his head slightly before answering, "We'll look into it."

He caught me raising an eyebrow at him. His body language said they had no intention of visiting. Too many families treated their siblings that way. I saw it too often in the Marines. The young Marine had to burn his vacation, his leave time, to visit family that never came to visit him.

"I think it's almost ready," Kate said, pointing to the kitchen. "Can you give me a hand, Jen?"

The women went through an arch into the kitchen at the back of the house. I stared the lawyer down.

"I swear to you on my life that I will take good care of your sister. You won't ever have to worry. We spend all our time together because we enjoy each other's company."

"But she completely disappeared, changed everything that was her life. She needs to be a teacher."

"Are you sure, big brother, that you know what she needs?"

CHAPTER FIVE

"United wishes and good will cannot overcome brute facts."
Winston Churchill

Jack Lawless clenched his jaw and scowled.

I leaned back in the chair and twiddled my fingers in my lap. "You could offer me a beer."

He didn't move.

I raised my voice. "Hey, woman. Get me a beer!"

"Get it your damn self," Jenny shot back from the kitchen.

"Can I rest my case that we're perfect for each other?"

"She's changed. I'm not sure I like it," Jack persisted.

"You mean, she's completely independent like she's been since your parents passed away. She changed back then. You weren't there for her. I wasn't there. But I am now. I will fight you tooth and nail if that's what you want, but it's not what I want. I *want* a beer, and you heard the good woman. I have to get it myself."

I stood up, finished with verbal jousting. By the time I

reached the kitchen, Jenny was popping the cap off a bottle of designer micro-brew. "You didn't have to get that. I was only trying to make a point, and you were magnificent, as always. Your brother thinks I'm not good enough for you. We may have to arm-wrestle."

"I think I can take you," Jenny replied.

"Not us. Me and him." She chuckled. "Dammit." I took my beer. She winked and returned to the counter, where Kate was cleaning up the dishes from the dinner's prep. "I can help if you need a couple more hands, and for the record, that smells magnificent. I don't care what it is. I'll eat it."

Kate looked over her shoulder. "He's warming up to you. I promise, or he'll be sleeping on the couch the rest of the month."

"I just want to say you look ridiculous in that shirt, but I know you'll beat this rather high bar *when* you come to visit us. I can't wait."

Now it was Jenny's turn to scowl.

"Direct flights from Reagan to Vegas," I added. I dodged the carrot slice Jenny launched at my head. "Another beer, please, for Jack."

Jenny pulled it out, popped the top, and carried it into the dining room.

She slammed it down on the table in front of him, making it foam over. He wrapped his lips around it to contain as much of the mess as he could.

"You listen to me, Jack Lawless. Ian literally saved my life. What more could you ask from my husband?"

He looked skeptical. I tried to look innocent, sipping my beer and gazing at random pictures on the walls. "Why was your life at risk? Was it because the mob found him?"

Jenny took a seat. "Yes. And Ian took care of it. Now we live in Vegas."

He crossed his arms and scowled again.

"Let's go. I'm not putting up with this crap." I looked at the beer, took a drink, put the bottle down, and headed for the door. Jenny grabbed her bag on the way. She wanted to slam the door, but I stopped her, closing it with a gentle click.

We could hear Kate yelling from inside. She wasn't being kind.

We strolled toward our car, but the black hoodies were there, leaning against the convertible.

"Not tonight, guys. Be on your way, and we'll be on ours."

"I don't think that's how it works," Mouthy Thug suggested. "We provided security for your car. You owe us for services rendered."

"No problem. Show me our contract so I can make sure I got my money's worth."

Three of them, all about my size. They had their hoods up. They thought it made them look bad. All it did was block their peripheral vision.

"Funny man. Three of us. One hour. That'll be sixty dollars."

I turned to Jenny. "You take that one. I'll take these two."

"How about we each take one and then see if the last one pees himself before running?"

The talker tried to pull something from his pocket, but he was far too slow. I delivered a heel strike to his face at the same time as Jenny delivered hers. Noses exploded, and the two bounced off our car and started to fall. I lined up a roundhouse, but Jenny spun ahead of me and delivered an elbow to the third young man's mouth. He slammed against the car before coming forward into my roundhouse.

He was unconscious before he bounced off the trunk a second time and crumpled to the ground. We dragged the three onto the sidewalk so no one would drive over the misguided youths. A quick check revealed a small-caliber pistol, a .25 semi-auto. I couldn't tell the brand with my fingertips. I relieved the young man of his weapon and stuffed it into my pocket. Each also carried a folding knife, lock backs with big blades. We tossed all three into the storm drain.

I dusted off my hands. "Nicely done, Miss Lawless. Excellent technique."

"Of course, Mr. Bragg. I compliment my teacher."

Kate and Jack walked toward us. "What the hell happened?"

"An attempt at extortion. They will regret the errors of their ways whenever they wake up." Jenny squared up on her brother. "I want to punch you in the face so bad right now. For how you always treat me like I'm a moron. How do *you* deal with filth like this?" She pointed at the bodies. "You pay them, don't you?"

Jack didn't answer, which was all the answer she needed.

"You missed it. Jenny took out two by herself," I noted.

"I'm supposed to say I'm sorry," Jack stated.

"That's horrible. Try again." Jenny poked him in the chest.

"I'm sorry."

"Once more. This time with feeling."

"I get it. I'm not good with change, and this is a big change."

"It's not," Jenny countered. "Not really. You will always think of me as if I were still ten years old. I'm not and haven't been since, well, since I was ten. That's almost twenty-five years ago."

"Nineteen," I corrected.

"Yes. A full nineteen years."

Two of the lumps on the sidewalk stirred.

"You broke my nose!" one young man cried.

Jenny surged toward him. He fell backward into a shrubbery. "I'm going to start breaking fingers one by one if you and your buddies don't get out of here. If you come back, fingers and toes, and I'll probably slice off an ear just to show that I'm serious."

He backpedaled on the sidewalk until he was against a low stone retainer wall. The other groaned as he stood, face wrecked. They helped the third, who was still unconscious. He was missing his front teeth from Jenny's elbow strike.

"Go on. Clean yourselves up and rethink your life choices."

"We're coming back, and you'll be sorry." The one I had leveled grunted and blood bubbled from his lips. I ran toward him, caught his hand, and twisted it around behind his back. His one friend failed at carrying the other, and they both fell into the short wall, then to the sidewalk.

I forced him onto his face, pulled his head back, and twisted his arm until it dislocated from his shoulder. He howled, so I shoved his face into the sidewalk until he stopped. I pulled him to his feet. "I don't like bullies. I should kill you where you stand. No matter where you go in life, be looking for me. You cross the line, I might show up to rip your other arm out of the socket. You keep trying to roll people, you're going to find out what's it like to be on the wrong end of a prison lover. Get the hell out of here and don't come back."

I let him go, but he could barely move. He had to hold one arm with the other.

"I need you to go, or I'll have to kick you in the balls," I told him. Jack and Kate looked aghast. Jenny helped lift the one struggling to return to the waking world. He doubled over. We dodged out of the way as he heaved onto the sidewalk. He wiped his bloody mouth on the back of his sleeve. I looked at the mess. "You shouldn't have eaten so many tacos before embarking on your failed crime wave."

The three limped and staggered away.

"I think it's about time for us to go," I stated. Jenny agreed.

Jack stepped close. "You aren't even breathing hard."

"I'd hate to think I wasted all my time in the Marine Corps. Jenny and I train every single day. These three were Little League. I hope they got the message."

"We have to live here, and now they know who we are!"

I shook my head.

"And you have the gall to think you're protecting me?" Jenny spat at her brother.

He sighed and hung his head. Kate gripped his arm. "I'm sorry," he said, finally and sincerely.

"Find yourself a dojo and train in self-defense. Both of you. The family that fights together, stays together," I advised.

"If you'll do me a favor?" Jack requested. "Don't hit so hard next time. That's going to leave a wicked bruise." He rubbed his mid-section before holding his arms out.

Jenny hugged her brother. I waved and held the door for her for when they finished. Kate was standing there in her ridiculous shirt. I tried not to stare, forcing myself to look away. I joined Jenny in the car.

We kept the top up because the evening air was cool. I set the GPS for our hotel, which was only a few blocks away.

"Your family is nice," I deadpanned.

Jenny settled for giving me the side-eye. We dropped

the car with the valet and waved off the bellhop to carry our bag and backpacks ourselves into the colonial-style brick-faced hotel.

We checked into the honeymoon suite and got ourselves settled before Jenny attacked me, ripping at my clothes. I was always game for a good throw-down, but I didn't know why. I fought her to a stalemate.

"We'll take this up again as soon as I know why the frenzy." I held her wrists and pinned her to the bed. We were both half-dressed. I wasn't sure the buttons had survived on my shirt. I thought I'd heard something rip.

Jenny finally stopped struggling and I let go, rolling next to her.

"Freedom and fury," she said. "He has always been mean to me, like a bully, but he protected me when I was growing up while also giving me a hard time. He never stopped thinking he needed to get me out of trouble. But he and his family were nowhere to be found when our parents were on the downhill slide of life. He still thinks he can boss me around. Used to think. We set him straight, Ian. We are free from his superior attitude. He is firmly in his place, and maybe what's left is a decent human being."

"I have high hopes. I wanted to play nice, but I'm not putting up with anyone demeaning you. You know what, huggy bunny?"

She chuckled. "What?"

"I'm pretty hungry. What did we miss out on?

"Homemade lasagna. Don't tell her I said anything, but you're not missing out on anything because she's not a very good cook. Neither of them is. That's why the kids left before dinner. The dining hall at the university will have better food."

"That's harsh. The so-called kids seemed to have a sense of urgency. I thought we were coming out here to spend time with your family, and here we are in the hotel, getting naked and then ordering room service."

"We came to see my family, but we're on vacation. I felt guilty about not coming because that's how Jack makes me feel. But not anymore. We can buy them tickets. They pay a fortune for their house and two kids in college, soon to be three. They don't have any extra money. He's too proud to say because he's a big jerk."

"I wish I had known we were coming out here to confront your brother."

"I thought he might have changed."

I gave it my best sarcastic tone of voice, drawing out the word. "Really?"

"I hoped. I'm sorry, Ian."

"Kate took it like a champ. He should listen to her more." I undid the next button on Jenny's shirt. She threw her hands over her head and closed her eyes. Her skin was soft and warm. I kneeled over her and confirmed that my buttons were gone. I threw the shirt toward the garbage can.

"Sorry about that," Jenny mumbled, not sounding sorry at all.

CHAPTER SIX

"If your opponent offers you a draw, try to work out why he thinks he's worse off." Nigel Short

The hotel's small restaurant wasn't crowded since we were early. We ordered breakfast and prepared for the day.

"Jasmine Underhill is the middle child in the Lawless family," Jenny explained. "She was usually the peacemaker, but then worked her way into a career as a wedding planner. She took today off to hang out with us. Her husband Anton works as a contract interpreter. He's working a conference in Orlando, so you won't meet him. Their two kids are Eomyr and Arwen."

"Your sister is a Tolkien fan. I can work with that." I rolled my finger. "Out with it. How old?"

"Ten and twelve. Sorry about yesterday. I swear it was an unintentional oversight regarding the ages of Jack's kids."

"I'm obligated to believe you, but I don't think I should." Our meals arrived, and we dug in. Eggs and bacon tended to cool too quickly. I finished before Jenny, with my bad habit of eating quickly when on a mission. That was what this felt like. Meeting Jenny's brother made me happy he didn't live closer or visit. I hoped Jasmine was nothing like her brother. Jenny deserved me to play nice, but I hated confrontation and internal family angst.

I selfishly wanted to be alone with Jenny and live free of external entanglements. I had little interest in her family but couldn't tell her that. I had to try, or at least look like I was. I hadn't brought my computer or anything besides a vanilla smartphone with nothing on it except access to the internet for inane reasons. And the phone to use to call for things like a hotel.

I'd ditch the phone after a few months. Couldn't leave a trail. I was still in the game.

And I had to play, even with two pre-teens and a sister standing in my way, a new obstacle since the overbearing big brother was in my rearview mirror.

"Why don't we pick up a couple gift cards for them to add in with the other things? By the way, what did you get them? I thought you had toys, but that wasn't what they were, were they?"

"So many questions, Mr. Ian Bragg. Are you finally taking an interest in my family? No. That's not it. You just don't want to be embarrassed like last night, and I understand that. I didn't want to be completely open about it because I was afraid it would turn out exactly as it did. I was afraid that if I told you that my brother was a bit abusive growing up, as big brothers are wont to be, you would have beaten the crap out of him."

I blew out a breath and took another sip of my coffee. It didn't taste like mass-produced percolator coffee. It had a slight nutty bite. I liked it. "You know me so well. I look at you and can't believe anyone would be mean to you. It makes my blood boil. And yes, I know how the real world works. I can't beat everyone up. But if I limit it to those who really deserve it, Jack would still be on the list."

Jenny chuckled before returning to her plate.

"What are the challenges I'll be facing today, and what did *we* get them?"

"We bought them books. A couple of my favorites, McCaffrey and Lackey." She took another bite and chewed slowly while I waited for her to fill me in. "Fine."

I was instantly on guard. "That word never means fine. I'm sorry, but I'm screaming down the highway of life, and you just threw an 'Under Construction' sign in front of me without any other context. I like your new hairstyle. That does NOT make your butt look big. Of course, a new pair of shoes makes sense. I'll do the dishes." I held my hands out and watched for cues. She gave me no hint. "I'm spitballing here to see if anything sticks."

Jenny took another bite and chewed slowly. I got up and borrowed a newspaper from the counter. I sat down and opened it fully in front of me. Jenny used her fork to pull down the newsprint barrier I had erected.

"Yes, dear?" I was still in the game.

"She'll be fine. We probably should have gone to Jazz's home in Woodbridge last night, which is bigger than Jack's. It's not in the high-rent district. Well, for this area, anyway. She's the peacemaker. She probably could have kept Jack from being a total jerk. But I wanted to see my niece and nephews, even for only a brief time. I think you'll like her. And we'll all get together again tomorrow since it'll be Saturday. Jazz reserved a local restaurant for a group lunch."

"I look forward to it," I lied most unconvincingly.

Jenny sighed and cocked her head as she looked at me

through the V she created in the paper. I put the paper down and folded it.

"I know you hate this, but you're doing it because it's important to me. I'll make it worth your while." She licked her lips with the tip of her tongue.

"I think 'hate' is probably the correct word, but as long as I'm with you, we'll be fine. Don't abandon me with one of your siblings again, please. Ever."

"I'm proud that you didn't hit him."

"You exploded the beer in front of him. I liked that."

"I didn't know you liked beer," Jenny countered.

"Only good beer, especially if it's expensive and someone I don't like bought it."

"So petty." Jenny shook her head before she stood. "We'll be driving against traffic, so it may only take thirty minutes to get there."

"Let's stop on the way and pick up a couple gift cards for the kids. And probably the older kids too, say, $500 each?"

"That's a lot."

"I want your status as the favorite aunt to be solidified for all time. And it's on our employer." I waved the gold card, which I was going to use to pay for breakfast. "Without a computer, we're not able to get any more cash than we have on us."

Hand in hand, we paid our bill and strolled out of the hotel. A twenty for the valet expedited the return of our car. We put the top down and cranked up the heat.

"You said thirty minutes?" Jenny looked at me as I scrolled through my various Rush playlists. I pointed at one and smiled as I tapped play.

Limelight.

Jenny rolled her eyes while I laughed demonically. The valet remained stoic, but I thought I saw him bobbing his head in rhythm as I pulled into traffic on my way to the interstate.

Traffic was heavy until we started heading south on I-95. After that, it was a cool ride in the morning sunshine on an unusually warm early fall day.

Jenny looked at the buildings and areas on both sides of the road in her search to identify the changes. DC was always changing while staying much the same. I watched my mirrors. Too many feds in Washington, DC for my liking. My job and theirs were polar opposites. If I did everything right, one person died. If they did theirs right, no one died.

Supposedly. At least, it sounded good. Damn politicians. Even after getting to know a good one, I still didn't trust them.

We took the first exit to Woodbridge, maneuvering our way into a commercial area, where we stopped at a grocery store to pick up a couple gift cards. One thousand dollars later, we headed into a residential neighborhood until we arrived at a nice standalone house, a little older but well maintained. The homes in this area had well-manicured front yards as well as full-sized backyards.

The driveway was open, and Jenny pointed to the right side. I hugged that side to give someone room to get out if needed. We put the top up but left the windows down. I scanned the area to see if anyone was watching. A heavier woman popped out the front door and screamed. Jenny screamed and ran to her.

Jasmine. I put on my game face and strolled up behind them, waiting for the happy sisters to unclench.

When Jasmine pushed Jenny aside, I put my knight into play, dominating the middle of the board. "I married the wrong sister. No wonder Jenny didn't tell me how gorgeous you are."

I held my arms out for a hug. The two sisters stood with their fists on their hips, giving me the Lawless judging stare before Jasmine turned to Jenny. "You're married?"

"Not her, too?" I tried to mirror Jenny's pose. She was on her heels. I moved my other knight into play. "We had a magnificent affair. Our planner could have been the best in the world."

Jenny slapped me across the arm.

"We got married by a fat Elvis," I blurted.

Jasmine started to laugh. "Is he always like this?"

I nudged my wife. "Tell her about last night. This is mild. But I admit, we *were* married by Elvis, where we declared a hunk of burning love before going our separate ways. By that, I mean we left the King a hundred buck tip and headed for the honeymoon suite."

Jenny wrapped her arm around me as Jasmine led the way into the house. We dumped our shoes in the entryway and made ourselves at home.

We had Jasmine to ourselves all day while the kids were at school. After two minutes of Jenny and Jasmine talking rapid-fire at the same time, I had to stop them. "You are such a breath of fresh air. Can I get a cup of coffee, please? I need to juice up if I want to keep up."

"Weren't impressed by our big brother?" Jasmine said as she took us into the kitchen. The pot was on, but she dumped the coffee that was in there before I could stop her. It smelled fine, but she insisted on making a fresh pot. I looked at the sink and tried to will the coffee out of the drain and into my cup.

But I had to wait.

"No. Jack is a wiener." I had stronger language that applied, but I wasn't telling them anything they didn't know.

"I think that's probably the best description of him I've

ever heard," Jasmine allowed. "I have to say that married life agrees with you, Jen. I have never seen you glow like this. You look so fit."

"We work out every day," Jenny said.

"You're newlyweds, you're supposed to."

"On top of that. But yes, so much of *that*," Jenny said slowly and emphatically. She wasn't wrong, but I didn't feel I needed to be in on the conversation since Jasmine appeared to be sizing me up to determine if it was the truth or not.

"I'll wait in the living room," I said and backed out of the kitchen. The women giggled at my expense. Jasmine wasn't wrong. Jenny glowed, but I'd seen it from the first moment I met her.

I played with my phone while I waited for my coffee. With a simple app, I was able to access my accounts and found two deposits made ten minutes apart for a grand total of seventy-five thousand dollars. I had gotten a good chunk of my money back, but the Archive wanted to talk to me.

It was important to call them and soon. Jenny brought my coffee. I showed her the phone screen. "I need to run to the store real quick," I said loudly enough for Jasmine to hear. Jenny pulled me to my feet and hugged me fiercely. I almost dropped my coffee cup. Jasmine swept by and relieved me of it without my having taken a sip.

The universe was conspiring against me. I suspected the Archive had reached a decision regarding the training. I didn't want to keep them waiting. On my way to the front door, Jasmine intercepted me to hand over a travel mug with a lid.

"What is this sorcery?" I took the cup and held it up with both hands as if worshipping the gods of the coffee bean.

"I see why you married him," Jasmine said, raising her eyebrows at me as she walked away.

Jenny opened the door. "I'll be right back, Miss Jenny. I'll call from the driveway so you can see that I'm here."

In the old days, I had been able to compartmentalize, focusing on one thing at a time to the exclusion of all else. When Jenny entered my life, that had changed, and I couldn't close doors as a tendril of my mind sought solace in thoughts of her. But I could see it coming back. Jenny was here, a warm embrace away. She would wait while I took care of that which needed to be taken care of.

I would reopen the door, and she would be there. I wanted that ability back, not because I was taking Jenny for granted, but because with focus, we'd both be safer. At the end of the day, that mattered more than any sharing of distractions.

I checked the deposits and tapped in the numbers in the order they were received. Jenny waved from the front window. I nodded back while closing out of my account on my smartphone, then put it on the dash of the convertible. I pressed send on the burner phone and waited while it rang.

"Ian. Congratulations on your first successful contract." It sounded like Chaz.

"That's good to hear. I haven't been following the news. I'll check into the Hollywood Reporter when I can."

"But that's not what I called about. We have thought about the training, and I agree it could be a very good thing to take the company to the next level. How you run this will be a template for other sessions. We think two a year are not out of bounds. Each run by a different person in a different place with different attendees, all singularly focused on making our operators the best in the world. Better operators means a smaller footprint. There are a number of ways we could be discovered. We need to reduce those pathways.

"It may seem counterintuitive to do that through having face-to-face gatherings, but if most people drive in, all under aliases, there will be no trail. Set it up for November if you can. We'll control the flow of potential contracts to make sure those in your region are available to attend."

"I've been looking into ways to make it happen off the grid. I'll come up with something that is worthy of the Archive. I won't let you down."

"The only reason we considered it was because of you. You aren't like the rest of us, Ian. That's a good thing. As for those other two potential contracts you've been sitting on, either get them out for bid or kick them back. We don't like telling potential clients 'no,' and we really don't like telling them 'no' after we haven't done anything with their proposal for two months."

"I hear you. I'll take care of it when I get back."

"You're not in Vegas?" Chaz asked. It made me wonder where the gold card charges showed up if he wasn't aware that it was being used outside of Vegas. Maybe they had the bank administer it anonymously. I liked that possibility.

"No. I'm in DC because that seven-oh-two area code burner was a bit spendy to set up a call. It's cheaper to fly out here and buy a couple two-oh-two burners. Plus, we're visiting Miss Jenny's family, as much as that grates on my soul. They know nothing about me."

"Keep it that way. You are the only married operator. Like I said, you're different from the rest of us. Let that be your strength, not your weakness. I'll be at your training while Vinny minds the store."

The phone went dead. I stared at the garage door but didn't see it. My mind raced from one thing to the next. I could accept one of the contracts and reject the other. I had an idea regarding the training and had a couple of months to get everything set up for an anonymous retreat. I hoped that was enough time.

A template for the future.

I felt the pressure to get this right, far above and beyond what I usually put on myself. I saw the syllabus in my mind. Two days, active training interspersed with classroom sessions. Keep the mind engaged. Fitness in between. Maybe four days. They hadn't put a limit on me. I was the only one with a family. Maybe we'd do it around Thanksgiving when normal people were doing normal holiday things.

The sessions came into focus. I saw in my mind a way to pull it together. We needed a dude ranch. We'd rent all the rooms and have the place to ourselves. Laser gaming. Surveillance systems. The dark web. So much opportunity.

I wanted my notebook but hadn't brought it. With two pre-teens in the house, they had to have a pen and paper. I hopped out of the car, shut the door, and strolled casually to the house. I knocked and waited.

Jenny appeared. "You could have just come in. You are family." She blocked the door so I couldn't come right in. I traced a line down the side of her face with my finger.

"You are so beautiful, Miss Jenny," I told her. An "Aw" from inside made me step back. "I'm a guest, so I don't walk into people's houses."

"Come on in, you big stud," Jazz called from inside.

"What did you tell her?" I asked. "And did you tell her?"

"That's your department, sweetie, for that other thing, but the first thing, just sisterly talk, nothing more."

"Good things come to those who wait," Jazz stated, giving Jenny a one-armed hug while continuing her appraisal of me as if I were a goose hanging in the butcher's window.

"Just sisterly talk, huh? I'll find out later what exactly that means. In the interim, we have something to tell you that you cannot tell anyone. We feel it's important for you to know because it's important that you don't ask certain questions, and definitely not online."

"I don't care," Jasmine said, standing and waving over her shoulder as she walked away. "As long as you keep *Miss* Jenny as happy as she is now, you could be a murderer for all I care. It's all good as long as you don't get caught because then she'd be unhappy."

"What if they were only bad people who no one would miss?"

"Depends on your definition of bad." She stopped in the doorway to the kitchen and leaned against the jamb with her arms crossed.

"Drug kingpins, terrorists, philanderers… You know, the usual destroyers of people's futures. But no one outside of that."

"You should be working in Hollywood with that imagination. They already did that with *True Lies*. You'll need to come up with something fresh." She poo-pooed me and left the room.

Jenny's eyes shot wide and her mouth dropped open. "See?" I whispered. "*True Lies* ruined it for us hardworking folk."

She play-pushed me into a chair and then climbed into my lap.

Jazz returned with mimosas.

It was barely ten in the morning, but I was ready for one.

Jasmine raised her glass. "A toast to the newlyweds. I'm already head over heels in love with my new brother-in-law."

Jenny remained in my lap while we made small talk. I tuned out when they devolved into reminiscing. I had work to do. I was ready to get on the plane back to Vegas.

I interrupted. "Would you happen to have a notepad and pen I could have?"

"No mincing words. You need it, you've got it." Jazz hopped up and disappeared upstairs.

"What was the call about?"

"Training session is a go. November. Chaz is coming to observe how to implement it companywide. Also, Guano is no more. Contract is complete already. There's the executive summary."

"The hit is done?" Jenny asked a little too loudly. I held my finger to my lips.

"Supposedly. I can't jump online and search for it without a VPN, but we can browse the Hollywood news without searching."

Jenny tapped her smartphone, vanilla like mine. She brought up the Hollywood Reporter and roamed from screen to screen, looking at the latest news.

Jazz returned with a pocket-sized Moleskine notebook and a Cross pen. "I get gifts from the wedding parties all the time. It's amazing what people give their guests when they get married. Ignore the imprint and engraving."

"This is nicer than I deserve. Jack and Diane," I read from the notebook's front. The pen was engraved, Bill and William, October 16, 2019. "Looks good. I'll use the heck out of these."

"Got it," Jenny said and showed me the screen. Julian

Guanore - Dead at 44. I continued reading the article while Jasmine tried to read upside down. I scanned until I found the alleged cause of death. Alcohol poisoning. I pointed it out to Jenny. That relieved more pressure than I thought I had been carrying about the contract. I could feel my muscles relax. "This calls for another mimosa."

Jenny climbed out of my lap so I could sit at a small writing desk in her sister's living room. I started jotting the notes that were at the forefront of my mind. With the first contract successfully behind us, my focus turned toward the training. What to teach hit men? The question would plague me until we pulled it off and probably far beyond.

I started writing a project plan to make sure everything was handled. An all-inclusive dude ranch was looking more and more optimal to make the logistics easy enough for the training to be of value. More notes. More checking on my phone. Back to notes.

Someone touched my back. "Honey?"

"Damn." I closed the notebook. "What time is it?"

"Lunch, but Jazz is cooking dinner, so we're going out for lunch. We'll take the convertible."

Jasmine waited near the door. They were both ready to go. Jenny called to her sister, "We're from Vegas and spoiled when it comes to chow."

"Chow?" Jazz's features contorted into a disgusted face.

Jenny laughed. "My Marine uses those terms. 'Chow' is generic for food."

"Then why doesn't he just say food?"

"Because he's a Marine."

"I thought you said he was out of the service?" Jasmine was getting more confused.

"Once a Marine, always a Marine, big sister. You can't win this, so you can stop trying. And the question still stands. Is there any good chow nearby?"

"How about Mexican? Or maybe a Brazilian steakhouse for dinner with the fam?"

"Both sound good. You have a Brazilian steakhouse nearby? Is it any good?"

"Less than five minutes away, and it's all kinds of good. It's expensive, so we don't go there often."

"On us," Jenny said. "Maybe you can talk to Jack and get our reservations changed. He can drag his sorry ass down here instead of us coming to him all the time."

"Drag his sorry ass?" Jazz shook her head. "You used to be cultured, a schoolteacher."

"I used to put up with Jack's crap, too, but I married a Marine, and now I'm hard as woodpecker lips."

I beamed like a proud parent. Jasmine had no reply.

Jenny glanced at the notebook in my hand. I nodded just enough to let her know I was on track. I stuffed it into my pocket, and we left to see what the world had to offer. I would enjoy lunch but was looking forward to the Brazilian steakhouse, where servers would roam the tables carrying skewers of meat for easy delivery to plates sporting a green coaster. I liked it when the buffet came to me.

Despite the fine dining and good company of the day, my attention was elsewhere. We set up dinner at the Brazilian place for the next day, Saturday. We spent a couple hours with the kids after they got home from school, and then we bowed out.

As it turned out, Jasmine wasn't a good cook either.

CHAPTER SEVEN

"In preparing for battle, I have always found that plans are useless, but planning is indispensable." Dwight D. Eisenhower

Our visit went quickly until Saturday evening approached. I was occupied within my own mind about things that neither Jenny nor Jasmine could help me with. Training was different from a wedding, but as a professional planner, I knew she would have insight into things that I wouldn't think about.

We walked into the Brazilian steakhouse to find that we had arrived first. "I want to sit next to Jazz and bend her ear on party planning and how to deal with divas."

"You think your attendees will be divas?" Jenny pursed her lips and studied my expression.

"It'll be alpha dog central. I need to make them all feel like there's no competition because that will devolve quickly. These people will do anything it takes to win. Much like a bridezilla who wants to dominate everyone and everything. So in simpler Marine terms, let's go with no leg-humping at the retreat."

Jenny smirked. "Don't frame it that way."

I arranged the chairs while Jenny watched. "I would be greatly obliged if you sat next to your brother since me beating him up isn't allowed."

"You want me to beat him up?" Jenny asked, cracking her knuckles.

"I want him beaten up, but not by you or me. We will have to let that go for now. Who knows, maybe he'll be a decent human being, having seen the light."

Jasmine arrived with her two kids. We spread them around the table, leaving five spots for Jack, Kate, and their three.

I figured he'd be late because that would reinforce my low opinion of him, but they showed up five minutes before our reservation time. It gave me hope. "Would you look at that? They're early," Jenny said. We stood to greet them.

Jack shook my hand and tried to hold my gaze, but he couldn't maintain it. There was a big difference between a corporate lawyer and a person who killed people for a living. He moved around the table and then sat next to the ten-year-old. They put the three kids between them, and Kate sat next to Jenny. In that arrangement, Jack was in my line of vision. I turned my chair to talk to Jazz.

"I'm running an event fairly soon. Can you give me some tips on how you deal with divas?"

"Are they paying you to run this?"

"Kind of, but not really."

"That makes your job a whole lot harder. I have clauses in the contract where I can double the charges after so many changes. They have to come to a decision sooner rather than later, or they pay me a lot more."

"That would be easier to tolerate, but how do you help other guests survive the tyrannical beast?"

"You mean, the aptly-named bridezilla?" Jenny was nudging me from behind. I put my hand around my back, and she held it. I nodded to Jasmine to continue. "Communication is key. You have to keep everything in the open and then play to people's strengths and limit their weaknesses. One of the best tips I have is to give everyone something to do, something important."

"I bow before the wisdom of your experience." In a few words, she had filled in all my missing puzzle pieces. It came to me clearly. Bid it like a contract, with each part a separate bid and the general details buried for whoever the winning bidder would be. They'd be able to present a session and be an active player in one of the hands-on sessions. There would be plenty of opportunities over the course of the schedule.

I had settled on three days as the optimal time. We could cover a lot of information in three days without leaving too big a footprint, as in, they'd still be in and out before anyone grew suspicious. It would be worth their while.

I'd get another contract out of the way between now and then. Maybe two. I thanked Jazz and turned in my seat to face the table as well as Jack. Jenny nuzzled her head against my shoulder.

"You two are so cute," Kate said, looking sideways at her husband.

He tapped his glass lightly with his knife since the conversations had stopped. He remained seated and spoke in a soft voice. "I'm sorry for not being a model big brother. For not being someone you could count on for support in your lives. I have to do better now that these three are growing older. I want to be the cool grandfather, not the grumpy one that no one likes to visit."

"Bring your dumb ass to Vegas and visit us," Jenny said.

"Not helping," I whispered.

She poked me. I poked her back. When we looked up, everyone was watching us.

"As I was saying, Funpa, not Grumpa. I'm trying."

Before Jenny could take another jab, I raised my glass. "Hear, hear." It was water, but the thought counted. Jenny conceded and toasted her brother. He seemed relieved.

Jenny leaned close to Kate. "How bad did you have to kick his ass? And whatever it was, thank you. That was a long time coming."

"On the couch the last two nights. This is a new couch, and it's not comfortable at all. That was just the icing on the cake. You'd never stood up to him like that before. You've changed, Jenny. Ian is good for you, and he won't say it, but we're both proud of you."

"I couldn't agree more. I always thought a partner was supposed to make you better, the whole being greater than the sum of the parts. I'm better than I was and improving with each new day. I love my life."

"Even though, you know, hiding," Kate said with her hand shielding her mouth.

"Makes you sharp, knowing that someone out there wants to kill you," Jenny replied matter-of-factly.

"A successful trip," Jenny said as we sat in the 737's first-class seats, waiting for the flight to take off. I pulled out my book. I had read a little bit in the hotel room but planned on finishing it during this flight. I needed to know the ending. "Don't you want to talk to me?"

A dangerous question. I made sure my bookmark was secure and put the book in the seat pocket in front of me before twisting to face my wife. "I always want to share life with you." One of my better countermoves because it was sincere. I didn't like to get into deep conversations in public places because people didn't need to hear our business. I leaned close and glanced right and left to highlight how close the other passengers were, even in first class.

She nodded to show she understood. "Thank you," she said, eyes sparkling with joy. "I think we might be more of a normal family now, thanks to you."

"I didn't know your family wasn't normal," I said, keeping my voice low.

"I fear we're all too normal, but at least now we won't be fighting over stupid stuff. What's next?"

"Let's wait until we're in the comfort of our own home to talk about next steps. We're going to be busy getting ready for all kinds of things, and I'll need your help every step of the way."

"Go team," Jenny replied with a smile, squeezing my hand and leaning back with her eyes closed. I pulled out my book and opened it with one hand. Reading about a hitman. In fiction. If they only knew the truth.

Alcohol poisoning. I got my money's worth on that first contract. Time to dig deeply into number two. I already knew I was going to cancel the third contract. I couldn't find enough on the target, and the client offer was less than forthcoming about the nature of the desired hit. The only thing it had going for it was the two million dedicated to making it happen. I refused to be swayed by the money.

What would someone pay to have another person killed? Were the benefits worth the risk? I wondered what the top end was. What was the most someone paid?

Rich people never believed they'd end up on the wrong side of prison. They counted on their money to keep them free. In most cases, that was true. The Peace Archive kept all conversations away from prying eyes. The Caymans provided a physical refuge, while the dark net delivered a shadow within which public personas could virtually hide.

I tried to read the book, but my mind wandered far too much. I kept rereading the same page. I gave up and fiddled with my Jack and Diane notebook instead. I added notes on questions I wanted to ask Chaz. I didn't expect him to answer too many of them, but anything he wanted to tell me, I'd be all ears.

CHAPTER EIGHT

"How do men feel whose whole lives (and many men's lives) are lies, schemes, and subterfuges? What sort of company do they keep when they are alone? Daily in life I watch men whose every smile is an artifice, and every wink is an hypocrisy. Doth such a fellow wear a mask in his own privacy, and to his own conscience?" William Makepeace Thackeray

"It's nice to be home," I said the second we walked through the door. I caught my wife from behind and hugged her, nibbling lightly on her neck. She faced me, but it wasn't to respond to my sultry advances.

"Tell me what you need help with, and I'll work on it while you do your other stuff. You're not going to take me for a roll in the hay just so I sleep while you work."

"Is that what you think I'm doing?"

"It is." She stared at my hands.

I stopped pawing her. "I need you to find a dude ranch where we can have three exclusive days and no other guests. We need to have it all to ourselves. A conference room with power. Internet. At least a dozen rooms. We'll pay for all of it. None of the guests will be paying for anything. It has to be in November, whichever days we can get."

"Is that all?" Jenny smiled at me. "I'll be done before you, and then you can listen to me watching TV."

"I guarantee you'll be done before me, but we have some time. I look forward to dessert. I think we've had enough dinner to hold us for a while, especially with the limited workouts while on the road."

"Two hours and then dojo," Jenny suggested. "It was invigorating beating the crap out of those punks. I still need to be better and faster."

"It's always good to put the misguided in their place."

"I see more and more why you did what you did, why you do what you do." Jenny took me by my hands, the look in her eyes promising that dessert would be worth waiting for. "Let's get a start on what needs to be done, shall we?"

I jumped online and navigated to the back end of the Archive's bulletin board to cancel the one potential contract. A new one had dropped into the queue. A major drug dealer. "What the hell is this?" Jenny stopped browsing potential retreat sites and joined me to look over my shoulder at the screen.

"What am I looking at?"

"A government hit. This doesn't look private."

Jenny read the page and reached past me to scroll down to read to the end. "If that is all true, this is a very bad man who has hurt a lot of people. Parents of missing youths probably hate this guy with every fiber of their beings."

"Possibly." I scrolled down and pointed to passages. "These look like a bureaucrat wrote them. *Community integrity. Flow of drugs. Society.* Distressed parents would be more tuned in to harm done to their children, wouldn't they?"

"Does it matter?" She tapped the bottom line of the page. *$2,500,000.*

"What if it's a setup, a trap to take down the Archive?"

"Then they would have had someone more convincing write this," Jenny replied, returning to the couch to browse locations for the training.

I needed to get back to the contract that I was still on the fence about, a hedge fund manager. I didn't want it to look too much like my final hit as an operator, but it was almost exactly like that.

Leading his company farther into a fraud where there would be no escape. There was a chance to save it, but that window was closing. I reread the proposal's language. *Brought back under SEC control before all investors lose their money.*

Would an aggrieved board member or investor talk like that? Everything else in the proposal went into the fraud details. Did I care if people were defrauded? They already had been. I couldn't fix that. Was this retribution or intervention? That was where I'd been stuck for the past month.

I dug into the dark web because the answers were nowhere to be found in the proposal. I had an idea that anonymous proposals made the process even more difficult. We needed counter-leverage to make sure we didn't get set up.

Maybe they weren't anonymous, only anonymous to me. Chaz and Vinny had been in this business for too long not to have leverage over those who hired the Peace Archive. They were savvy enough to protect themselves. Government contracts would help keep them out of the fire. The perfect balance.

I put my Moleskine on the table and jotted a note in the section with questions for Chaz. Named requestors?

Who, indeed? I already knew the answer. That was the next level up in the organization. *For services rendered, both public and private, contact the Peace Archive.*

The dark web showed even more allegations against the hedge fund than what was included in the proposal. I couldn't see how it could be saved since the fraud was serious. Much of the money had been funneled to questionable projects overseas. It was probably unrecoverable unless those projects had not yet started and the managers had funneled the money elsewhere, but those in power couldn't trace it to its final destination with the manager in the way.

They had offered two million dollars to clear the way. I felt better thinking it was the Securities and Exchange Commission looking out for the investors by handling matters outside of public scrutiny. It almost made me renew my faith in the system, except that it was probably a rogue department of regulators using its budget to take care of the investors rather than punish the instruments of the investment.

I chuckled. It was the opposite; it was the ultimate punishment. They had delivered a death sentence. We make the hit, or all the investors lose their money and the government has to prosecute, which would cost far more than the two million offered.

My speculation was closing my mind to other possibilities. I went to the window and looked out with my hands behind my back. Not even Rush could help me through this.

To assess the proposal and award a contract, I needed to know the source. The Archive wouldn't tell me the source. Otherwise, I would already know. How much trust could I place in them?

Their lives were as much at risk as mine. They had to know that if their regional directors were taken down, they would spill what they knew. That would expose the back end of the bidding board. There was little there, nothing that said contracts for execution. Only how bad people were, a date, and a dollar amount.

I trusted the Archive. They'd missed on the Tripplethorn contract, but they had made amends. One bad regional director did not make for a bad company.

With my template from the Guano package, I put together a new package on the manager. I double-checked the addresses and schedules I could find for him and fleshed out a dossier. With the proposal intact, I posted it for bids with a minimum of three-quarters of a mil.

I closed that window and dug into the new package. Felipe Gomez lived in a veritable fortress in the Catalina Foothills overlooking the city of Tucson, Arizona. He was as clean as a person could be. Nothing ever got to him, although dealers associated with him were arrested with great frequency. None of them rolled, but they were all too small to be in business on their own.

"We need to go to Tucson." I was convinced I'd find my answer closer to the target.

"Fine. When do you want to go?"

Jenny's reply made me realize I had spoken aloud. "Give it a couple days. Let's enjoy being home for a bit first."

"I have a place lined up for November. The week before Thanksgiving is their slowest time. Monday arrival and Friday morning departure. They have twenty rooms, all-inclusive. They insisted that we take the horses out at least once a day."

"I don't know anything about riding a horse," I grumbled. "Why do we have to ride the horses?"

"It makes us look less like a bunch of people hiding from the law and more like a team-building group avoiding corporate America."

"I shouldn't be surprised that you found what sounds like the right place. Where is it?"

"Outside Flagstaff. We can stop on our way to Tucson to shake some hands, kiss a few babies, and sign a contract."

"The stars must be in alignment, Miss Jenny. What time is it?"

"Dinner time," she replied. I returned to the table and checked the clock on the computer. Four hours had come and gone in a flash. Inwardly, I was happy to have my focus back, but we had missed our dojo time. Jenny knew what I was thinking.

She stripped to her underwear and moved the coffee table out of the way before sliding the dining table aside. "Grab on." She bent over one side of the couch. I took the other, and we moved it to the far edge of the living room. Jenny started to stretch. I stripped to my shorts and joined her.

Breathe in, breathe out. We ran through the tae kwan do sequences, ending with a face-off. We bowed to each other, then assumed our positions, dominant foot and hand forward. We smacked the backs of our hands off each other before jabbing and blocking initial probes.

Jenny was in the zone. Wary. I was getting there and happy that my defenses covered me as my mind cleared and engaged in the chess match of hand-to-hand combat. I started to move more quickly, back and forth, lunge, retreat, trying to get Jenny to overcommit and give me an opening. I feigned while she spun. I jumped over the sweep as she transitioned to an uppercut that I barely blocked, twisting at the waist to avoid most of it, redirecting it with a forearm that I turned into a strike.

A backhand caught her on the top of her head. She stumbled, not from being dazed, but from getting knocked off-balance. I rushed into the opening, caught her arms at the elbows, and wrapped her up. I picked her up but caught myself before bending over backward to pile-drive her head into the carpet. This wasn't the dojo.

"Give!" I said, which was our word to end the fight. I found my face buried between her breasts. I slowly let her down. She was breathing heavily, with a slight sheen of sweat on her body. "Nicely done."

"I left an opening." She shook her head as she undid her bra and tossed it at me.

"If your leg sweep had been a couple inches higher, you would have had me. It was close." I followed her into the bathroom for a shower.

She stopped me. "Why don't you order some Chinese for delivery? I don't feel like going out."

"I'm not ordering egg foo young. You never like it."

"Please? My search for the perfect foo young continues."

"You don't like it from this place."

"Then order from a different place," Jenny countered.

"But I like the Tso's from this place."

"You might like the Tso's from a different place that could have the perfect egg foo young, and we'll never know unless we try it."

"You're going to hate it," I replied over my shoulder on my way to the living room to make the call.

"Probably," she conceded. I heard the shower turn on.

I had already prepared a list of places and put it in the kitchen drawer. I'd call the next on the list and hope for the best. She'd been clear from day one when I bought a disgusting concoction and she didn't like it. I smiled. Unrepentant honesty. We both embraced the ideal, between us anyway. I made the call, ordered three entrees, and hurried to join my wife.

CHAPTER NINE

"The world consisted of predators and prey. You were either hunting or running." Charlene Weir

The ranch was nearly thirty minutes outside of Flagstaff at the end of a series of winding roads. We followed the GPS on the smartphone, which we would have to soon destroy and replace. We couldn't carry around a record of where we'd been.

"I already like this place," I said as we made the final turn onto little more than a cart path. The sprawling ranch-style building near the end looked rustic but by design. It had a newer construction feel. I checked my phone. The ranch had its own Wi-Fi. "Two thumbs-up."

The sign said Circle B Ranch. We made it to the right place, parking in a small lot with four other vehicles. A thin layer of red dust dulled their shine. Jenny pulled me toward the entrance while I tried to take in the surrounding area. I gave up and hurried along with her.

Inside, we were greeted by an extensive Wild West

collection displayed on every available surface. Horse tack hung front and center in the entryway. It even smelled like a horse to add to the allure.

At the counter, Jenny was all business. "I'm Jenny Lawless, and I spoke with the manager a few days ago about an exclusive retreat. We were in the area, so we thought we'd stop by."

"Make yourselves at home while I find him," the young man replied. "He could be out on a ride. He goes every day."

I wandered around the small lobby, trying to take an interest in the western flavor. Small brass plates affixed by each item shared the glory of what made it important, extolling the virtues of the hard men who'd opened the west to the rest of America. From settlers to gunfighters to cattle punchers, horses were critical. There was one picture of a young man, bare-chested with an Army cap, smoking with a buddy. It was labeled *Tan Son Nhut Air Base*.

Boot steps announced the arrival of a cowboy.

A grizzled old man stepped from behind the counter, offering his hand to me first before bending to kiss Miss Jenny's hand. "You want to rent my place for a group training?"

"We do," Jenny replied. He looked at me, and I nodded at her.

"We have the dates available. It's all yours if you want it. Will there be a buncha pretty gals like you coming?"

I chuckled at the old man's Western charm.

"I'm afraid it will probably be a bunch of rough single men," Jenny replied.

"Veterans," I added. "We're a bunch of independent personal security consultants."

"Makes sense. Why do you want to work a horse ranch?"

I looked at Jenny, and she explained, "We want to be out of the way, not necessarily work the horse ranch. We will avail ourselves of some of the extras, but generally, we would like to use your meeting room for directed training and then use your land for a few physical training exercises, one being a laser training live-fire."

"Part of staying here is you have to work the ranch, clean out stalls, haul feed, those kinds of things. If you had more pretty girls coming, I'm sure I could arrange to have that taken care of."

"Stop with that nonsense." An old woman walked in, looking like a refugee from a Louis L'Amour novel. "I want to meet our future guests, especially since I'll be doing the cooking. I'm Mabel, and this cantankerous old coot is my husband Buck."

"I see who's in charge." Jenny winked at the old woman.

"Damn straight. I'll work with you on the menu, and he can reserve the horses and set up the work schedule."

I rubbed my chin. "If no one was going to be here, then you would have had to take care of the horses. I'm not sure we want to do that. We're not here for the ranch experience as much as to be off the beaten path and enjoy what you have to offer."

"It'll cost you extra." Buck tipped his head back as if he'd played a trump card.

"Done!" Jenny declared without negotiating before she caught herself. "How much extra? And the menu?"

Buck answered first. "Five percent kicker if you don't help clean the barn."

"Beef, beans, and greens. Some beer he makes that isn't drinkable, but we have tea, too, and coffee."

"Sounds perfect. Bacon and eggs for breakfast?"

"Either that or biscuits and gravy. We didn't get to looking like this because we don't eat well. There you go. We've worked on the menu, and it's set." She waved and walked away.

"Your meeting room?" I asked.

Buck led us to the first door down the short hallway to the kitchen and dining room. He showed us a space currently set with three round tables. Without them, it would easily seat twenty. We'd configure it as needed when the time came, depending on how many showed up.

"I'm ready to sign the contract," Jenny said. "And we'll pay in full up front. I hope you don't mind."

"I'll take that deal every day of the week and twice on Sunday." He gestured for us to follow him behind the counter.

From the looks of Buck's office, filing and organization were not his strong suit. Piles of papers and books occupied the single desk in the middle of the room. He sat behind it, reached into the drawer, and pulled out a simple piece of paper with blanks to fill in. He confirmed the dates, hand-wrote them in, then asked for the name of the group.

Jenny looked at me. "Security Enterprises, Inc," I replied, not knowing if it was real. Buck wrote that in. Poked numbers into the old calculator he dug out from under a pile. "Four nights times twenty rooms times two hundred dollars a night…" He stopped and looked at Miss Jenny. "You two can have your room for free."

"We thank you," I replied. "You assume we're together."

"If you're not, then you should be. Stop pussy-footing around and marry this gal!" He stopped calculating and stared at me.

"I already did because there was no way on God's green earth I was going to lose her."

"Good!" Buck returned to his ciphering, having to cancel everything and start over after the interruption. "That'll be fifteen thousand, two hundred dollars, and adding the state hotel tax, it'll be an even nineteen thousand."

I tried to hand over the gold card, but Buck held up his hands, refusing to take it. He pointed at his desk. "Do you think anyone lets me handle the money?" He pointed at the piles of papers. "We'll do that up front."

We stood. He looked me up and down. "You look like you can handle yourself. Ever been hurt?"

"In the Corps." I pulled up my shirt to show my scars. The .45 was tucked into the back of my waistband. "Good for a Purple Heart, or in other words, a bad-guy marksmanship badge."

The old man lifted his shirt. Lines, white from age, traced up and down his back. He had a holster at the small of his back, too.

"When Charlie thinks you have information and they want it..." His voice trailed off before snapping back to the present. "Marines got me out of that mess. Made for a long two days. Semper fi, bud."

"I see why you wanted to get away and start a horse ranch and why you ride every day. There's freedom in these hills, isn't there?"

"All a man needs is a job and a good woman by his side."

"Something like that," I agreed. Jenny wrapped her arm around my waist.

"Purpose and partnership," Jenny clarified.

"She's the smart one." Buck raised his eyebrows. "Every couple needs one. You know who holds that title in this house." He pointed at the wall where the kitchen was on the other side.

At the counter, I told the clerk to run the charge for twenty-five thousand.

"You don't need to do that," Buck complained.

"I know. You're helping us out. Do you have any rooms for tonight? I don't feel like getting back on the road." Jenny nodded and hugged me close.

"Give them the honeymoon suite," Buck told the clerk. "No additional charge, of course."

"I heard dinner was beef, beans, and greens." I looked at the old cowboy for confirmation.

"At seven sharp. Don't be late." Buck clumped back into his office.

"Would you like to go for a ride?" The clerk offered. His nametag said Jed. "Dusty is out there right now. He has a couple horses saddled and ready to go. These horses are more docile, shall we say."

I knew the implication. "You mean, horses that even a moron like me could ride?"

"We try to be careful in not offending our tenderfoot guests." He grinned broadly.

"I'll wear the title proudly. What do you think, Miss Jenny?"

"I think we'll dump our stuff in the room and be right back. I'd love to go for a ride."

Once outside, I had to share my secret. I looked around before I said it. "I've never ridden a horse before."

"And after today, you still won't have ridden one, not real riding. These horses will follow the leader. It's like a camel ride at the fair."

"I have ridden a camel, which is something I prefer not to do ever again." We had thought it was a good idea when on liberty in the Middle East. It wasn't.

"I'm sure this will be better than a camel ride."

We had one small bag, being experts in packing light.

Even Jenny because she knew we could buy whatever we needed, although reality had shown that we didn't need much.

"I'm glad we wore jeans," I said sarcastically. Both of us were in shorts and with the weather, we hadn't brought any jeans with us.

"I'm sure they'll have a soft cushy for your tushie." Jenny was less than sympathetic.

"Don't tell me you're an old hand at riding."

"Okay. I won't tell you." She smiled before holding her head high and walking briskly.

"I suppose November is going to call for a whole new horse-babe wardrobe."

She glanced over her shoulder at me. "You know it."

I caught up and stopped her. "This is perfect. Thank you for getting it." I kissed her but pulled away quickly. "You taste like rock dust."

"It's called sexy cowgirl."

"I'm not a fan."

She shrugged. If that was the worst problem I had that day, life wasn't too bad.

Dusty was an aptly named young man since he was covered with the fine red particles common to the area. Three roans, already saddled, stood in a small corral. He opened the gate and invited us in.

"Welcome to the Circle B. We provide horse training for our guests, but we also breed horses for sale to other working ranches."

"We just came for a simple ride. I'm not a horse guy."

"Teaching you about horses is done a little at a time. You'll find with each ride, you learn more about the graceful animals allowing you to sit on their backs. Be one with your trusty steed."

"That's what I meant to say."

Jenny gave me the side-eye. "I've ridden before. A lot. Please watch him to make sure he doesn't kill himself. I like having him around."

"Your wish is my command." Dusty swept his cowboy hat off while bowing deeply.

I waited while Jenny expertly mounted her horse by grabbing the pommel on the saddle, putting her left foot in the stirrup, and bouncing a couple times to jump and throw her leg over the horse, settling easily into the saddle.

"I needed help the last time I rode."

I followed Jenny's lead and was able to mount the horse on the second try. Dusty made quick work of getting into his saddle. He rode to the gate, where his horse turned sideways, allowing him to flip the latch. It backed up, and he pulled the gate inward to open it.

He pranced out and our two horses followed, heads down, walking at a measured pace. I stroked my mare's strong neck. "Aren't you a good horse?" I cooed.

A tan appaloosa galloped past with Buck in the saddle. He ran a short way ahead before stopping and trotting back to us. Dusty saluted and kept going. Our horses dutifully followed.

"Dusty will take you on a short walk around the property. Maybe thirty minutes. Any more, and you won't be able to walk afterward. Or sit. Or be comfortable in any way."

"Thirty minutes sounds just about right."

Buck loped ahead and disappeared into the low trees. We passed a barn and a second stable on our way to another gate that Buck had left open for us. He rode farther ahead, trotting easily. He looked to be one with his horse. I could see the allure, but it wasn't for me. My roan kept a steady pace. The mare had one job and was doing it. Follow the trail. No excitement.

We started climbing a low hill. The trail narrowed as the trees closed in. A commotion in front of Dusty caused his roan to rear. He held on, shifting his weight as he needed to. The riderless appaloosa crashed through the trees beside us, going the other way. Dusty spurred his horse to a lope, but ours maintained the same slow pace. I jumped off and sprinted past Jenny and up the trail.

Buck was on the ground, while Dusty's mount jumped up and down, hammering the ground with her front hooves. I saw the movement before I heard the rattles.

The horse was in the way. There was no more time. I dropped to a knee, aimed, and fired.

Dust kicked up between the prancing hooves as the round split the rattler in two, flipping it to the side of the trail. I got up and ran, hoping that Buck hadn't been bitten. I checked the area before kneeling beside the old man. Dusty worked to calm his mount.

"Hey, old fella," I called while checking his legs and arms for a snakebite. He was clean except for the bump on his head.

He stirred. "The older you get, the farther away the ground gets. Harder, too. Help me up, young fella."

"Army head, hard as a rock," I replied.

"Damn straight," Buck agreed. Once on his feet, he was able to see the area. He scanned the ground for the snake, stopping when he noticed what was left of the rattler. The old man snapped his fingers, and Dusty rummaged in a saddlebag to bring out a burlap bag. Buck drew a knife, cut off the head, and put the rest in the bag. "These are good eating."

Jenny finally rode up leading my horse, and I said, "Hop

on, Buck. I'll walk. Me and horses aren't quite on speaking terms, but they'll see it my way in the end. If they don't, then it's clearly not the end."

Buck did not feel like himself because he didn't argue. I helped him onto my old mare. Dusty took the lead horse's rein and pulled his head around. I gripped my former mount's reins and headed back toward the ranch.

"You have a nice piece of property, Buck. I look forward to bringing my people here to enjoy it."

"Sure," Buck replied before nodding toward my back. "Is that an M1911?"

"A1. Yep." I pulled it out, unchambered the round, dropped the magazine, and handed it to Buck. He looked it over well before giving it back. It still smelled of gunpowder. There was a faint layer of dust on it already. I needed to clean the weapon.

He pulled his hand cannon out, made it safe, and held it by the barrel to offer to me. "A Desert Eagle. Nice piece of gear, Buck." I admired it before handing it back. It was almost brand new. I guessed he hadn't fired more than a few magazines through it, if that many.

"I never had time to pull it out before General Patton tossed me."

"Do we have to go looking for your horse?"

"Nah. He'll be at the corral, wondering what happened. He may be a beauty, but he's about as dumb as a box of rocks."

I snorted and kept walking down the trail. Mud tendrils trailed down my legs from the dust clinging to my sweat. I wasn't sure if any washing machine would get the dust out of my clothes. I'd tell the operators that on the invitation. *Be prepared to burn your clothes at the end of the event.*

We could make the property work for all the events I had in mind. The lower area contained an open pasture and included a lightly wooded area. Within that space, tactics and maneuvers could be taught. A short class on not being seen. The possibilities rolled through my mind as I walked. Feeling the ground beneath my feet was much better for my mind than riding. We'd already accomplished everything I wanted from this part of the trip.

"There's my dumb horse," Buck grumbled. The appaloosa waited at the gate to the stable. I pulled the mare to a stop, and Buck slid down. He steadied himself and strolled toward his horse, clicking his tongue as he got close. The beast whinnied to welcome his master back. Buck pulled something from his pocket to feed the horse— a sugar cube. He gently stroked the stallion's nose.

Despite the names he called it, he loved that beautiful horse.

Jenny slipped down the side of her ride. Dusty gathered up the reins and wished us well. Hand in hand, we walked back to the main house.

"I could use a shower."

"That's an invitation I can't turn down," I declared as I patted her backside.

"Shameless." She slapped at my hand. "Are you ever going to grow tired of being with me?"

I thought that might be a setup question, and I didn't know what kind of answer Jenny was looking for, so I gave her the truth with a twist. "Not a chance in hell. And don't get yourself killed because I enjoy having you around, too."

CHAPTER TEN

"The greater danger for most of us lies not in setting our aim too high and falling short; but in setting our aim too low and achieving our mark." Michelangelo

Mabel wasn't kidding. She threw down slabs of beef that could have been roasts, a steak, or some hybrid. Slow-baked beans and steamed green beans were the foundation of our evening meal. Gravy and buttermilk biscuits were on the side. Jenny looked at the quantity of food, knowing that she couldn't eat it all. The three families with a mess of kids ate family-style.

"We have our work cut out for us, Mrs. Bond." I did my best Sean Connery, but it fell flat.

"I'll see what I can do," Jenny conceded. We hadn't eaten lunch, so there was that. She whispered, "Did you check the bids?"

"Not yet. I will as soon as we're done. We had two when we left, but both were underwhelming."

Jenny already knew that I wanted better.

Buck strolled in, clumping in his cowboy boots, and joined us. Mabel put a plate in front of him.

"Here you go, Buck. Take half of mine," Jenny said, and she started to cut.

Buck sized me up. "What do you really do, Ian?"

"Security," I lied in an even tone.

"Dusty told me about that shot you made. A winding rattler between a bucking horse's legs. That's not something your average mall cop can do."

"I learned to shoot in the Corps, a lot better than average. I like staying sharp. Private security, Buck. Anonymous clients, so don't ask questions that I can't answer. Just celebrate another day of life."

"You old coot!" Mabel exclaimed before rushing away.

We chuckled together.

"She keeps me on the straight and narrow. How about a special treat? You ever had rattler?"

"Can't say that I have." I looked at Jenny. She made a face and shook her head.

"You'll like it. You're meat and potatoes people. I have to run off those vegans. We can't accommodate them. I send them down the road to those hippie places in Sedona."

Jenny snorted and then coughed to try to hide it, but Buck was onto her. "Not you, too?"

She took a bite of her steak and started to chew.

"Good." Buck examined the portion Jenny had deposited on his plate.

I glanced over, and she was still chewing. It was my turn to laugh. Buck produced a bottle of Heinz 57 and dumped a generous portion on his plate. He put the bottle on the table. Jenny immediately helped herself and then shoved the bottle into my hand.

We'd been spoiled by five-star steakhouses and filets

that melted like butter. This was a completely different world. Earthy beef cooked hard. Welcome to the dude ranch experience. I started with the beans. After one bite, I was convinced they were the best I'd ever eaten. I cut the steak into smaller-than-normal bites to limit the amount of time I had to chew it.

Jenny finally managed to swallow her first bite. She started on the beans and nodded to me in agreement with the smile on my face.

Every place has its specialty. What Mabel lacked in steak-cooking finesse, she made up for with a kettle of slow-cooking great northerns, seasoned to perfection.

When she returned from the kitchen, she carried a small platter with a center dish of a honey-mustard dip surrounded by breaded and deep-fried circlets of snake.

"I would have let it soak overnight in buttermilk, but Buck wanted to have it with you. Don't be shy with the dipping sauce. There's more where that came from."

Buck took one in his fingers, but it was still hot. He tossed it back and forth until he dropped it on his plate. He stabbed it with a fork and dipped it deep into the sauce. He popped the whole thing into his mouth as if he were eating a scallop. He chewed with his eyes closed, a smile spreading across his face.

Mabel grinned at us. "I tried one back in the kitchen. This was a good kill, not too young, not too old, most of the meat intact. Enjoy!"

She bustled away to handle the other tables.

Jenny and I looked at each other. Buck caught us making faces. "Damn city folk!"

I surrendered and dug my fork into one, dipped it in the sauce until it was completely coated, and stuffed it into my mouth. The sauce had a tang that covered some of the different taste of the meat. It wasn't bad. I wouldn't go out of my way to eat more, but I wasn't repulsed.

"Go ahead. It's fine," I told my wife. "To the victor, the spoils. In the Old West, we have a tendency to eat the loser in life and death fights."

"Exactly." Buck took another one and then started eating them like potato chips. Jenny had one, and I ate one more in solidarity with my fellow veteran.

"I thank you for the use of your place in November. We'll make you proud and won't be busting anything up. I'm not sure any of our people are drinkers. We have to keep our wits about us at all times."

"It's better that way. If you'll excuse me, there's a lot of work to do cleaning up the kitchen."

"Do you need a hand? We can help." Jenny agreed with my offer.

"You'd do that?" Buck asked before shaking his head. "I'll have to turn you down. Mabel would tan my hide if I didn't carry my weight. I do appreciate it. You're the only guests who ever offered to help clean up the kitchen. I knew you were special when I talked with you on the phone, little lady. Both of you. We'll make sure your event goes off without a hitch. Think about a horse ride or two. Everyone loves those."

Buck stood, tipped his cowboy hat to us, and headed toward the kitchen. He pinched Mabel's butt as he passed.

"I want to be them when I grow up," Jenny remarked.

"I want a good bidder on the fund manager and good info on our friend from Tucson," I replied, getting back to business. I ate barely a third of the meat but devoured everything else. I started getting antsy.

Jenny saw it. "To the room and the internet for my urban cowboy."

"Got work to do to afford this lavish lifestyle of ours." I

took in the entirety of the rustic dining room. "I'm not belittling this. I think Buck and Mabel are great. This is going to work out perfectly as a location, which means the rest is up to us. We'll need to gear up with laser games and presentations and successful contracts."

Jenny leaned close. "Making the world a better place, one contract at a time. Makes you sound like a lawyer."

"Bringing justice where it otherwise wouldn't be found."

"Live for today but plan for tomorrow," Jenny replied with yet another of our one-liners.

"Lots of work to do." I pushed back from the table, sorry to see so much leftover. I'd have to ask Mabel to cut back on the portion size for the retreat. I didn't need everyone in a food coma because the Archive would be asking for their full attention. If we got it wrong, the domino of bad things that could happen would start falling, and nothing could stop them.

We retired to the honeymoon suite, where we found a box of local chocolates on the turned-down king-sized bed. We set them aside for later. I pulled the laptop out of my bag and accessed the Wi-Fi, then used my VPN to make my computer and me disappear from prying cyber-eyes.

I raced through the labyrinth of memorized access pathways to get to the back side of the Archive bulletin board. Still only two bids on the hedge fund manager. I double-checked to make sure they were the same. One bid for two million by an operator with eight prior contracts. He appeared to be fishing for the max payout. My guess would be an operator getting ready to leave the game. The other bid was for the minimum but had zero successful contracts. Experience or exuberant youth?

Neither. Maybe give the first timer a chance. If that

contract was an SEC hit, it wouldn't be scrutinized too much by the feds. That's what I hoped. It would give us over a million of overhead for the company coffers.

I didn't care about my bonus. I was making more money than I ever had. I looked at Jenny, who was sitting cross-legged on the bed, searching for a television station showing something interesting. This wasn't a smart TV, and the place was barely wired for electricity, let alone snooping or subterfuge. We had checked and found it clean of bugs and other devices. I was amazed at the quality of the internet. It was probably the desk clerk's doing since he was from the younger generation, and the internet was a critical component of his life.

"What?" Jenny asked when she caught me staring.

"We're not in this for the money." It was a theme I was embracing more and more as time went on. As I matured.

She smiled at me. "Forego our lavish lifestyle? I kid about a new wardrobe and stuff like that, but you know none of that matters to me. We're fine if we never make another penny and have to live off your savings."

"*Our* savings." I chewed the inside of my cheek as I studied the bids. I almost impulse-clicked the approval for the newcomer but decided to wait. "We'll give it another day. I want these in the rearview mirror so we can focus on the future."

"I think you will constantly have one or two contracts in the queue."

"There can't be that many rich people mad at other rich people."

"What if it's government agencies? There will be an endless stream of applicants. Hiring the Archive is an easy way to shortcut the process. I know you're right, and I'm afraid that we might be able to prove it. I don't think we want any of that action."

"The wisdom of youth," I said, shutting my computer and joining Jenny on the bed.

"I'm a year younger than you."

"Forever twenty-nine." I looked at the chocolates but didn't think I had room for one. "The government angle will be a new tightrope that we'll have to walk. You think the new hedge fund manager was because of the other guy?"

"I do. It makes the most sense. The SEC sees a way to clean up the bad actors without looking like they're going on a crusade. It gives them leverage to coax those about to go over the ledge to stay on the right side of the law."

"I'm Marshall Dillon," I said.

"Maybe a less wheezy Doc Holliday," Jenny countered.

I adjusted how I was lying. The bed became less comfortable with each passing moment. "Uh-oh." I could feel it building up inside of me. The pressure became unbearable. "I may have to take a raincheck on sexy night. I think I went too hard on the baked beans."

I bolted for the bathroom and locked myself in. I heard Jenny chuckling. I was about to find out how not funny it was.

The University of Arizona dominated a part of Tucson, with "A" Mountain sitting majestically on the western side of the city. According to the Drug Enforcement Administration, the DEA, Tucson was in the primary corridor for high-intensity drug trafficking between Mexico and the United States.

Otherwise, it was a pleasant city with a decent museum scene, a world-class observatory, and plenty of nature preserves as a testimonial to life in the desert. It was also the home of the military's largest airplane graveyard. I had never been there and wanted to see it. We couldn't get access because it was located on Davis-Monthan Air Force Base, but we could drive by the perimeter and ogle the planes.

Felipe Gomez lived on the other side of town, and that's where we'd spend most of our time observing from afar.

"What do you expect to get from this?" Jenny asked for the twelfth time.

"That this is a bad dude that has some vulnerabilities. We need to be able to make the hit. I need to personally see what kind of security he travels with. He might not have a vulnerability that a single operator could exploit and then escape from."

My answers were getting better with each iteration. "I'll buy that. What if someone bids two mil and two months?"

"I would give them all the credibility in the world and award them the contract."

"What happens if they disappear after getting the first half?" Jenny wondered.

"Then I'll have to handle it personally." I took her hand. "It's the law of the jungle, baby."

"What if they try and miss?"

"Then it'll make their job that much harder for the second try. The way it works is we only have to get lucky once, while the target has to be lucky all day, every day."

"I can't see too well," Jenny said, squinting through the windshield past the overlook across a cut at a house surrounded by a high wall.

"We need to buy binoculars and a book on bird-watching."

"Bird-watching?"

"For when the cops ask us what we're doing watching

the house across the valley. Expect to be stopped, be clean when they stop us."

I pulled out after we'd only been there for a couple minutes, not long enough to arouse suspicion. Watching the house was going to be a long-term effort. A young couple watching desert birds would be innocuous.

Plan for the worst. That was why I had left the M1911A1 with Buck, a .45 caliber piece that Jenny's dad had acquired. It was a classic and a good shooter. I'd put enough rounds through it that I was comfortable with the weapon. I would always be more comfortable packing, but there were times when it wasn't optimal. Like now, in the drug capital of Arizona, while casing a kingpin.

As long as we didn't get too close to Mr. Gomez, when a heavy-caliber weapon would probably come in handy.

We drove to a Walmart to pick up the supplies we'd need for our observation. Binoculars, a guide to the desertscape, a book on birds of the Southwest, a blanket, a case of condoms, and snacks.

I hoped we wouldn't need any of it but didn't want to leave anything to chance.

It was still too early to check in at the hotel, so we drove around the neighborhood, avoiding passing the same location twice.

Gomez's homestead dominated the end of a lane. We didn't enter because there was only one house with a gate and a long driveway at the end of the road. We stopped around a corner where I could look for places to see the gate, which was tucked into an arroyo, hiding it from casual observation.

A white SUV with dark windows passed us, heading for the end of the lane. I let the car roll backward until we could see. The vehicle stopped, and a driver stuck an elbow out. A cactus prevented me from seeing the intercom, which probably also included a camera. The gate retracted, and the SUV drove through. The gate closed after it passed. A person appeared on the other side of the gate and faced down the lane.

I felt like he was looking directly at us. I put the car in gear and drove slowly away. There was no need to draw additional attention to us by burning rubber on our way out.

"Why the intercom if someone was there?"

"Redundancy. If the guy on gate duty can't make any decisions, then he can't be swayed by a good story. Only the faceless voices from a security room can let people in and out. The gate guard can keep people from sneaking in when the gate is open."

"That's next-level paranoia."

"Not something your average real estate developer puts into place."

Jenny looked out the window. "So much brown here. It's like Vegas without the bright lights."

"One desert looks like the next, but only kind of. They're all different. Saguaros down here break up the brush and sand. Vegas doesn't have much of anything that grows."

"Some realtors have enemies because they develop land where people want to keep it for nature."

"Felipe develops the desert, and since he's not a real developer, he buys desert land and bulldozes a road to it and through it. That's about it from what I've read."

"Surely the feds have to be curious where he gets enough money to afford his fortress and the army to man it."

"It's not against the law to be rich," I replied. "As long as he never had to show how he became wealthy in the first place, he'll stay out of the legal system's sights."

"I expect the DEA tried to get the IRS to investigate him. An audit, maybe?"

"I wish I knew what had been tried to see where his pressure points are. Maybe he could be lured into something. What the hell?"

In the rearview, a squad car closed with its lights flashing. I pulled over to let them pass, but they pulled in behind me, front end angled toward the road to give my car space.

"Get out the registration and insurance card," I said.

Jenny dug through the glove compartment until she found the title and an insurance card from a fly-by-night company that took my cash and didn't ask too many questions. I pulled my license out of my minimalist wallet.

I put the three items on the dash, rolled down the window, and kept my hands on the wheel.

A sole uniform eventually exited the car and strolled up beside my window. He stayed well back. "License and registration, please.

"I have my driver's license, insurance card, and the bill of sale on this vehicle. I haven't changed over the registration yet." I handed them over my shoulder. The officer took them and returned to his car. He tapped stuff into his computer and talked on his smartphone.

Not the radio.

"I think we have ourselves a policeman moonlighting as private security for our Mr. Gomez," I suggested, watching every move he made in the rearview mirror.

"Can he pull us over for no reason?"

"No. But to prove he's in the wrong, we'd have to take it to court, which I'm not about to do. But this helps shape the dossier. I'm not forming a lovingly wonderful opinion of Felipe."

Jenny opened a snack and started eating. "Will they take the car?"

"I don't think so because then he'd have to answer a bunch of questions at the station, starting with the probable cause on why he pulled us over. I'm sure he has a standard phrase he uses. Here he comes."

We both sat straight and waited for the lifetime it took for him to get from his car to my window.

"Mr. Lawless. You had ten days to register your California vehicle. That was three months ago."

"I remembered that I had forgotten that until I saw your lights in the rearview. We live in Vegas but picked up the car on a whim in California. It's been a great vehicle. We'll register it as soon as we get home in a couple days."

I kept my hands on the steering wheel where he could see them. I was happy to have two IDs in my wallet, one with my Lawless persona that I had never used before.

"What are you doing in this neighborhood, Mr. Lawless?"

Straight to the point. I preferred that.

"We look like trailer trash driving through the high-rent district. We can dream about being able to live in a place like this. It's the closest we'll get to this kind of lifestyle. I'm between jobs right now. There are prospects, but none of them would put us into a place like this. Just dreaming, my man, before heading back with the riffraff where we belong."

He handed back the title, my driver's license, and the insurance card.

"Get your car registered as soon as you get back and don't bother coming back up here. Dreams about homes like these won't do you any good. You have a nice day."

I didn't bother to reply. I started the car, checked for traffic, signaled, and drove out.

"That kind of top cover is going to make the hit extremely complicated." I headed straight for our hotel, a ranch resort that wasn't part of a chain. I wasn't upset about getting pulled over. At least they didn't have any record of Ian Bragg. "How can we surveil the house if we can't be seen in the area?"

"You've always wanted to try one of those drones," Jenny said softly.

"I have. We'll take the overland route on foot, come in from the far side. Let's see if we can buy a drone with a range of a mile or more. We're going to need a few bottles of water. Are you up for a hike, Mrs. Bragg?"

"I am always up for experiencing life with you, Mr. Bragg." Jenny tapped on her phone. I followed my GPS to the hotel less than a mile away. "We may not have to hike very far. How about a drone with a range of more than five miles?"

"Well, now, that offers a completely different set of options." We pulled into the hotel's meandering parking lot.

Jenny took my phone, typed in a new address, and pressed Go. "There's a dealer in town for the DJI Mavic Zoom 2. They even have one in stock."

"We could be up and running in no time." I turned up the music. *Hemispheres* was playing. Not my favorite album, but Rush is Rush.

CHAPTER ELEVEN

"Time spent in reconnaissance is seldom wasted." Philip Marsden

Our test flight in an open area behind the hotel proved that our drone was an advanced piece of gear. It wasn't as easy as an on-screen video game. It felt like flying a plane, but the four rotors made it seem more stable than a winged craft. I took off and landed several times before taking it out for an extended flight, mainly beyond where I could see it, but just barely. I didn't want to scour a neighborhood looking for an expensive crashed toy.

Plus, it was their only one in stock. I watched the screen on my phone linked to the video feed from the drone and reversed course, both hands on the control pad in my lap. I guided the drone back over the field and descended slowly to land it before us.

Jenny shook her head at the stupid smile on my face.

"Nice to know it worked. That'll save us a fair bit of walking, I think," she noted.

"Yes, but we still have to maintain some line of sight to the drone. Otherwise, we could lose the signal. Then drone fall down and go boom."

"Is that your technical evaluation?"

"It is my learned opinion. Let's recharge this thing and check the boards. We'll have a full day tomorrow. I'll build out the first parts of a dossier. This one is going to be complex, to say the least. I still can't tell you if he's good or bad." I looked around to make sure no one was near. "Maybe he's a good guy on the run from a cartel. We have to be sure."

"We have to be sure," Jenny parroted. We carried our prize back to the room, then settled in. Jenny checked out the room service menu while I jumped online.

"Another bid, thank goodness, and it's the woman." I didn't know what else to call her, but she was already my favorite. Her bid was one and a quarter million this time. We had room to maneuver. I accepted her bid without further delay. "Damn."

"Isn't that what you wanted?"

"I think she's the one I want for this gig."

"Maybe she'll finish the hedge fund quickly, just like the last one."

"Two days. That was amazing. She's feathering her nest at a high rate of speed, and I'm good with that. Maybe she likes what she does."

Jenny frowned. "You never *liked* it."

"I accepted it as a job that had to be done to make the world a safer place, but no, I never liked it. I was good at it. I am good at it. I do it so others don't have to."

"I know, sweetie. I love you for it. I love you in spite of it. I will love you if you keep doing it or if you retire. I will support whatever decision you make because I know your heart is in the right place. A hitman with a conscience who judges more harshly than any person could."

I knew Jenny supported me, but it was always nice to hear. The simplest words sometimes had the biggest impact. I needed to figure out what made Felipe Gomez tick. I wanted the woman to be quick with the hedge fund manager, so she'd be available for this job. This guy wasn't clean, but I didn't know if he was dirty enough for a death sentence.

Just like pornography, I'd know it when I saw it. If I did, I'd publish the request for bids.

The next morning, drinking my first cup of hotel room coffee before Jenny awoke, I dug as deeply as I could get through the dark web looking for anything incriminating on Mr. Gomez, but it all ended with speculation. None of the go-betweens turned on him. No street dealers named him; those leads stopped at dead ends.

Other arrested dealers gave up their suppliers, but not Gomez. The others remained elusive, some living outside the States, all of them staying out of the public eye.

Which suggested that Felipe Gomez had his meat hooks into law enforcement, both local and federal. Getting stopped for no reason convinced me that at least the street patrol had been infiltrated. I wished I knew who put up the money for the contract.

Screw plausible deniability. If we were to do this right, I needed as much information as possible.

They didn't care about right. They were paying for results. They were buying an individual to be sacrificed on the altar of expediency. Even though I hadn't met any of my operators, they were my people, and I had to protect them.

I leaned back in the chair to stare at the screen in the dark of the early morning. I kept circling back to my responsibility. Dead operators tell no tales. Captured operators spill their guts. Would they know enough to finger me? Not now, but once we trained, they might.

No. Nicknames for all the players. Chosen at random. No pictures. And we'd go in and scrub the contract to leave no record of Ian Bragg. The nice guy next door that Buck wouldn't give up, no matter how hard law enforcement pushed. Could the same be said of Dusty?

We'd do some name changing sleight of hand and bury the records as soon we got back to the ranch. Until then, we had the minions of Felipe Gomez breathing down our necks. I did a map study of the area and came up with a viable entry point from the other side of the hill. It meant walking but would be outside the jurisdiction of the Gomez neighborhood.

I expected the same policeman wouldn't be around to confront us since it was ten miles out of his way to get where we'd park. Peaceful bird watchers, doing nothing to nobody. A couple of crazy kids carrying their toy drone up the mountain on a trail.

A fourteen-hundred-dollar drone with a range of eight kilometers and a total flight time of thirty minutes. One man's toy was another's surveillance system, like using a baby monitor to record a conversation.

Or using a magnetic GPS tracker on a potential target instead of on a teen driver taking the family car on a date.

I continued dabbling with various search phrases to find anything I could on Felipe Gomez but continued to come up empty. Maybe there was no Felipe Gomez. I set my VPN to act like it was coming from Mexico City and started searching for the property records. Someone had to sign the dotted line, and it had to be notarized. Who bought that land? Who filed the building permits?

It didn't add up. A Rachel Smith had paid for the property and was the name on the background documents. That was too easy. A front? A lackey? An alias? It led to more questions than answers.

Searching Rachel Smith led almost nowhere. Almost. A blog by a reporter wannabe connected the same dots I had found. Antoine Hernandez had gone more in-depth, detailing a string of connections that tied Rachel to Felipe. His final conclusion was that they were the same person. He opined that the person shown in grainy pictures was a bodyguard or stand-in and that the blonde woman next to him or trailing behind was the kingpin.

How could I have missed that?

Because I was looking for who proposed the contract more than I looked into the target. I searched for information on Antoine Hernandez. He worked as a line chef at a local restaurant. After our first flight, we'd head out for lunch and speak with Mr. Hernandez. I wanted to see how scared he was or if he was simply a conspiracy theorist. From what I saw, he was the only one who had an opinion of what was really going on.

Maybe that was why Felipe Gomez had never been arrested. The personality was buried, and without probable cause, the police could never get a face-to-face meeting. Lawyers held them off. Local cops kept people away from the property.

If there was a woman at the heart of the organization, it changed nothing, but the contract was for Felipe Gomez. Another instance where it would be nice to have a conversation with the requestor. I wasn't a fan of getting set up to fail.

I dug more but came up with nothing. Jenny stirred, slowly opened her eyes, and looked at me. She patted the bed next to her. I joined her so she could hug me while waking up slowly.

"Whatcha working on?"

"I don't think Felipe Gomez exists."

She chuckled. "That changes things. Can we go home now?" She waited for the rest of the story.

"I think Felipe might be the alter ego of a woman named Rachel Smith."

"Then why didn't the DEA place the call for her instead of the guy?"

"That's where law enforcement stopped. They discounted the link and went right for the name they kept hearing instead of rooting out a secretive individual. I don't think they'll ever find him unless they get too close, then a convenient lackey will get sacrificed for the cause while the organization lives on."

"Devious. Are we still hiking into the mountains?"

"You bet. I want a closer look at that compound for the sake of the dossier. And we need to find a journalist called Antoine Hernandez. I know where he works. I hope you don't mind Mexican grill. It is Tucson, after all."

"It's for work, so we do what we have to." She threw the back of her hand to her forehead. "Shower time."

She climbed out of bed, naked as usual. "I don't get tired of this view."

Jenny looked at me. I had put on shorts since the fake leather desk chair was cold from the constant air conditioning. "Neither do I."

I looked at my computer, but it didn't have the allure of

life's other priorities. My stomach growled. I couldn't remember if the place had breakfast included or not or what the hours were. I checked the clock before catching myself. *You must be getting old when you put your stomach first,* I told myself as part of a cautionary tale.

The road to the back side of the hills surrounding the Gomez fortress was little more than a dirt track for a planned expansion. The far side only had views of a small valley and the mountains, unlike the southern face, where the city sprawled beneath the foothill mansions.

We parked at a place where the track was wide enough for someone to get by if they wanted. I checked my phone —no reception. I packed all our water into my backpack. Jenny carried the controller in her pack, and I carried the drone in my hand.

We headed out and up, climbing as much as walking. We went slowly because of our recent encounter with the rattlesnake. I didn't have the pistol this time. I would be hesitant to throw the drone at it, but getting bitten in a place where phones didn't work wasn't my idea of how to conduct a surveillance. We walked in silence while navigating to a point on the high side of the mountain directly behind the Gomez fortress.

Behind as well as a couple of miles distant. I was restricted from making a low pass because an intervening rise blocked our line of sight. I'd keep it just above and use the camera's zoom and pan features to get the views I wanted.

I put the drone on a rock, turned it on, and stepped back while Jenny removed the small control console. She clipped her phone into the bracket at the top, checked that the camera image was coming through the direct feed from the drone's camera, and gave me the thumbs-up.

With the city of Tucson before us, cell service had returned. I wondered if the drone would work without it. I hadn't checked the literature. Then again, it didn't matter. We were using it where we had service, not checking on nesting eagles deep in the mountains.

With the power on, the four blades spun nearly instantly to their flight speed. I thumbed the levers to lift the drone skyward and sent it skimming over the ground toward our target. I gained altitude to keep it clear of the saguaros. It raced across the valley and was soon little more than a dot at the edge of what I could see. I gave it more altitude and started watching the image from the camera.

I rotated it thirty degrees forward to get a view of where I was going. I raised it higher as the drone cleared the final ridge. The mansions and neighborhoods spread before me. "Can you tell where the hell I need to go?"

Jenny had been leaning over my shoulder, watching. She pointed at the upper left side of the screen. I took it easy, sending the drone in that direction. I slowed to a stop and rotated the drone through three hundred and sixty degrees. I saw where we were but couldn't see us. We were no more than specks in the distance.

"Is that it?" I stopped the rotation and zoomed in on the compound. The entry gate was clear beyond it.

"That's it. I think if you keep this altitude, you'll be able to fly around it. No one should notice. There's enough jet traffic." She ended with that hopeful thought. The drone had a high-pitched whine that sounded like an annoying bee. It forced people to look for it.

I flew toward the compound, rotating the camera and

circling the perimeter. Men with rifles walked inside the wall, stopping to look through strategic openings in the blockwork. The house's main section was three stories tall to get the best view of the city from the top floor balcony. In the back, a mother-in-law wing and pool house wrapped around an oversized kidney-shaped pool with a hot tub at one end.

Someone was sunbathing. I tried to zoom in on the individual. A woman, lightly tanned, wearing a bikini. An individual stood in the shade beyond. The sunbather turned to look in the direction of the drone. I kept it still. She talked briefly to the individual in the shade and then strolled to the pool, dove in, and started to swim laps.

I moved the drone to get a better look at the entire perimeter. Movement from around front alerted me—a couple of men with guns. I strained to see.

Not rifles but shotguns. They took aim at the camera. I almost fell over yanking the controls to bank the drone and bring it back at ninety degrees to where we were. I sent it skyward, rotating the camera backward while I climbed. Puffs of smoke suggested the men had fired.

"That was interesting." Once the drone cleared the last of the houses and came over the ridge, I dipped it low over the valley and turned it toward us, skimming the tops of the cacti on its way back to us.

"How did you know they were going to shoot?"

"Sense of urgency, and I've been shot at before. There's a feeling you get when someone is raising their weapon."

"I applaud your reactions." Jenny slow-clapped before shielding her eyes to look for the inbound drone. The high-pitched whine signaled it was getting close.

"I almost fell down." I slowed the drone as it approached and descended carefully, jockeying to land on the rock from which it had launched barely fifteen minutes earlier. "I want my toy back."

I powered it down, and the props stopped spinning. Jenny looked it over. "No worse for wear. They didn't hit it."

"And now it's time for us to hit the road because I'm sure the locals will be trolling the streets, looking for the evildoers." I tried to sound ominous. There wasn't another vehicle as far as the eye could see. This was a remote area of the desert hills. We scrabbled down the hill a lot faster than we climbed it. The drone and our backpacks went into the trunk. We hopped in and bolted away, bouncing down the dirt track at a blazing ten miles an hour until we made it to the newest construction and paved road.

We turned down the side roads to work our way into town. On a loop back, approaching the main road, a police cruiser raced by on its way toward the end of the current subdivision and where the dirt road started. When the unit was out of sight, we hit the road, speeding out of the subdivision and onto a high-speed access road.

"Point to note on this dossier. Once you're spotted, you'll be fighting everyone to get a clean shot. I don't see how anyone could get close enough to take her out, and I am convinced it's her. Rachel Smith and not some dude named Felipe Gomez. I hope we got a good enough picture of her when she stood up."

"She seems to keep herself in good shape, from what I saw," Jenny offered.

"Seems?"

"It's a shape that could be bought and paid for."

"Ah. I hadn't noticed." That earned me a gentle punch on the arm. I forced myself to relax my grip on the wheel once we entered normal city traffic. "What do you think about lunch?"

Jenny checked her watch. "It might be a little early still."

"Back to the hotel then, lovely lady. I'd like to take a closer look at that video."

We drove on main roads, then side roads, looped around in circles, and finally came to the hotel from the opposite side of the Catalina Foothills. I was certain we hadn't been followed.

We parked close to our room and intercepted the cleaning crew before they entered. "Would you look at that! We made it back early. No need to clean the room since we're just going to go in and mess everything up." I slipped the cleaner a five-dollar bill. She tried not to look at the drone in my hand.

"Fresh towels?" she offered.

"Do you have any coffee? I drank what we had."

She dug into her cart to find two new cups and four extra coffee pouches.

"You are the best!" I took them with a big smile as Jenny held the door for me. We disappeared inside with our backpacks and the drone, closing and locking the door. I dug the computer out of the safe and plugged in the SD card from the drone, which recorded the flight at the highest resolution.

We scrolled through until we came to the Gomez compound. Two men patrolling with two more we hadn't seen standing in the shadows. The wall around the compound had no gaps, only two pedestrian gates beside the main entrance. Driving meant one way in, one way out. A security system was prominently displayed on the corners of the house and outbuildings.

At the pool, the camera took high-resolution images of the woman. With a quality freeze frame, I cut out a number of pictures, both straight-on and profile. The look on her face said she was not amused by the interruption in her day. She did keep herself in good shape, but she wasn't young.

"How old do you think she is?"

"Let's start with the fundamentals. She's about five foot six, a hundred and twenty pounds, enhanced breasts, at least a D cup. I suspect she's easily forty, maybe forty-five."

"That old?" I couldn't keep the surprise out of my voice.

"Easily. Look at the skin on her arms. She's in shape, but there's age on that skin. We call them water wings, but not to anyone's face. I'll get them too soon, I fear. And from what we can see close up, there are the telltale wrinkles at the corners of her eyes. This is where some women are more successful fighting the good fight than others."

"That old?" I tried to see what Jenny was seeing, but it eluded me. I trusted her judgment. "Fine. Forty-five, looks thirty."

"You think she looks younger than me?" Jenny's tone left no doubt in my mind that I was in the danger zone.

I touched the side of her face and asked her to hold up her well-toned arms. "You are," I leaned close and whispered, "thirty-five." I sat back. "I do see the difference. At least forty, maybe forty-five."

Jenny smiled. I had extricated myself from a predicament of my own making. But Jenny had shown me a way to more precision. There were some important things a bikini couldn't hide.

We scrolled through the rest of the video to collect other details about the house, the property, and the security. The valet. The shotgun blasts. They had fired but had missed the drone by a wide margin. The quick juke had foiled their aim. I had felt as if they were aiming at me personally. I don't play video games because I can't separate myself from the action on the screen.

I closed the computer and locked it in the safe. I didn't have the thumb drive to store information for the dossier, and with access to the back end of the Archive bulletin board, I didn't need it. I could store everything there in the security of their digital vault. It was a necessity to put the contracts out for bid.

A good hacker couldn't break through. It was in the Peace Archive's vested interest to be secure from all eyes at all times. I trusted that and also expected that a good hacker wouldn't be able to link any of it to a specific person or location.

In our line of work, security and anonymity were paramount. In Rachel Smith's line of work, her personal safety was critical. Similar in how we each flew on the wrong side of the law. It was time to talk to Antoine Hernandez. We changed clothes and headed out.

"Getting hungry?" I asked.

"A little." Jenny rolled down the window and hung her elbow out. It was desert-pleasant, still in the 80s temperature-wise, not oppressive. "I can feel the strain on this case. Are you going to bid it out?"

I slowly shook my head. "Unless something changes, I'm having a hard time rationalizing putting someone into that line of fire."

"Plus, the proposal is wrong, if you are correct in that there is no Felipe Gomez. Will they complain if the woman is hit and not the man?"

"The Archive already has their money. Will the Archive go to bat for us if the woman isn't what they want? The ubiquitous 'they.' A quick conversation would help settle things, but I sure as hell don't want to do it. It was tough talking to Jimmy, but bureaucratic middlemen? I don't trust those knobs as far as I could throw them."

"Do we still need to meet with Antoine?"

"I think so. I want to clarify a few details in case the Archive talks to the folks who want the hit. Maybe they'll appreciate the lengths we go to in trying to get this right. They shouldn't take a death sentence lightly, and neither do we."

CHAPTER TWELVE

"Patience is not the ability to wait, but the ability to keep a good attitude while waiting." Anonymous

The restaurant could have used a new coat of paint and a new sign. Inside, the lights were dingy, the paths between the tables dirty from too much food dropped and not enough mops scrubbing it clean, and the few tables surrounded by a variety of chairs that looked like they'd been purchased at a second-hand store. It was a total dive. The servers yelled the orders at the kitchen. The customers yelled their orders at the servers.

And the aroma made my mouth water.

"What do you want?" a young girl shouted at us from behind the register, her finger hovering over the buttons. We went to the counter because I didn't feel like yelling to show that I didn't have the menu memorized.

Jenny pointed at me to go first. "How about a burrito and two tacos? One beef, one chicken."

"We might be out of chicken," she advised.

"Then two beef."

"And if we're out of beef?"

"Then it'll be really hard to make a beef taco."

She shouted over her shoulder as she tapped. "Chef's preference, one b, two t…"

Jenny stepped close. "Just a taco salad, beef if you have it, or vegetarian if you don't."

"Taco salad," the clerk yelled at the ceiling. "Grab a seat. I'll bring it to your table. Here are our world-famous nacho chips and salsa. Self-serve drinks over there." She pointed into the darkest corner. My eyes hadn't adjusted yet. Jenny headed over, and I selected the only open table. I tried the chips and salsa before Jenny returned.

She put two glasses of water on the table. "Self-serve drinks means there are pitchers of water on a table and a bunch of empty glasses."

I would have chosen water in any case, but I found the humor in the claim.

"Cuts down on overhead. I have no idea how world-class is defined, but these aren't bad." Jenny tried a chip and agreed.

We plowed through only half the plate by the time our food arrived. The server placed a couple of bottles of sauce on the table. I held up a twenty-dollar bill. "Is there any way we can talk to Antoine Hernandez?"

She took the money and tucked it into her bra before shouting toward the kitchen, "Antoine, customers on four."

"Thank you," I told her. She winked and walked away.

"Subtle," Jenny noted. "I like it."

I looked around the tables. No one watched. No one cared. It was the perfect place for an illicit meeting.

A line cook emerged from the kitchen, wiping his hands on a dirty apron before using it to wipe the sweat from his brow. I waved at him.

He sat down and hunched close, casting furtive glances at the customers. He looked at me. "I'm Antoine."

I spoke barely above a whisper. "I want to know more about Rachel Smith."

"You read my blog. Nice. Can you hire me as an investigative journalist? I could use some extra work."

"Rachel Smith. What aren't you saying in your blog that you know about her?"

"Flight of fancy. I put that out there to show how you can make certain facts fit any narrative you'd like. I want to be a journalist." He sat back and gestured toward the counter and the kitchen. "This isn't exactly what I had in mind as my life's ambition."

"They've gotten to you. That's fine. It'll help keep you safe. I do need more investigative work." I turned to Jenny. "Can you bring up her picture, please?"

Jenny tapped her screen to scroll through the captured stills. She brought up the best picture and adjusted it until the face filled the screen.

Antoine's face went white. "Where'd you get that?"

"Can't have you being afraid, Antoine. That's not how investigative journalists do their best work. Cautious, yes. Afraid, no. This is who we are focused on. This is the person we need more information about. And ultimately, this is the person we need to talk with. I am not with the government in any way. I'm with a private consortium that would like to talk with this individual." Jenny put her phone away.

Antoine struggled with relaxing. His head jerked back and forth at every sound.

"Antoine. I need you to focus. Give me your phone number, and I'll be in touch."

"No way. Give me yours."

"That's not how it works. I found out that you worked

here. How hard do you think it'll be to find your home and a phone number? That's not a threat. I'm not going to hunt you down. I mean you no harm, but we have a mutually beneficial interest in seeing this through. I will start paying you, but I need more information. I'll give you a thousand dollars today to thank you for your work to this point. If I get nothing else, it will still have been worth my money."

"I need two grand," he said, leaning close again, his eyes perking up.

"What makes you think this is a negotiation? You haven't agreed to do anything for me. I need something, Antoine, to demonstrate that you aren't going to disappear. You're the only one who has shown any desire to do this research and do it in the right way. What motivates you, Antoine?"

He gave us a half-smile. "Money." He laid his hand on the table, palm up.

"Then why did you look into Rachel Smith in the first place when you weren't getting paid? How much does it cost you to keep your blog going?" I looked at him from my position of power. He was afraid. I wasn't. He was desperate. He was out of his league. And he was the only one who tried to do anything about a notorious drug dealer who lived a lavish lifestyle on her drug business.

"I want to be a journalist."

"Then damn the torpedoes! Full steam ahead," I quoted. "I can hire you for one article, but I need a bit more. I will remain anonymous, and so will you until this breaks and the right people do the right things about it to make sure that you remain safe. Safer than you are now."

Antoine nodded. A gruff voice called his name from the kitchen. I reached into my pocket and took out my stack of hundred-dollar bills. I had fifteen of them left from my travel cash stash. I shoved them into his hand. "I'll split you the difference to show you that I'm serious. I need your phone number."

Jenny produced a pen and the pad of notepaper from the hotel. He wrote down his number and nodded as he walked away.

I sniffed the food on my plate. "Better than nothing," I suggested.

"The food or the cook?"

"He didn't tell us not to eat it, so I'm going to go with that as a good sign. He would know."

She chuckled. "Always so calm. How can you do that?"

"I'll think about it later. I'm already rerunning it in my head. That's how I give the appearance of calm. I'm not quick enough to understand the implications now. I'll be a nervous wreck later, but with the love of a good woman, I'll get through it."

"Uh-huh." Jenny didn't sound like she was convinced. I had just hired a research assistant. How was I going to keep him in the dark about me while getting what I needed from him?

"Let's finish and go home. There's no reason to stay here any longer."

Jenny dug into her taco salad, humming with pleasure at the taste. I tried my taco and then took too big a bite of the burrito. A total dive, the best place for down-home food. It was magnificent; I thought it might have been the best Mexican food I'd ever tasted. I expected I would pay for it later, but for that brief moment in time, life was good.

We drove the speed limit on the interstate highway that took us through Phoenix. We needed to stop by Buck's place to pick up the .45.

The drive was easy. We had Rush playing in the background, but when we passed through Phoenix, Jenny flipped on the radio and looked for a pop station. A little bubblegum music to go with the drive. We only got caught in one minor holdup.

"I'm happy to be out of Tucson."

"So am I, sweetie," Jenny replied. "Something didn't sit right about that place, all of it after we were pulled over, oddly enough, and it intensified when the cops came after us following our drone escapades."

I nodded. "We have a new toy. We'll play with it more back home. That thing is a bash!"

Jenny faced me, lifting her sunglasses to make sure I knew she was looking at me. Judging.

"I stopped maturing at twelve. You knew that when you married me. Now you're stuck." I smiled beatifically as I flopped my head sideways to meet her gaze, but only briefly. I was driving.

We continued north out of the big city. As soon as the radio station started to break up, I switched back to my music player. I dialed up *Dreamline* to make sure Jenny saw the wisdom and sound philosophy of listening to Rush. She gave me the side-eye before reaching for my hand. I held hers as we drove, thinking about communication with the Archive to make more informed decisions that protected everyone's interests.

I had a list of things I wanted to talk to them about. I also had three two-zero-two area code phone numbers with the sixth and seventh digits being low numbers. I could send the message for a phone call for the low price of thirty-one thousand dollars. I needed to talk to them.

What would they be willing to share with me? That would be something completely different. But I had to know.

I'd give them the address and dates of the training, along with the name Security Enterprises, Inc. for a private event. It wouldn't be anything that could be traced to anyone. The operators wouldn't write anything down. There would be no paper trail. They couldn't trace the gold card because it was securely linked to an anonymous account in the Caymans. No trail there, either.

Anyone digging would find themselves in dead-end after dead-end. Like the search for the real Felipe Gomez. I was convinced there was no such individual.

"I wonder how the hedge fund manager is faring."

Jenny shook her head. We couldn't check as long as we were on the road. That was something best done behind the security of a VPN that showed an internet link from Outer Mongolia.

"Then we'll be down to nothing in the queue and can focus on the training session."

"Where are you going to practice?" Jenny asked.

"The desert. Our house. Some laser games with you so we can get the tactical scenarios right."

"You want me to go into the desert and play Army with you?"

"Play. Army." I poked her arm. "It's important to me."

"I know, and I'm sure it'll be a good time. Will you be able to handle it if I win?" She poked me back.

"Setting up scenarios. It'll probably bore the snot out of you, but when the operators are on the clock, wasting time is the last thing I want to do. I think we can fit a lot of quality training in a short window."

"You have your heart set on this, don't you?"

I dialed up *Closer to the Heart* on my player. "You know me. Now that Gomez is behind us, I am focused on this. Is it crazy that I want a higher level of professionalism for those in our business?"

"Since those who lost their way tried to kill us, I understand why you don't want that to happen to anyone else."

"How not to get lost in the moment and stay true to the purpose. We deal with bad people, but there is a limit to the risk to ourselves and the company. Damn! This is going to be a good time." Jenny watched me while I smiled and bobbed my head to the music, thinking of the opportunities and challenges of working with however many operators might show up, in addition to the boss.

The remainder of the drive to the Circle B was uneventful, just like all travel should be. Jenny and I had enough excitement in our lives without adding to it unnecessarily.

When we walked through the door, the counter clerk waved and hurried away.

"Going to get Buck and Mabel?" I wondered. We waited at the counter and were soon rewarded by the sound of Buck's heavy tread. He thrust out his hand for a hearty shake before taking Jenny's hand gently and bending over to kiss it. She held her head high and gave me a look that challenged me to do better.

Treat her like a princess? No. Revere her as the other half of my own soul? I winked at her. I could do that. Buck straightened.

"It gets harder and harder to bend over to kiss a pretty girl's hand." Buck sighed.

"What I hear you saying is that I should get all the hand-kissing out of the way now while I'm young?"

"That's it. That's exactly what I meant." Buck chortled on his way into his office behind the counter. We followed him in. He opened a gun safe between two bookshelves.

"Here's your piece, young fella. If there's anything you ever need, you let me know. Mabel will give me a hard time if I don't take care of you good people. She's kind of sentimental like that."

"An Army dog beholden to a Marine. Say it ain't so, Buck." I loaded the .45 and tucked it into the back of my shorts. "We all have our crosses to bear. Do you have any rooms available? I don't want to drive into the night to get back home, not if I don't have to."

"You don't have to. Jed!" Buck yelled at the doorway. The counter clerk appeared. "Set up my friends in the honeymoon suite. Their money is no good here. You take care of them."

"Will do, Mr. Buck." He waved for us to follow him out. Once at the counter, he tapped on the screen to register us. "The name's Jules, but he can't get himself to say it, so he calls me Jed. I guess it blends with the theme more."

"Jules. That's fantastic." Jenny was pleased. I didn't care as long as I knew what to call him.

He handed us a skeleton key. Those were the only types of locks in the place. No digital access passes at the Circle B.

"They're showing an old John Wayne down on the side of the barn. You sit on hay bales and eat popcorn and drink sarsaparilla while wrapped up in a stinky old horse blanket. It's worth doing."

"Thank you, Jules. We didn't go last time, but I think we'll take advantage tonight," Jenny replied.

"Stinky horse blanket?" I wasn't sure of the draw.

"Get there early and take one off the top. You can thank me later."

"That's what I'm talking about," I exclaimed. "An ounce of gouge is worth a pound of knowledge, and that is some gouge right there."

Jenny and Jules both looked at me like there was a mushroom growing out of my forehead.

"We'll get there early." I took the key out from under Jenny's hand and strolled away.

She caught up. "Aren't we going to grab the bag?"

I rolled my lips between my teeth and took her hand as we hurried to the honeymoon suite. With the stress of Tucson well behind us, we were in the mood to celebrate.

And dinner wasn't for another two hours…

CHAPTER THIRTEEN

"What you are is what you have been. What you'll be is what you do now." Buddha

Back in Las Vegas, we stood in our living room and looked at each other. "What do we do now?" Jenny asked.

"I've been thinking the whole ride back, and my thoughts are everywhere. I'm going to have to sit down and actually be organized on two tracks. One for the sessions themselves, making sure I have the material correct, and the other will be on the logistics of getting people there."

"Can't you just tell them to be at the Circle B sometime after check-in on Monday to be ready for the start on Tuesday morning?"

"I guess we could if we wanted to do it the smart way. And tell them to give a phony name at check-in, one that we'll call them for the duration. Aliases for everyone!"

"Okay, Boris," Jenny replied. She waited for it. She knew it was coming.

Who was I to disappoint her? "Doris?"

"No! Natasha, of course." Jenny looked smug while opening the suitcase to chuck our laundry toward the washer. "Maybe you tell them to pick their favorite western character. This doesn't have to be glum, does it?"

"A little alter ego action. I think you're onto something. There's no reason it can't be fun. An annual convention of operators where we all get together, but no one knows anyone. They can't track us in or out. I'm jiggy with it."

"Jiggy?"

"Let me know when you want to go to dinner, and I'll close down for the day. I want to capture my thoughts while they're still fresh, and I need to talk with the head shed. I'll drop the first half of that deposit this evening." I put my computer on the table, plugged it in, and opened it.

Jenny snuggled up behind me to kiss my ear. Then she left me alone so I could focus on my work. She fired up Rush for me and went into the bedroom. She returned in her workout gear, grabbed the keys, and headed for the door. She called over her shoulder that she was going to the gym. She was out the door before I turned to answer.

I committed to getting back into the gym tomorrow. I had jogged at the ranch, but it wasn't the same since I ran on tiptoes, wary of snakes, not wanting to die on a dude ranch in the middle of nowhere. I needed to lift, but I wanted to do it with a clear mind.

I dug into the system and started taking notes. I plugged my thumb drive into the USB port and started saving my notes. Sessions on dark web exploitation, open-source research, and personal observation. I started downloading pictures to use as examples. I grabbed stills from various movies where they got it right and wrong. The net made it easy to find everything.

For the user originating out of Dubai in the United Arab Emirates, thanks to my handy VPN redirect.

Tactical exercises with fire and movement. Exfiltration. And sometimes the right answer was to run as fast you could. How did you know when that was the best choice? Conditions of the engagement.

How to shape a target location in the operator's favor. Boobytraps. Exit strategies. Critical elements to the survival of the operator so they could fight another day.

I thought of them as warriors in the underground battle against evil. It was easier to see the world in those terms when we were the ones ending lives. *Buffy the Vampire Slayer* as an allegory of real life.

There are monsters out there, and sometimes they sunbathe by their pool wearing a skimpy bikini. Other times, they drive a Porsche with the music blaring. When Daniel Nader tried to run me down, I could see it in his eyes. No remorse. Only anger masking his fear.

The outlines came together. Three days, eighteen indoor sessions and four outdoor scenarios. Thirty hours of training time over three days. A quarter of that time was dedicated to conversation and input.

I didn't know if any of the operators would add their experience to the shared pool of knowledge. Maybe not, but I hoped so to follow Jasmine's advice and get everyone involved. Operators tended to be secretive for self-preservation. If they didn't share, my eight total hits would have to suffice unless I could get Chaz to provide his insight. He should have seen it all during his years in the game.

He still was in, collecting the potential contracts—a different game, but every bit as dangerous. Maybe I had the best job in the company, with almost no exposure when it came to the hit and no exposure from vetting the potential contract.

I crossed my arms and looked at my computer screen. The clock said it had been four hours since I started. Jenny had not yet returned. I jumped up and grabbed my phone to immediately dial her number. We were growing lax. I hadn't destroyed the phone yet following the last trip. I needed to do that. Today.

Jenny picked up on the third ring. "My lover miss me?"

"A whole lot. Are you okay?"

"Yes. They had a full spa treatment available, so I helped myself to that, and now I'm relaxing with a bottle of water."

"Where are you?"

"The bedroom."

I carried my phone in my hand and stalked down the hall. Jenny was on the bed, holding a book in her hands. She waved a bottle of water at me. I turned back toward the door. I saw the car keys on the counter. I lifted my phone to my head. "I didn't hear you come in."

She talked into her phone. "I was quiet so I wouldn't disturb you. You looked like you were completely immersed in your computer."

"How long have you been home?"

She tapped her screen and ended the call. I realized I was still holding the phone to my head. Jenny patted the bed next to her. I crawled in to find that she was naked.

"Honey, I've never seen you focused like that. I've been home for an hour. I showered at the gym before the spa."

The scent finally hit me: sandalwood. "You smell good." She put her book down. "You look good, too."

"Why, Mr. Bragg, are you trying to earn favors from me?"

"I already have you in my bed. What else could I want?"

"Dinner. There's a new Chinese place the nail artist talked about, and do you know what she said?"

"I'm all ears." I propped my head on my hand.

"They have egg foo young to die for."

I deflated. "How much do you want to bet that it isn't?"

"If it's not, I'll dance naked for you."

I pursed my lips. I was willing to take that bet. "What if it is? On the very remotest of remote chances that it's not disgusting, what would you win?"

"You dance for me."

"You sure know how to take my mind off whatever it is I was doing. I can't remember anything except back to Seattle and that nasty garbage that cost me my General Tso's."

"When you get to the perfect foo young, Grasshopper, you'll find the journey was worthwhile."

I have to admit that the new restaurant was good, but the egg foo young left a lot to be desired. Jenny admitted defeat graciously, and she danced for me.

I dropped the second deposit and waited with my burner phone. Time passed, and I started to pace.

An hour later, they responded. I answered it before the phone rang a second time.

"Ian, what can we do you out of?" I think it was Chaz on the line.

"I have a few questions regarding a variety of topics. Are you free to talk for a few?"

"We'll see. Depends on the questions."

"Fair enough." I gathered my wits and started with the most important things first. "How can we ensure that the people dropping the request are square?"

"I'm not sure what you mean."

"This last job. There is no Felipe Gomez. That personality is a creation of one Rachel Smith, who is bottled up in a fortress. I sure as hell wouldn't take that job for only a couple mil. It would take a long time to pull off that gig."

"That's interesting. The requestor has upped their marker to five million dollars on that job."

"Still for Felipe Gomez?"

"It is."

"I'm rejecting it right now. There is no Felipe Gomez, at least not one who runs a drug cartel in Tucson."

"That's interesting. I expect you know this because you went there and checked it out."

"I can't put any of my people in harm's way for a DEA contract on the wrong person."

Silence on the other end of the line.

"Do you have any other questions?"

"Switching to the training…" I no longer needed to fight that battle because Chaz had given me the answer I had been looking for. "Would you like to review my plan, outlines, and logistics? Then, who will take care of getting the word out?"

"We'll take care of letting people know. Once you have that package ready, drop it in the back end. You'll find a spot in the lower left-hand corner of the screen. If you let your cursor hover for five seconds, it will come up with a link. Click that, and it'll take you to an encrypted input form. You can send anything that way. You don't need to burn up your money making deposits to request phone calls."

"Isn't an open contact system like that vulnerable?"

"We have the best people guaranteeing our cybersecurity. No one will be checking our email anytime soon, if ever. And we trust that those who know this is available don't share it with anyone else, no matter the circumstances."

"There's no way I'll crack. Deny, deny, deny. That's the only way to deal with any kind of law enforcement. You don't have to worry about me. But for the training, I hope that you'll be able to share your experience, assuming you'll be able to make it."

"I think I will. Needless to say, I haven't talked about most of it with anyone, ever."

"Time to bring the next generation up to speed," I suggested.

"I think you're right. It is time if we're to grow. It's looking good for new work. Lots of new work. Would you be able to handle three new packages if I dropped them on you?"

"I'll do my best." It was the most I could commit to.

"How could we ask for anything else?" The tone suggested they would be willing to ask for a lot more. "Are you sure you'll turn down four mil on Gomez?"

"Absolutely. If your contact is willing to make it the one who runs the Gomez drug ring, then I can move it forward. I am in contact with someone who will be researching more on one Rachel Smith. We won't be going in blind, but this will be an extremely difficult contract. It's worth two to three mil, and I'd suggest a six-month timeframe to be on the safe side."

"I'll see what I can do. Look for that one popping up, too. That'll be four new packages you'll see in the coming days."

"I'll be watching for them. Pick a good Wild West name to go by when you check in to the Circle B. I don't want you coming unprepared." I took a breath. "I want to make sure we're doing the right things, so thank you for the opportunity. I appreciate your time, Chaz."

"That's what we want, too, Ian. I look forward to talking with you. Do they have a good single malt at the bar of wherever we're going, do you know?"

"It's a dude ranch and there's no bar, only beer that the head cowboy brews, but it's not fit to drink. I'll bring a nice bottle of Scotch for you."

"You may want to put that in your logistics plan, that it's a dry ranch."

"You're not kidding. We'll be eating a lot of dust while we're there. Makes a man mighty thirsty. Thanks for your time, Chaz." I hung up before Chaz could tell me that wasn't what he meant.

He was going to chime in on the classes. That was what I wanted to hear. I could feel the calming effect it had. I was mostly ready for November. Three packages were inbound, with a fourth imminent.

"All done?" Jenny asked, dressed in her gi and ready to go to the dojo.

"I dropped that I knew the DEA was paying for the Gomez contract. Chaz iced over instantly, but he's going to see about adjusting the target to be the head of the Gomez drug ring."

Jenny followed me into the bedroom, where I put on my gear.

"And then he intimated that he'd have it back within a day or so."

"That's a pretty fast turnaround for an organization that is supposedly hard to find."

"Supposedly, unless you're the right people." I slapped Jenny on the butt as I hurried past. "Time to get back at it. It's been too long!"

CHAPTER FOURTEEN

"A good plan today is better than a perfect plan tomorrow."
George S. Patton

The two months flew by. The only thing I did besides work out was live on my computer, researching and building dossiers. Every time I felt like taking a shortcut to finish a project, I stopped, and Jenny and I would go hiking or go to the movies. We even went dancing once. When we came home, I'd get back to it and resolve the issue that was holding me back.

I felt like Paul Atreides preparing for the attack on House Harkonnen. Assassins lurked in the dark corners of a shadow world rife with conspiracies.

Four contracts dropped. Three contracts approved, and one of those was on Gomez the drug lord. I dropped an additional three thousand dollars on Antoine Hernandez to find more information on Rachel Smith, anything related to her leaving the fortress compound. He discovered three high-profile charity events she was attending on behalf of some non-profit as a concerned private citizen willing to make a generous donation.

The charities were little more than vehicles to funnel money into the pockets of those supporting certain politicians so a further donation could be made. The rallying cry was always, "Think of the children." That clinched it for me. I put out the proposal with a dossier that included my personal observations. Minimum bid was two million dollars with a timeframe of six months.

We had nine bids the first day. I didn't think they knew what they were getting into, but the big numbers were a strong incentive.

The woman bid on it, but she bid five million. I couldn't take her bid. I also wanted her to be available for the training session. I selfishly wanted to meet her, shake her hand for finishing that pig, Dr. Guanore.

I'd find out soon enough. Six months into the gig, I had executed four contracts. All I needed for the year was three, but Chaz had indicated the direction the company was going during our last phone call. The Peace Archive was getting busier.

We'd put out the proposal for an operator training retreat. Each participant would get twenty-five thousand if they showed up. Eleven had bid the contract. I accepted all eleven. With Chaz and I, that made thirteen.

Maybe not the luckiest of numbers, but I didn't worry about that. It was going to be a good training session. That meant I needed a dozen sets of laser game gear. The good news was the ArmoGear came in a set of four. I only needed to buy three sets, but then I needed to get a crate of AAA batteries as each set of four took twenty-four batteries. The blasters had a range of one hundred and fifty feet and kept track of limited ammunition or other game constraints that could be set ahead of time.

Of course, Jenny and I went out to the desert to test the systems. There was much running and diving and juking. We had to buy another set after I dove on a rock and broke the vest part of the getup. In my defense, it was my only choice to avoid getting taken out on a clean shot as I approached Jenny's position. I declared that round a draw while Jenny claimed victory, so we compromised and she won.

With a trunk full of gear, we pulled into the empty Circle B parking lot a full day ahead of our attendees. I wanted to set up and be ready. Jenny and I could ease our way into it.

I checked in as Doc Holliday and Jenny signed in as Big Nose Kate. "Do I call you Big Nose or just Kate?"

She made a face at me. "Depends where you want to sleep, Doc. Katie Elder's the name."

"Mum's the word, Jules," I told the ever-present counter clerk. "Just us and our party over the next few days. We shouldn't need anything besides Mabel's fine cooking. We will be low maintenance, with no room cleaning for our people."

"No room service?"

"Nothing at all, my man. We'll be ultra-chill."

It was Jenny's turn to be surprised. "Ultra-chill? My God. I married a teenager."

"You did?" Jules was instantly confused.

"No! Yes, if you count maturity. But...nothing." She stopped digging the hole.

"Mister B has you in the honeymoon suite. Do you want to designate the rooms for your other guests?"

"First come, first served. Put them wherever. Three hots and a cot is our bit of paradise. No one will complain. If they do, send them to me. I'll have them killed. Do you have a place where you bury the bodies?"

"Bury the bodies? No. If it's okay with you, I'll handle any complaints, Dr. Holliday."

"That'll work, too. I'm not a good complaints department guy. We'll tell them not to complain, so you won't get any." Jenny elbowed me. I pulled her close and hugged her tightly.

Jules, aka Jed, handed us two skeleton keys. We headed for our room, carrying nothing but our backpacks.

We dumped our trash in the chair before heading back out to get the lay of the land. We picked the spots for the tactical exercises while casually strolling through the area. We had gone over the game plan so often that within thirty minutes, we had completed everything I thought we needed to do. I had a pad of paper that would be burned at the end where I'd take down the western names so I had a running tally of who was who, at least by their alias.

I wasn't sure that even Chaz knew who the operators were who were coming. Plausible deniability. No one person knew too much.

An hour to dinner. I had nothing to do. I started pawing Jenny.

"Stop it. You're bored, aren't you?"

"Is that a bad reason to, you know, do it?"

She rolled her eyes.

"Oh, no!" I dropped my chin to my chest. I continued in a low voice, "The honeymoon is over."

"The honeymoon is most definitely *not* over!" Jenny declared. With her hands on her hips, she studied me. "How about chess?"

"I'm game. I think they have it in the lobby."

We were not disappointed to find a set, the board burned into the lid of a wooden barrel with both chess and checkers pieces available. We set it up, and Jenny went first. I had been studying different opening moves and put a new one into practice. Jenny raised one eyebrow but responded in kind.

She had been studying, too. We played to a draw before joining Mabel, Buck, Dusty, and Jules in the dining room, where we sat around one big table. After Buck said grace, we ate family style, passing the serving dishes around the table right to left until everyone had filled their plates. We didn't start eating until Mabel took a bite and declared the food fit for consumption.

I noted that she did not start with the well-done steak.

"Any of your people have food allergies?" Mabel asked.

I shrugged. "No idea. I never asked. We're a self-contained bunch. If someone needs something, they'll let you know. I shared the menu, and no one batted an eye." I unloaded the Heinz 57 on my steak. Jenny waited for me to cut a piece off mine for her. "How's your horse?"

"Dumb as ever, but he's looking good. Coming into some nice musculature. He'd be one to sell based on looks alone, but I can't do it. He's my boy."

"See any more snakes and critters in the area?" I didn't know if we would be getting any urbanites who would have a hard time with a rattler or a stray coyote.

"Nothing more than usual. The deer have passed through on their way to lower ground. The predators followed them. We have a mountain lion in the area, stirring up the chickens on occasion. It's keeping the rabbit population down."

"No threat to humans?"

"Depends if he's hungry enough and how vulnerable the human is."

"I didn't hear a 'no.' I'll tell our people not to wander the hillsides alone." I started to eat. The steak was nowhere near as tough as it looked. Maybe that was from the sauce I had bathed it in. I wondered if Mabel wanted any tips on cooking a good steak. Probably not. She had her way, like all of us who were comfortable with our daily lives.

After dinner, we went for a short, twilight ride in the low area surrounding the ranch. A casual ride on gentle horses with Buck up front and Dusty in the rear. We returned before it got too dark. Once locked into our room for the evening, Jenny let me know in no uncertain terms that the honeymoon was still going strong.

The first guest to arrive declared himself to be Wyatt Earp. I had thought about it but didn't want to be presumptuous. The Black man was short, wide-shouldered, and looked like a powerlifter. He wore a polo shirt and jeans that were belted tight, two or three sizes bigger than what his waist called for to fit around his massive thighs. He reminded me of an NFL running back.

Jenny and I intercepted him after he got his skeleton key. "I'm Doc Holliday, and my better half here is Katie Elder."

We shook. His hand engulfed mine. I was thankful he didn't use the full extent of his strength. My hand would not have survived. He had a quick and easy smile, white teeth standing out against his darker skin.

"Wyatt Earp. How long you been in this gig?"

"A while, but it's been a good run so far. I was looking for a way to give back and the company agreed, so here we are."

"How many?"

I assumed he meant successful contracts. I imagined us as fighter pilots checking out enemy planes painted on each other's fuselage. I didn't know what was kosher to share.

"A dozen, give or take," I replied ambiguously.

"I only have two. I'm looking forward to this to help me get over the hurdle. I'm not very low profile if you haven't guessed."

I looked him over. "It's your shoes, isn't it?"

He laughed, deep, from his diaphragm. It sounded like thunder. "No, I was in the running for a Heisman. You don't know who I am?"

I started to whisper. "I have to confess that I don't. If you're that well-known, how can you be an operator?"

"Famous people can get in where others cannot. Making a hit look like an outsider did it? That's the real challenge. That's why I only have two. I've taken four contracts but couldn't get to the far side of the others."

"Master of the gym accident." I gripped his shoulder in solidarity with my fellow operator. It felt weird. He came across as a happy guy. Reality said that he was okay with killing people. It was sobering.

I felt like Eliot Ness and the Untouchables fighting organized crime in Chicago. It made more sense in my mind to think of us as the good guys. The alternative was one reason we were here. The first-ever meeting of professional operators to make sure they had a sound moral compass.

For my peace of mind. After having met Wyatt Earp, I knew that I had made the right decision and was on the right track.

The next person to check in was nondescript. He could have blended in anywhere: a fan at a ballgame, the person in a seat on the subway, the guy in the next cubicle at work. Easy to describe and hard to identify.

He checked in as Marshall Dillon. Jenny and I introduced ourselves by our aliases.

Marshall Dillon came across as soft-spoken, not

making eye contact, his body language submissive. He stayed closer to my side, away from Jenny. She didn't push it. After a quick but surprisingly strong handshake, he excused himself to find his room. I didn't expect to see him until the next day.

The next in was a taller man, well-built with a confident walk. He introduced himself to Jenny first as John Wayne. He bent down to kiss her hand. When he stood up, he still had her hand in his. She extricated herself and pointed at me. "Holliday and Kate."

"Doc! I got this tooth that's hurting me something fierce," he claimed, opening his mouth and sticking his finger in to highlight the offending area.

"The last person you want digging in your mouth is me." I laughed.

"I figured. It's not really hurting me, but how's your healthcare in this gig? Is HR going to talk to us about the different plans that might be available?"

"HR? Your time in the corporate world has led you far astray. If you see someone who looks like Human Resources, they won't be. I think you're SOL."

He leaned close. "You brought your woman to this?"

"My partner. We're a package deal."

"That info alone has made this whole week worthwhile. I have to keep fighting off the women." He looked at Jenny. "You can imagine why, but I don't want to be a hound dog, not all the time. I'm going to have to contemplate this. Are you going to talk about what it's like working as a husband-wife team?"

"I hadn't planned on it," I replied.

"Maybe over a beer after dinner." He picked up his bag and waved stiffly before leaving, his brow furrowed from the revelation.

I recognized the next face to roll in. My old first sergeant. He gave Jules the name Audie Murphy.

I chuckled softly. Of course, he would.

He strolled over and shook my hand. I told him our names. He turned to Jenny. "You're her. Nice to meet you."

She fixed him with a hard gaze. "I'm sure I don't know what you mean."

"He was a great shot and a tough kid when I knew him about a million years ago. Ready to fight anyone if he thought they were wrong. But he was missing something. Judging by his face, you were it. You're her." He whispered, "The one who made Ian whole."

"Big dog! I wasn't that bad, was I?"

"Bad? Not in the least. It put you on edge and made you sharp, but the next level would have remained out of your reach without your better half. Congratulations."

"Thanks, Audie. I appreciate the kind words. Why are you here?"

"We might want to do this across all the regions. I'm looking at it from that perspective, but," he dipped his head toward mine, "Chaz will be here, too."

"Good. I hope you don't mind that I'll draw on your experience to supplement the classes."

"I figured. We'll help out where we can, but only what we don't have to prepare. I'm more than happy winging it. Doing a PowerPoint for review up the chain is a non-starter."

"I'm with you on that. For the record, I do have some PowerPoints, and you're going to love them."

"Doubt it. It was nice to meet you, ma'am." He bowed his head and walked away.

"*Ma'am*. You military guys are easy to spot."

"They're lonely," I said. I hadn't contemplated the attention Jenny was getting.

She took my hand. "It's impossible to miss that."

"We should have brought a bunch of hookers."

Jenny tightened her grip. "We're not in Nevada."

"Good thing we didn't bring those hookers you insisted on," I blurted a little too loudly.

Buffalo Bill strolled up. "Am I to understand there *won't* be hookers?"

"My apologies. The entertainment committee failed to close the loop on that detail, it appears. You'll have to make do with egregious amounts of full-on Western chow."

"*Chow?* Uncouth barbarians inside the gates! Somebody call room service." He twirled a hand in the air while wearing a devilish grin. Middle-aged and handsome with gray at the temples, he could have been sitting on the board of any Fortune 100 company, and no one would have batted an eyelash.

I instantly liked him. That was probably his gift and a key to his effectiveness. I wondered about everyone's preferred method of carrying out the contract. *Buffalo Bill in the study with a letter opener.*

A young man was next to arrive. He looked to be little older than a newspaper delivery boy. He came up to us before checking in.

"Are you the head honcho?" he abruptly asked.

"I guess for the next three days, I am, but," I whispered behind my hand, "they'll be watching everything I do."

"Good one! You can call me Billy the Kid." He shoved his small hand toward me. His Brooklyn accent fit him perfectly.

"I guess you're in the right place, then. Why don't you check in and get your room?"

"Cool, pops. Did I hear something about hookers?"

"No! There are no hookers."

"Crap. If there's a next time, consider bringing them in.

I'll take two, for reference." He winked at Jenny and strode to the counter.

"I'm starting to regret not getting the hookers," I quipped. Jenny settled for shaking her head. "You're a big hit at this party. Everyone's envious of me, bagging the prom queen."

"I wasn't the prom queen. I didn't even go to the prom."

"That's garbage!" I kneeled next to her and held her hand in both of mine.

"What are you doing?"

"Will you go to the prom with me?" She pulled me to my feet for a kiss.

"Give her the tongue!" Billy shouted from across the lobby.

"Isn't it past your bedtime?" Jenny called back.

"Ouch!" Billy tried to look hurt, but he couldn't hold the expression for long before a grin split his face.

He performed a modern multi-part handshake with Jules before taking his key and whistling his way to his room.

"Where did they get the kid?" I wondered. "I guess it takes all kinds."

The next person to stroll through the door seemed to stop time with her presence. She walked like a CEO while looking like a professional model. She was dressed rugged but classy. Jenny sized her up as only another woman could.

"She's too skinny for you," Jenny whispered at me.

"She's the one. I want to thank her for taking care of Guano and the hedge fund guy. She's making me look like a genius."

She walked to the counter, abundantly aware of her effect on people. Jules stared until she tapped the counter with a perfect fingernail. "I'm Jack Palance."

Jules fell over himself to check her in, giving her the second nicest room in the hotel. First come, first served—unless it came to Jack, who probably got the best wherever she went.

After our introductions, I had to say it. "Thank you for the good work this year."

She didn't answer.

"Welcome, Jack. I'm glad you could make it."

Jack Palance strolled away, a simple overnight bag carried casually over her shoulder.

"That's more what I expected. Operators not wanting to talk about their work."

"She's trouble," Jenny suggested, crossing her arms and staring after the other woman.

"She's extremely good at her job, gifted even, and one of the deadliest people here this week. Don't forget that. You don't want to get into a catfight with her."

Jenny frowned. "You're right. She's the prom queen who ruined it for the rest of us."

"I don't think she was the prom queen. I think she was probably too busy being an adult to be bothered by high school stuff. I bet she can turn it off as quickly as she can turn it on. No wonder it only took her one day with Guano. She probably crooked her finger at him, and he came running."

"Straight to his untimely demise." Jenny loosened up and nodded toward the door. "Look who's here."

Chaz entered and waved but went to the counter and checked in as Stephen Austin.

"Who's that?"

"Early governor of Texas, I think. The city is named after him."

I met him at the counter. "*Stephen*. Good to see you again."

"And you are…"

"Doc Holliday and my better half, Big Nose Kate."

"If you picked that, I'd say you like to live dangerously and not in a good way." He took Jenny's hand. "Miss Kate, always a pleasure to see you."

We eased away from the counter.

"The others are wondering about having a family and staying in this line of work." I wanted to see his reaction.

"We are evolving as a company. I hope you two don't mind being our guinea pigs. There was a time when I would have become apoplectic at the thought of an operator having a relationship. But times change. Some of our people are better alone, but some may be better with a partner."

Jenny nodded slowly before interjecting, "How will you know?"

"We trust our people with all of it. This is something else we'll trust them with. I'll make an announcement during one of the sessions. Vetting a partner before our people tell them what we're all about, that's something we do want to have a say in. Of course, you were already fully into the program before we could get involved."

"Trust," Jenny said, leaving it at that.

"Indeed," Stephen replied. "I hope dinner is everything you said it would be."

"You're in for as much of the Old West as you can stomach." There was nothing like being frank with the boss.

He grunted noncommittally at the truth.

"I have a bottle of Scotch for you. It's in our room. Let me get it for you."

"No need. You stay here with your lovely lady. We'll share a drink after dinner." He excused himself.

It was another hour before the next person arrived.

Jack strolled through, flirted briefly with Jules, and continued outside.

When the doors opened, I expected it to be Jack, but it was a Hispanic man, medium build, nondescript. He introduced himself as Geronimo, had a firm grip, and offered nothing else. I left it alone. Half of the group wanted to talk, and the other half didn't. They put themselves in their own boxes. I didn't have to do that.

Another operator strolled in, a tall, distinguished older gentleman. I suspected he might be older than my father if the old man was still alive. He told Jules to call him Ringo, short for Johnny Ringo.

After he had his key, he offered his hand to me. "Doc Holliday and Katie Elder."

"Are your sons at the barn causing trouble?"

"I don't have any sons," Jenny replied.

"Ah, the sons of Katie Elder would be something to make a movie about, I'm sure."

"Wyatt Earp is already here," I said softly.

"Heathen! He shan't get away with this." Ringo smiled and walked away.

"They seem to be enjoying the theme," Jenny suggested.

"I'm pleased that people are getting into the spirit of it. It's going to be a great week, Miss Jenny."

"Kate," she corrected. "I agree. Well done, *Doc*."

The second to last attendee, strong with well-muscled arms and broad shoulders, presented an average face with untamed black hair. The start of a beard gave him a duskier complexion than was natural. He introduced himself as Roy Rogers before asking which way to dinner.

"In an hour, at seven sharp or Mabel will tear a piece out of your backside."

"I won't be late. I love down-home cooking, just like my ma used to make. I'll probably cry real tears when I eat it."

"Was your mom a good cook?"

"Not in the least."

"Prepare for the waterworks, my man, because Mabel is more like your mom than not." I tried to be ambiguous in case Mabel was listening. No one complained because she fed everyone, but it was going to be a long week if we didn't improve her steak skills.

"Damn!" Roy left, already half-blubbering.

The last one to arrive was a little overweight, the average looking guy who lived next door. He was the kind who would bring cupcakes on Friday, the type who was quick with a kind word of support when people needed it. He introduced himself as Chuck Wagon.

Jenny and I both laughed at his creation. He shook hands with both of us but didn't say much. He was the kind of guy we would forget ten seconds after we met—a perfect persona for an operator.

"There we are, an even dozen students, ready to improve their game and get their continuing education credits."

"I thought of it more like professional development. PD is different from the CEUs we had to get as teachers."

"I'm completely besnoggled."

"What does that mean?"

"It means that I'm more than happy to call it professional development." I took her by the hand. "Go for a little walk?"

"Missing your Jack already?"

"I don't want to start with twelve and end with eleven. That wouldn't look good on the old resumé."

We walked outside and followed the path toward the stables. At the gate, Jack and Dusty were locked up, lip to lip. He held her butt cheeks tightly in both hands while she clawed his back. I coughed. She broke free, almost falling over because Dusty wasn't as quick to release his grip.

"If you'll excuse me." She curtsied before throwing her hair over her shoulder and sauntering back toward the main lodge.

"I'll join you at dinner," he called after her.

"Maybe. I might have other company."

"That one's a bucking bronco that ain't ever been tamed, not by the right man, anyway," Dusty muttered.

"Don't get your hopes up, Dusty." I slapped him lightly on the shoulder. "Are we ready for tomorrow? Early afternoon, fourteen horses."

"I'll be ready. Don't you worry about that. Is Jack coming?" Dusty stared after her.

"As far as I know." We left him to his thoughts.

Once we were alone, Jenny was dying to talk about it. "Overactive libido?"

"Maybe she's always on, unable to turn it off. She's the type who can tear an organization apart from within. She's also the type who best works alone."

"She may not have found the right man yet. It could be Dusty," Jenny quipped.

"It's not Dusty." I had no doubt about that. "It's not anyone here. I don't know if there's anyone on this planet who could make her turn it off. She might like it."

"Sounds like the prom queen."

"I'm going to ask." I gave Jenny the side-eye.

"Don't you dare. It'll sound juvenile, and you'll make me look petty. You don't want that, do you?"

"I'm kidding. I won't bother her with that. She could be the best of us because no one would suspect her."

"I would." Jenny saw past the polished veneer, surprised how many could not. At least she gave me credit for understanding the woman had the bite of a black widow.

CHAPTER FIFTEEN

"But that afternoon he asked himself, with his infinite capacity for illusion, if such pitiless indifference might not be a subterfuge for hiding the torments of love." Gabriel Garcia Marquez

Mabel delivered the exact same meal we had had months prior, but the portions were cut in half. Roy hugged her as if she were his own mom. He inhaled his dinner and held his plate up for more. Mabel was more than happy to oblige.

Buck looked oddly at the strange collection of individuals we'd brought together. He leaned past Jenny to talk to me. "Security, huh?" He shook his head.

"That's all you'll ever know us as, Buck."

The dining room was less than half full, with people eating quietly. Thirteen operators. Jenny, Buck, and Mabel. Dusty hovered at the doorway, unsure of whether to join us since Jack was at a table without an empty seat. My first sergeant talked to her in hushed tones I couldn't make out.

The men going by Wyatt Earp and Marshall Dillon had joined them and were listening intently.

I gestured at Dusty to join us.

At the table next to us, Chuck Wagon, Roy Rogers, Billy the Kid, and Buffalo Bill had started a game where they all took a bite of steak and raced to chew it enough to swallow it. I blamed the unrepentant Billy the Kid. It would have been embarrassing if it hadn't been so funny. I fought with myself not to watch.

At the bigger table with six seats, Buck, Jenny, Chaz, and I started with the baked beans.

"Take it easy on those. I remember what happened last time," Jenny suggested while innocently studying the Old West décor of the dining room. The guests at our table didn't have to ask what she meant.

Dusty took one of the empty seats at our table but didn't bother putting anything on his plate. He snagged a dinner roll and chewed it absentmindedly while Jack ignored him from the next table.

"What do you think, Dusty? Any coyotes we'll have to chase off?" I asked in an attempt to wrench his attention away.

"Nope."

"Rattlesnakes?" I tried.

"Not since the last time you were here. Been pretty quiet in the hills."

"Scorpions? Zombies? Jehovah's Witnesses?"

He finally broke his reverie. "No. You won't have to shoot anything or anyone on this trip, but we are sporting iron when we go out. For *your* protection." Dusty chuckled. He and Buck had been armed last time, but neither had been able to get a shot off. "I expect you'll be packing as well. What about these others?"

"I don't know, but I doubt there's anything out there

that we can't handle, not unless you get raided by a marauding band of Apaches in the middle of the night because I need my beauty sleep. I can't be bothered in the middle of the night."

"Middle of the night is relative. That's when he gets up," Jenny noted.

"Early bird gets the worm." I smiled.

Jenny returned to eating. I needed less sleep than she did, but when I was tired, I slept. It bugged her as an unresolved mystery of the universe how someone could fall asleep so fast. I didn't like wasting time.

"Are you going to say something to the collected masses? Tell them the schedule for tomorrow?" Chaz asked.

"Sure. I can do that." I glanced at Buck and Dusty. I'd keep it ambiguous. I took a bite of the coleslaw, wiped my face, and stood. "Welcome to the Circle B for the first-ever gathering of Security Enterprises professionals. Over the next few days, we'll share some techniques that have worked to ensure our personal safety while improving our overall process for delivering to our clients.

"And that is our two-way commitment. When we take a contract, we're assuring you that our interests are secured and that you will get a contract worthy of carrying out. The company is nothing without its people doing the right things for all involved. We'll start at nine in the morning. Breakfast is at seven, something light like biscuits and gravy, pancakes, and slabs of ham."

"Slices," Jenny suggested.

"Slices of ham."

"And bacon and eggs, scrambled, none of that over-easy city trash." Buck spoke loud enough for everyone to hear. Billy laughed heartily and pointed until he found everyone looking at him.

"Hey!"

"All I'll say is that if you go hungry this week, that's on you." They'd take care of themselves. "You are on your own to explore and enjoy what the Circle B has to offer." I turned to Dusty. "Are you spinning up a movie this evening?"

"I can if you want. I hadn't planned on it."

"Fire up the popcorn machine and play it again, Sam."

Dusty nodded. "Movie starts at eight."

I looked back at the group. They were watching me since I was still standing. "I want to thank you all for coming. Movie starts at eight down by the corral."

"You should be a politician," Chaz told me.

"I shouldn't, really."

Jenny chuckled. "He shouldn't," she agreed.

"Ian here saved my life," Buck said into the silence.

"Doc, you mean," Chaz clarified. "Why am I not surprised?"

"*Doc.* Yes, that's it. He shot a rattler's head off while it was crawling between a bucking pony's hooves. It was the damnedest thing I ever seen."

"Of course, it was. Those in the security business tend to have an aptitude toward that kind of thing, but our Doc Holliday is special," Chaz remarked.

"Damn straight," Buck confirmed. The others started talking, generally small talk. They were too used to saying nothing even among their peers, and especially not here with outsiders present.

Dusty played with his food more than ate it, all the while watching Jack.

At nine in the morning, all were present and accounted for except for my old first sergeant. We started the first session without him. The role of the contract and that it wasn't sacrosanct. The session went quickly since no one seemed surprised by the overview. I only wanted to lay the groundwork for a session on the last day about ensuring that the target was a bad guy before going all-in.

I knew Chaz would back me because I had asked him at the movie. To my surprise, it was *Kelly's Heroes* and not *Casablanca*. A favorite of mine, so I was good with it. Everyone watching had fun, even with the old horse blankets and fresh-made stale popcorn.

The second session was on using the dark web to do research. Half of the attendees had never accessed it, and the other half hadn't taken it to that degree. We started with the critical VPN approach. Even Chaz took mental notes. I had never considered myself to be a hacker, but I had learned a thing or two.

Seeing how little some of the operators knew about internet security, it was surprising that they had not been caught. Maybe some of them had, but we hadn't heard about it. In my opinion, it was better to risk an all-hands meeting like this and learn how to limit exposure than for one of us to get caught.

If one lost, we could all lose. That session extended into the next one, taking it over. Two hours on the dark web. Many took notes, writing down pathways and programs and resource books for further research. Afterward, I realized that the entire effort I'd put into bringing the operators together had already been worth it and would pay off with the internet security training alone.

Audie had still not shown up. On the break, I went to the counter to find it empty and a handwritten sign that Jed would return in time for the group's checkout. Buck wasn't in his office, so I helped myself to the master keys. Jenny raised one eyebrow but didn't say a word. We hurried to Audie's room and pounded on the door. When there was no answer, I let us in.

The first sergeant was in bed, but his color was off. I touched his neck to check for a pulse, but his skin was cold. Jenny remained by the door while I looked him over. I didn't see any injuries on his torso. I rolled him over to check his back, finding nothing that would indicate what he'd died from. When I rolled him back, I noticed a spot on the pillow under his head. I rolled him again.

Jenny cleared her throat, watching my clumsy machinations.

I used the flashlight on my phone to shine on the back of his head. At the base of his skull was a clean puncture, filled with a plastic-y version of blood. Not dried and not scabbed over.

I left him where he was, and we locked the door on our way out. I leaned my back against the wall and closed my eyes. "This sucks."

"It's worse for your friend," Jenny replied matter-of-factly. "What do you think happened?"

"He was killed by an operator. There is no doubt about that."

Jenny exhaled heavily. "It's not your fault."

"It happened on my watch while these people were here. I can't help but feel responsible." Jenny leaned her forehead against mine. The touch of her breath on my face helped me think through what I had to do, at least in the next few minutes. I failed to see beyond that.

Once in the conference room, I pulled Chaz into the hallway for a quick sidebar.

"Audie Murphy has been killed."

Chaz pursed his lips and looked deep into my eyes as if trying to discern if I was telling the truth.

"That sucks," he said, but his first thought was the same as mine, as evidenced by his glance toward the room where the operators waited for the next session. I handed him the master keys and told him which room it was. He took the keys, nodded, and headed down the hallway. Jenny started to go with him, but I caught her arm.

I didn't know who had done it, and I wasn't going to leave Jenny alone with any of them until I was certain. Despite all the training we had been doing, I couldn't be sure she would kill one of them to save herself. I knew that I could.

In the conference room, I closed the door behind us and started the session on disguise, being invisible in a crowd, and being unnoticed when alone. I shared what I knew, but Billy the Kid raised his hand. When I recognized him, he stood and started talking. He changed accents five times in the first five sentences. He lost his smile and tossed his bully cap on the table.

I sat down while Billy the Kid talked about the most important element of being able to blend in, and that was believing in the character you were trying to be. At the end of it, I realized that Billy could have been thirty years old, not much younger than me. I had assumed he was a teenager based on his manner and speech. He showed us that we were all wrong to assume. It was the perfect class. I pocketed my notes but could think of nothing besides the first sergeant, dead in the middle of Nowhere, Arizona.

CHAPTER SIXTEEN

"A snake will always be a snake, even if you put a chain around its neck and try to make it walk upright." Lisa Alther

The disguise session was supposed to end with lunch, but Chaz returned and asked everyone to stay put while he talked to me. The operators started whispering among themselves before we left the room. Jenny joined us in the hallway.

Chaz didn't give her a second look. "I'm sure you're right. What has to happen is that we need to take care of this ourselves."

"What are you saying?" I suspected, but I wanted to hear it.

"We need to find who did it and sanction them. Period. End of contract."

"I think we have to tell them, but we also need to make sure they can't leave. No one will tell the truth, least of all the one who did it." Jenny rested her hand on my shoulder. She didn't have anything to add but wanted me to know I had her support. I knew neither she nor I had done it. That was the extent of what I knew. That left us with ten suspects, all of them confirmed killers.

"You have something in mind, don't you?" Chaz's eyes darted around the area as if watching for the police to break down the doors and come storming into the area.

"We tell them a half-truth for now." A plan was forming in my mind. "What do we do with the body?"

"No one needs to know that he passed. None of us have any ties, so we need to find a final place for him in the hills. An arroyo, somewhere that will go undisturbed for the next fifty years. After that, no one will care. And Ian, first and foremost, no one in that room is who they seem to be."

"Tell me something I don't know, boss." I clapped him on the shoulder and headed in.

When we returned, everyone quieted and intently watched us. I looked from face to face. Some seemed confused. Others kept their expressions neutral. I cataloged them into two lists based on that criterion. It didn't mean I could discount anyone. Billy the Kid's presentation had shown me how easily we could be misled.

"The individual we called Audie Murphy passed away quietly in his sleep." I scanned the crowd looking for guilt, but that would have been too easy. No one in that room was shocked by the loss of life, not even Jenny. Surprised, yes, but not shocked. "And it makes me ask the question as this isn't my area of expertise. Does anyone know how to get rid of a body?"

Jack and Wyatt both raised their hands.

"I don't want to know why or how, but if you could give us some advice, I'd appreciate it. Great morning sessions. I appreciate the engagement, and besides that one little thing, it's been a pretty good day!" Most chuckled at my upbeat close to the first part of the training.

That also told me what I had already known. Instilling a moral compass in people who took death lightly was going to be a challenge. Despite my outward calm, the murder bothered me. I wanted to trust the people who worked on my contracts.

As the old saying goes, one does not want to know how sausage is made.

All of a sudden, training had become a bad idea. There was a certain peace that came from not knowing. Plausible deniability at the personal conscience level. It was another way to cope. Then again, what if one of the operators was a psychopath? Wouldn't it be better to take care of it ourselves than having them running loose in the world as a mass murderer?

That would draw a level of scrutiny that would not be good for the company. Where did they get their money? Even the Caymans would find it easier to turn over banking records of someone the entire world had grown to hate.

Even though they said they wouldn't. Trust no one. Leave no thread linking one thing to another. This was training at an entirely different level. And Chaz was backing my play.

Jack and Wyatt remained behind while the others filed out.

"What's the deal?"

"Audie Murphy is dead. We need his body to disappear. He's in his bed. We need to get him from there to somewhere else not associated with here or us in any way, where no questions will be asked."

"Like the cleaning crew from *Pulp Fiction?*" Wyatt Earp asked.

"We don't need to scrub the room, just move the man to his final resting place."

"That's much easier," Wyatt admitted.

"The key," Jack started, blinking slowly, her lips slightly parted and the tip of her tongue visible, "is to move when no one is watching and return before they know you've left."

"There's a couple people who know this area well enough to help make that happen. We need to bring Buck in on this."

"No way," Chaz stated, hammering his fist into his palm. Jenny stiffened.

"He was a prisoner of the Viet Cong for two days. They tortured him. He survived without telling them anything."

"According to who? Him?"

"Yes, him. But I believe him, and I believe we can trust him. And he doesn't know anything about us. Nothing at all. He gives us the local knowledge to deliver the result we want. Bottom line is we need him."

Chaz hung his head before lifting it back up and nodding.

Jack slapped Wyatt on his broad shoulder. "You hide bodies? I would have never picked you. Billy the Kid definitely, but not you."

"Dead men tell lots of tales," Wyatt offered. "Missing men tell no tales at all."

Jack stood taller than the Heisman finalist, easily leaning against him with her hand on his shoulder. He seemed immune to her presence.

Good for him.

"Any recommendations?" I wondered.

Jack didn't hesitate. "Lime within triple plastic sheeting buried deeper than six feet, vertically, with a dead animal buried between the body and the surface."

"That's nice, Jack. Thank you for being creepy." I rolled my eyes at her. "But I understand. When you detail it like that, it makes a lot of sense. We'll make it happen. I'll talk to Buck and see what we need to do next."

Wyatt shook his head. He didn't have anything else to add. "Good one," he told Jack and worked himself out of her clutches.

Jenny strolled in behind me, interjecting herself between Jack and me. I suspected she had done it on purpose. We detached ourselves from the conversation.

We went looking for Buck. He wasn't in his office, but it was lunchtime. We found him in the dining room, hovering over a plate of beans and greens.

We joined him but waited until he was finished before taking him outside to field our request.

"What's so important we gotta be out in the sun?"

"One of our people died, but our claim to fame is that we have no families and no record of our existence. We can't report his death because we're not going to be answering any uncomfortable questions, and definitely not if it's the local authorities. So, we need a spot in the nearby national forest where we can bury him where he won't be found."

"What is this?" Buck stomped one foot and glared at us. "I won't be a part of any murder."

Buck was no fool and deserved the truth. "You're right, Buck. He was murdered. And the worst part is, it was one of us who did it. When we find out who, we're going to end him and put him in the ground right next to the one who was going by the name of Audie Murphy."

"You're planning on killing another of your group?"

"We don't want to do it, Buck, but we have to. We cannot have a rogue in our midst, and that is exactly what we've uncovered. Unfortunately, it cost us one of our good ones, the second most senior person here, to find that out."

Buck took off his Stetson and slapped it on his thigh to knock off the dust. He rearranged it on his head.

"I'm not sure about this."

"I know that you'll keep our secret, Buck, but no one is going to randomly show up and ask about this man. We'll take care of his vehicle. There will be nothing to tie it back here."

"You saved my life, and you're calling in your marker. I'm good with that. It's how real men do business. Saved me in 'Nam, and it's the way I'll always be. I'll get some bags and duct tape. You can wrap him up, and then I'll lead you out the back. We'll take a few horses into the hills. Digging a hole will take effort, but you boys look plenty strong. I'm not helping to dig a hole. I'm a little old for that crap."

I found it easy to laugh with Buck. He was as straightforward as a person could be.

I waited for the bags that Buck pulled from under the counter. He snagged duct tape from his office. He called it his repair kit. "Do you have any lime?"

"Sure. Down by the stable. I'll bring a bag along with a couple shovels when I return with four horses. You know where the cleaning staff's office is?" I nodded. "Take him through there, and I'll meet you outside."

Buck clumped away. I returned to the dining area to snag Wyatt Earp and Chaz. Jack smiled with a bat of her long and full eyelashes. She knew what we were going to do.

Why hadn't I asked her to help dispose of the body since it was her advice we would be following?

A narrow hole suggested only one person could dig at a time, and I made the judgment that she wasn't the hole-digging type. This took brute force, and she tended toward a more subtle approach. Alcohol poisoning versus a broken neck. Jenny made eyes at me and joined me even though I gestured for her to stay there because I wouldn't be going into the hills. I had the afternoon's training to conduct.

"What are you doing?" she asked, not harshly, her hand gently cupping the side of my face. I put my hand over hers.

"We're giving the first sergeant a decent burial." I looked into her eyes. "Where no one will find him."

She changed to a whisper. "What about the person who killed him?"

"We'll be digging two graves. I'm not going, but you and I need to start figuring this out without directly asking people. Operators lie for their very salvation. It would be natural for them to be evasive when it came to finding our killer so asking directly will get me nowhere, and I have to find who did it because I'm taking this personally."

Jenny kissed my cheek and took my hand. We went to the first sergeant's room and watched as Wyatt Earp and Chaz wrapped Audie in black garbage bags, double-taping the seams. Wyatt pointed at the bloodstain on the pillow.

That told me that Wyatt wasn't our man. Chaz removed the pillowcases and threw them aside. If Chaz did it, there would be no retribution. I would want to know why, but his reaction had seemed sincere. I discounted him out of hand. That left nine candidates.

I had no plan on how to whittle them down. I hoped it would come to me by the start of the next session.

Once Chaz and Wyatt finished, they looked to me for the next phase. Jenny went into the hallway first to make sure it was clear before we followed. I led the way through the cleaning staff's area, happy that we had given them a few days off. Buck was already there, horses snorting and slapping at flies with their tails. Wyatt manhandled the body into the saddle Buck designated. He made quick work of tying the body in place, making me wonder if he'd done it before. There was a shovel on the other two saddles and a bag of lime behind Buck. If anyone saw, there would be no doubt what was going to happen.

It was high noon

Chaz turned to me. "Hold down the fort. We'll be back."

"I'll take care of it."

Jenny hurried into the cleaning area and snagged as many bottles of water as she could carry. She handed them to Wyatt and Chaz. "You'll probably need these."

"Wouldn't that be irony?" Wyatt quipped.

"Forgive me for not laughing now, but I know that's going to be funny later." I shook his hand. "Thanks for helping us."

He tipped his chin at me and climbed onto his horse, making it look easy even though he was short. Chaz followed suit, vaulting into the saddle and settling into place.

"Has everyone ridden a horse except me?"

Chaz shook his head. "I can't help it if you were raised wrong."

Buck clicked his tongue at his beautiful appaloosa and led the way out. The packhorse, tied by a rope to Buck's saddle, trotted along behind. Both Wyatt and Chaz pulled their horses around and nudged them up to speed.

"How can they make it look so easy?" I asked.

Jenny shrugged. "Not a car. A living animal that responds to standard commands, and they know if you don't have a clue."

"I feel horrible. As if I've taken advantage of Buck."

"Don't be. If he didn't want to do it, he wouldn't have. You guys are square now. And that is how he strikes me— as someone who would rather not be in anybody else's debt."

I knew she was right. It still bothered me. "Why couldn't we have an easy training where everyone learns, then one round of Kumbaya, and we all go our merry ways?"

Jenny laughed while shaking her head. "There are too many variables in your line of work. Nothing can ever go how you want it to. In the short time I've known you, what sets you apart from anyone else who might try to do this job is your ability to flex to the situation, revise your plan, and make sure you get the job done. So, my sexy husband, adjust on the fly and save the day. It's what you do."

That was the difference between working alone and having a partner. In a former life, I would have had to give myself the motivational speech. It wouldn't have sounded as good. Of that, I was certain. And the delivery wouldn't have come from sparkling green eyes that mesmerized me.

"Yes, dear," I replied, my pat phrase when she was right and I didn't want to admit it.

The others were in the hallway, and Mabel was cleaning up the dining area when we returned. "Meet us in the conference room. We'll start the afternoon session on time, but we'll adjust on the fly depending on when we are ready for a hands-on session."

I entered the dining room with my hands held together in prayer and worship. "Dearest Mabel, could we impose upon you for buttered buns and some baked beans. Maybe a chicken breast?"

"And some of those green beans if you have any left over," Jenny begged.

"You miss the dinner bell, you pay the piper." Mabel shook a handful of utensils at us.

"Damn!" I exclaimed, holding my heart and staggering toward her. Jenny picked up a few dirty plates and headed for the kitchen. "Paying the piper, aye-aye, ma'am!" I followed Jenny's lead.

Mabel continued clearing the tables. In the kitchen, we helped rinse and load the dishwasher. Three plates sat on the prep table, covered with plastic wrap. They had been there the whole time.

"Are these for us?" I wondered.

"Of course. No one goes hungry at the Circle B, even if they can't tell time." She put the third plate filled with meat in the refrigerator. Tape across the wrap had "Buck" written on it.

"You're the best, Mabel." We trapped her between us, and we each kissed a cheek before running off with our lunches.

We plopped down in the first available seats. I wolfed my lunch while Jenny took her time. I finished in three minutes flat and carried my plate and utensils into the kitchen where Mabel took them and shooed me away.

Jenny picked up her plate and followed me out of the dining room. She was going to finish in the conference room. She took a seat at the back while I checked my notes. After everything that happened, we started the afternoon session only two minutes late.

"No fear! We have work to do."

John Wayne shrugged. "What's there to be afraid of? Aren't we as snug as a bug in a rug at the Circle B?"

"We are mostly, I guess. Maybe I'm the one who is trying not to be afraid, thinking that I can teach you guys anything."

"You're doing great so far, pilgrim," John Wayne replied.

"Thanks, Duke. Where were we? How about casing a target? What can you do to improve your chances of getting the opportunity you want by finding where a target is most vulnerable?"

My small class of professionals made themselves comfortable and prepared to listen.

"In the last session, we talked about being invisible in a crowd by blending in. For this one, we're walking through an internet search, using VPN to create a profile and then establishing physical surveillance to identify vulnerabilities and refine opportunities."

Buffalo Bill chuckled. "You sound like a business consultant. No one would ever suspect you of anything. Do you leverage that?"

"My best disguise is as a homeless guy. I can get into character in milliseconds. But that's not what we're talking about here. Risk versus reward. How can we minimize the risk to ourselves while maximizing the opportunity for success?" John Wayne rolled his eyes. "At least I didn't say synergy or core competencies." John gave me the side-eye. "Throw me a frickin' bone!"

With the laughs, I was free to continue the session. In the back of my mind, I envisioned four horses heading to a distant arroyo to find an area in the shade to dig a deep hole.

CHAPTER SEVENTEEN

"The cunning of the fox is as murderous as the violence of the wolf." Thomas Paine

After two more sessions, we were ready for tactical movement time, but Chaz and Wyatt weren't back yet. I moved a second-day class into its spot. I tried to put myself into the right frame of mind during a long break, but the right words eluded me. My brain kept circling back to the murder.

An old Marine Corps saying came to mind. *No plan survives first contact.* It could not have been more true. My plan was done for. I had a trunk full of laser game gear that we probably wouldn't use. I planned to donate it all to a secondhand charity outlet.

When the group returned, I sat on the front table. There were two things I wanted to talk about: the murder and the morality of our work.

"We sanction only bad people. All of our contracts must be for people who society is better off without." No one scoffed, but most seemed less interested than I had hoped. "Let me tell you the story of why this is important to me.

"A while ago, I bid on and won a contract that seemed like every other one I'd had. I couldn't find any dirt on the target while I was looking for a vulnerability, the standard stuff we've been talking about and what you've done as part of your work. I kept digging, but something was off, way off.

"And then I committed the worst thing we can do. I contacted the target and had a conversation. A few conversations, actually. He had been set up. I pulled that string until I found where it had come from. I leveraged that person to cancel the contract, and then we had a come-to-Jesus meeting.

"Seems simple enough, but then the regional director got their panties in a bunch and came after me. That resulted in another come-to-Jesus meeting. I had to disappear for a while before the company and I were able to have a candid conversation. I had been put into an impossible situation because the regional director had become compromised. Why am I telling you this? Because you are the final safety valve to make sure the company keeps doing the right thing. We're the good guys."

"I like that," Johnny Ringo stated, his silver hair remaining firmly in place while he nodded. "Are you sure about the premise? I've never heard that before, and I've been doing this for three years now. And what's a regional director?"

I contemplated his question and how much I could tell them. I decided they needed to know, just like I wanted to know where the requests came from to better determine the veracity of the targets.

"The organization structure of the company contains three layers. The operators are the front lines. Regional directors vet the proposals, build the dossiers, and shape the contracts. The head shed takes care of working with the clients on their proposals and payment, of course. All the targets are supposed to be those who society will not work too hard to investigate regarding their loss."

"Or they die of natural causes," Jack interjected.

"Under ideal circumstances, yes. Natural causes where no one is looking for a third party."

"The targets are vetted by two different elements within the company before they go out for bid and dossiers? I've never gotten a dossier." Johnny Ringo looked skeptical.

"I do them on all of mine. You wouldn't see one until you won the bid."

"I've gotten a couple." Jack stretched languorously. Her shirt pulled up to show tight abs. "I like them. Makes the job so much quicker and easier. I hadn't seen one until a few months ago. Is that you, big guy?" She ended with her lips parted, head tilted slightly. She tucked the hair on one side of her head behind her ear.

"You can turn it off, Jack. Save it for the clients," I told her. Jenny's muscles tightened as she sat upright and scowled at Jack's flirting.

"As you wish." She leaned back and twirled her hair around a finger. Buffalo Bill, Billy the Kid, and Marshall Dillon watched her intently. "For the record, I like the dossiers."

"I'd hate all the research I do to go to waste. No sense in duplicating effort, right?"

"No sense at all," Johnny agreed.

The lip chewing and contemplative expressions suggested they were mulling over the information.

"Questions?"

Geronimo raised his hand. "Who pays money for these?"

"I don't have the answer to that. I have my suspicions. Leave it at those people who are willing to pay to circumvent our legal system."

"Avoids all kinds of sticky situations," Chuck Wagon commented.

"And that's why we vet these thoroughly. Removing a competitor to improve one's position in the marketplace is *not* a good reason. A disgruntled father following an attack by a high-profile individual on one of his juvenile kids? Oh, yeah. There's no shortage of bids when it comes to pedo targets." I took a few deep breaths before continuing, "Not all targets are as cut and dried. I do as much as humanly possible to satisfy my conscience that the target is viable."

Marshall Dillon spoke up. "Not all of my targets have been bad people. I do the job. I move on."

Billy the Kid nodded. "I don't even check."

"Neither do I," Roy Rogers added.

"This was the primary reason I wanted to host this retreat. I want you to check, and so does the head shed."

"That's twice you've said that. What does it mean?" Roy asked.

"I use that term to mean corporate headquarters. I'm a grunt at heart, a Marine, so I've always been less than complimentary of those who worked out of air-conditioned offices, delivering their orders from on high with little regard for those who have to do the real work. That being said, it's my term, and those in the so-called company's head shed have done the work. All of them were operators first. There is no corporate high-rise with a sign and a circular driveway out front. Our headquarters is more of a process to protect us and insulate our clients from outside scrutiny without alerting those who are the subjects of our contracts. The head shed is critical to our work, and we wouldn't be here without them. We wouldn't be who we are."

The group sat there in silence until it became uncomfortable. I looked at Jenny in the back of the room, her empty plate on the table in front of her. She blew a kiss before twirling her finger for me to keep talking.

"I listen to Rush. All the time. It drives my wife nuts," I blurted. Jenny threw her hands out and made a face. That wasn't what she had in mind when she so confidently encouraged me to say something.

Most of the group turned to face Miss Jenny. She stared at me, slack-jawed.

Chaz and Wyatt Earp walked in, no worse the wear for their adventure. They stopped at the silence. "What did we miss?" Chaz asked, using his Stephen Austin persona.

I whispered into his ear, "They wanted to know the process by which contracts get from start to finish. I told them what I do. Is there anything you're able to share? I didn't tell them who you were."

"It's okay." Chaz gripped my arm easily and smiled. He strolled to the front of the room. I joined Jenny at the back, and she promptly punched me in the shoulder.

Geronimo snickered from nearby.

"She loves me," I whispered to him.

When Chaz spoke, everyone focused one hundred percent of their attention on him. "Good afternoon. I'm Stephen Austin for the duration of this retreat. I've been with the company for a while. I came here as an observer to assess the viability of this program. Even though I missed a couple of the sessions, I think there's a lot that can be done to improve the overall professionalism of our organization while not compromising any of the anonymity we need to do our jobs. When you get better at what you do, you decrease your risk, which is high, but the rewards are substantial. I have no doubt we have a few folks in here who have earned eight figures or more in a very short time."

No one nodded or smiled to give themselves away.

"What can you tell us about how we get contracts?" I asked.

Chaz winced but was honest. "Not much. We have a separate liaison department that handles bringing the work in. Those potentials are vetted through the main clearinghouse before getting forwarded to the regions for development, bids, and management."

A separate department. More overhead, but there were probably only a few people in non-operator positions. I couldn't imagine how the Peace Archive solicited for work because a full-page ad in the New York Times would draw some potential clients, along with a whole lot of the wrong attention. "How many regions are there?" I wanted to know.

"There are five. Northwest, Northeast, East Coast, West Coast, and the middle of the country. There's also a potential international branch, but we're not exploring that one yet. It takes a great deal of effort to get the logistics in place before opening up anything outside the States."

Johnny Ringo raised his hand. He looked to be the oldest in the group. "Is there a career progression to move into different roles?"

"Invite only, based on performance. You don't call us. We call you." Chaz's answer allowed for no conversation. I was happy about the enlightenment. "Thank you for coming and helping us test this concept. We're not doing a written evaluation but let me know directly what you liked and what you'd like to see more of. Can I get a hearty round of applause for Doc Holliday and Katie Elder, who set this up for you?"

Chaz led with a soft clap that the others mirrored. The exuberance was underwhelming, but the smiles suggested this group would never cheer loudly for anything. They seemed to be pleased, and Chaz nodded at me after the round of applause.

"Take fifteen. We'll regroup and see what's next for the final session of the day." Jenny and I pulled Chaz aside. "That didn't take as long as I thought it would."

"There was a crevasse where Buck had been dumping deer carcasses for decades. No one is going down there. So, it's taken care of. We're a little dusty, but we didn't break a sweat."

"Any thoughts on who might have done it?" I wondered.

Chaz shook his head. "Could have been a personal vendetta, although I don't like our people going rogue and killing outside of paid work."

I kept my expression neutral. I had accepted a million dollars for a hit outside the Archive. I wanted to think they knew about it, but it wasn't my job to enlighten them, either. That hit had been paid, and none of it had gone to the Archive. That wasn't what Chaz was talking about. He was okay with killers, but not murderers.

"Press forward with the training, then?"

"As if nothing had happened, yes," Chaz replied

"Then it's time for some outdoor activities. I have a quick move-and-fire scenario. Everyone can score their gear for the session and hang onto it through the end."

He nodded before leaving the conference room. Jenny and I remained there alone.

"I could use a cup of coffee." All of a sudden, I felt bone-tired.

"It's like how you feel after you've done a job. It's the letdown after the rush." Jenny hugged me. "Let's get some water."

"I'm sure that's it, but I could use a cup of coffee."

Jenny didn't joust further. We headed to the dining room, where she poured a glass of ice water for herself, and I scored a cup of coffee. I added an ice cube so I could chug it. I finished it in two drinks and put it in the dirty dish bin.

"Feel better?" Jenny asked. She slugged her water, shaking her head vigorously to ward off a brain freeze headache.

"Not really, but we got stuff to do." I found our operators scattered between the dining room and the conference room. "In the parking lot to get your battle gear!" I trolled the hallways, bellowing for all hands to follow us outside.

Jenny led the way out to our car. I tried not to look at the other cars in the lot to see where they came from, but if the operators were doing their jobs, nothing would tie them to a home location.

We popped the trunk where the laser guns, vests, and gross of batteries were located.

November in northern Arizona delivered cool weather, enough so that I found it refreshing, and the operators wouldn't sweat too much beneath their gear.

One by one, they strolled past and picked up a laser blaster and one vest each. I looked around before handing over the equipment, acting like a drug dealer making a delivery, but no one was around beside us. Some saw the amusement. Others looked at the equipment as toys, unimpressed by the game. Jack was the least impressed. I ignored the expression on her face. Jenny scowled.

We walked as a group to the lightly wooded area beyond the stable and the corral. Dusty was taking the saddles off the horses, unhappy with the change in schedule. He had expected the group to take a ride. Not only were we an hour late, but the ride wasn't going to happen.

I took a side trip to see him.

"I'm sorry, man. We had a massive schedule change. Events beyond our control. I don't want to jag you around, and we ended up doing just that. Tomorrow morning, second thing. Ten to noon for a nice ride, if that's okay."

"Of course, it's okay. Why wouldn't it be?" He was angry, scanning the area looking for Jack, but she had disappeared on the other side of the tall man calling himself John Wayne.

"Thanks, man." Money talked. I handed him a couple hundred-dollar bills. He took them without comment. I didn't need Dusty to be hostile to the group, but Jack had done us no favors with her face-sucking game, played at Dusty's expense.

She was not a bridge builder. I didn't need her to be, but I also didn't need her tearing down the bridges that I had built.

That was the problem I had when I served in the Corps. The best warfighters were not the best Marines when it came to time in garrison or on liberty. They were good in the field fighting the enemy. They created chaos when bored.

Maybe Jack and I had more in common than I wanted to admit.

Jenny had continued to the exercise kick-off point and started briefing the operators without me. We had run through this particular exercise four or five times. She knew it as well as I did. She talked through the mechanics of it. Two teams facing each other across an open area. There was a flag in the middle. First to get the flag won. It was the usual paintball scenario. I wanted to see the variations on tactics as we switched up teams between each iteration. We'd run through iterations until we ran out of time.

Once Jenny was finished with the basics and everyone had their equipment on, I stepped up to pick the teams. I put Jack in charge of one team and Chuck Wagon in charge of the other. I randomly added people until both sides had five each.

Chaz and I stood aside to watch. I gave both sides five minutes to get to their positions and come up with a plan. Jack pulled her team into a football huddle, where she grabbed the butts of the men on either side of her.

I wondered if she had a filter or how she could operate in any public setting. Then I thought she might have been abused to the point that she became the aggressor as the only way to control the situation.

Chuck talked to his team, asking questions for input, and making a decision. He raised his hand in the air to show he was ready. His people spread out, putting a good ten feet between each.

Jack's team started close together. She nodded that she was ready.

I pulled a whistle out of my pocket. Jenny had been waiting for it, plugging her ears next to me. Chaz followed suit. I blew one short blast.

Chuck's team turned and ran to the nearby trees. Dropped behind them into kneeling positions and started firing their laser beams at Jack's team, which had formed a wedge and was running toward the flag. The running team fired from the hip, but that was ineffective. The blockers were lit up, and their lights flashed and buzzers sounded. They stopped and laid down, leaving Jack to run, dodging and juking, but it was over in a hurry. Five lasers danced across her body until one hit the sensor on her vest and another triggered her gun. She slammed her gun on the ground and stormed away.

Chuck strolled out until he reached the flag. As he was about to put his finger on it, one of Jack's team fired from the prone position, lighting him up. The shooter ran, crouching, using Chuck's body as a shield. He reached the flag and yanked it from the ground.

Jack started dancing from where she'd gone, distracting everyone from the one who had dropped without having been activated.

The double feint.

She walked back to pick up her blaster, but it was broken. She made a pouty face on her way to Jenny to get a backup. Jenny was less than amused, scowling as she slapped it into Jack's hand.

"I'd do you," Jack told her.

"I wouldn't let you," Jenny replied.

"Saucy! Just how I like 'em." Jack smiled demurely.

"I thought 'breathing' was your standard."

"That too, but breathing and saucy? It's a win-win." She tossed her hair over her shoulder as she strutted away.

I waved my arm in the air to rally the teams. I picked the two operators who came across as submissive to lead the next two teams—Marshall Dillon and Roy Rogers. The teams dutifully took opposite sides of the field.

At the whistle, Dillon's team dropped to one knee and started firing, while Roy's team started running serpentine, firing from the hip, twisting and juking. One was hit, and he sat down.

Two of Dillon's team jumped up and ran forward while the others fired. They made it five steps and dropped again, providing covering fire for the rear group, who leapfrogged them, moving closer and closer to the flag.

Roy's team closed with the flag, but the snipers on the other side were firing better-aimed laser beams. Hip-firing was doing nothing. Within a step of the flag, the second-last operator was lit up. Roy dropped to his stomach and tried to pick off Dillon's team. They leapfrogged to the flag, only one getting tagged before Marshal Dillon declared victory.

The rounds went so quickly that we gave everyone a chance to lead the teams. In thirty minutes, we were finished, but everyone was breathing hard. There was a lot more running and engagement than I had expected. I figured there would be low-crawling or other more deliberate maneuvers, but there wasn't. The operators preferred aggressive action.

We had a lot of time available to us, so I ran a couple of suicide rounds. The five "losers" spread out, equidistant from the flag in an every-man-for-himself scenario. Billy the Kid fired sideways, dodged, dove, rolled, and fired again, clearing space on either side. He maneuvered toward the flag, then turned perpendicular, dropped, and took another shot, activating the one who had tagged the second last operator. Four units buzzed. Billy walked to the flag and tapped it with his blaster.

"Well played, Billy the Kid!" I shouted. Effective. I liked him and his adopted persona.

We put the winners in another circular firing squad and turned them loose. All four turned their blasters on Jack, ending her bid to be the supreme winner. Then they turned on each other, standing and firing Clint Eastwood-style until only one remained.

Johnny Ringo. "I was born a gunfighter," he drawled. "And lucky."

"You two for the final win. Winner has to eat one of Mabel's steaks."

"That could be the crappiest prize I've ever heard of," Billy remarked. He took one side opposite Johnny. They saluted each other. I blew the whistle, and they both turned and ran into the trees, setting up behind a trunk and taking potshots at the blasters' max range.

Billy moved along the tree line. Johnny stayed put, opting for the sniper approach.

Jenny leaned close to me. "I don't think either one wants to win."

After ten minutes of it, I walked to the flag and pulled it out of the ground. "You both lose!"

"Thank God!" Johnny Ringo declared. Billy the Kid stood and blew "smoke" from the barrel of his weapon.

"Take off your gear and keep it for tomorrow afternoon when we have a different scenario. Think about the different tactics folks tried today. There are all kinds of lessons we can learn about human behavior. We're operators, the best of the best when we're in our element, but out here, teams changed everything. What if it takes two operators to take out a target? That day is coming. I can sense it. Dinner at seven. See you there."

Judging from the way everyone held their toy blasters, not a single one of the operators was unfamiliar with firearms. They all showed trigger discipline, keeping their fingers outside the trigger guard unless they were aiming to fire. Even a toy laser gun.

Because it was second nature. Professionals.

Even the two who came across as submissive, Roy Rogers and Marshall Dillon. They were just fine, and surprisingly, those two operators were able to lead others.

I didn't know if that added any value to how Chaz and Vince ran the company. In case of a multi-operator job, we could count on our people to work together. That was a breath of fresh air for the time when a team operation was called for.

Jack pouted, bolting away from the group on a beeline toward the stable. It looked like Dusty was in for a treat.

Jenny rolled her eyes at me. I hugged her and whispered in her ear, "Steer clear of her, please. For me."

She understood, nodding tightly. "I'm not afraid. She kills men, but there's not a woman alive who would trust her enough to let her get within arm's reach. I can see how she's effective against men. Extremely effective because men are dumb around pretty girls."

"Was I?"

"You were masterful," Jenny conceded. "That's why you won the race for my affections."

"You seduced me with the old untie-the-robe trick."

"Because even smart men…" She left it hanging.

"And there I was, thinking I was suave and debonair." We followed the others toward the lodge. I took Jenny's hand. "Today salvaged nicely, but I cringe thinking about what tomorrow might bring."

CHAPTER EIGHTEEN

"Amateurs talk tactics. Professionals talk logistics." USMC version of General Omar Bradley's saying

In the honeymoon suite, I maneuvered my way to the back end of the Archive's board to find five new proposals waiting for review.

"What the hell, Chaz?" I scowled at the screen. Jenny leaned on my neck to read over my shoulder. "Gomez, AKA Rachel Smith, is back, and it's up to six million."

"I thought you dropped that contract on a bidder."

"I did. This must mean the operator either pulled out voluntarily or was killed during the attempt. Whatever the reason, it's back."

With a few mouse clicks, I rolled it back into the active bid pile, attaching the dossier I had built, which would be delivered to the winner. I didn't think it was necessary to add more to it since all I had was speculation.

I gave the other requests a cursory glance. An accused

pedophile ex-husband. A loan shark. A mobster. A builder who was cheating his high-end clients.

I looked hardest at the last one. It read like little more than a disgruntled homeowner's association with enough money to punish the developer. I doubted it warranted the death penalty. I'd look further, but my initial impression was to kick it back. It would take something spectacular to change my mind, but I'd dig deeper when I was fresh.

I already had four complete on the year. I had met my quota and then some. I'd made a little over two million dollars for the Peace Archive. And I wanted to think we made the world a safer place, too. I was good with that.

"They took it easy on you while you were preparing for this shindig. I think they expected you not to see these until you returned home."

"I think you're right. We can call it the price of success. I shouldn't have looked, but here we are. It gives me a running start before we get back home."

"Shall we?" Jenny asked, pointing at her watch. Six fifty-eight. Dinner started promptly at seven.

I shut my computer and tossed it in my backpack to carry to dinner. We arrived as Buck rang the bell outside the dining room.

"Thanks for your help today, Buck," I told him.

"It's all good, my friend," he replied.

I was happy to see pork chops on the menu. They were a far more manageable size than the roasts Mabel tried to pass off as steaks. Typical beans and greens accompanied the meal. There was a solid din of voices replaying the outside exercises.

I smiled to myself until I thought about my old first sergeant, dumped into a deer graveyard because one of ours had murdered him. That took the shine off my reverie. I looked from face to face but didn't see any guilt, no remorse. I shouldn't have expected anything different. Hitmen with consciences? I was unique, Chaz had said. Maybe I was the only one.

At a quarter past the hour, Dusty opened the door and held it so Jack could stroll in. She winked at John Wayne on her way to a single empty chair at his table. Dusty stopped and stared at our table, where there were two empty seats.

"No one likes us," I whispered to Jenny.

"I'm the boss," Chaz said from my other side. "They're giving us space. It's just how it is. You'll get used to it."

"Do any of the operators try to work you to get a contract?"

"Not anymore," Chaz replied. "But I expect you'll get some back-door offers from this. Do what you want with them. They're your call. Did you see the new stuff?"

"I did. Why'd you drop a bucket of spew on me in the middle of this?" Chaz raised one eyebrow and chuckled.

"We couldn't wait anymore. We wanted to give you time, but the business is growing, and you're a key player. We like how you think."

"What's the turnover like?" I wasn't about to waste my opportunity to bend Chaz's ear.

"We tend to keep people once they join us by tempering the contracts to one or two a year. Particularly aggressive new folks will hammer out six in six months." He pointed at me.

"I might have done that, but I was ready to walk out after that."

"For the right reasons. As long as the people are taken care of, they'll be there for you." He clapped me on the shoulder before turning back to his meal. He ripped the meat from the center of the pork chop and ate it with his fingers. I looked around to find I was the only one using my knife and fork. Even Jenny was holding hers up to her face, gnawing on it.

"When in Rome…" I put my utensils down and went to work, all the while watching the operators for any sign that they were the one who'd killed the first sergeant. I had no idea what that sign would be. I hoped I would know when I saw it.

We didn't go to movie night with the others, even though Buck promised *Casablanca* would be showing. I was tired but wanted to work on the next packages. Jenny and I were both tired of being around people. We usually had little to no interaction with the throb of humanity, keeping to ourselves, and that was sufficiently fulfilling to the point that we could have retired to a mountain getaway, going completely off the grid, as long as we still had access to nice restaurants.

That had become our Achilles heel. We loved that part of our lives. It tied us into living in a place like Las Vegas, which was the epitome of a wide variety of quality restaurants within a small area. We were spoiled, and we knew it. We accepted what we liked, and that gave us access to the other half of our lives: gym, dojo, home, hikes, and modern conveniences.

Jenny put on my music. Rush's *Time Stand Still* echoed softly through the room. She turned on the television and selected closed captions so the sound wouldn't bother me. I got up to sit on the bed and kiss the side of her face. I didn't have to say any words. I tingled when I touched her, and she responded to me for the brief moment of my enduring gratitude. I returned to vetting the proposals, relaxed and focused.

HBO was playing *Starship Troopers*. I had to turn my back on it; otherwise, I'd watch. It was significantly different from the book, but I considered it to be quality entertainment in its own right.

I disappeared into the world of reprehensible human beings who were potential targets. The movie ended, and I was out of gas. Jenny was sound asleep. I closed out the packages and checked the bids one last time. The woman going by Jack had bid on the Rachel Smith package. She bid three and a half million versus the five million of last time. I accepted her bid, which automatically closed the bid process. I wondered if she would leave before training ended.

I was oddly okay with that. I didn't need her yanking Dusty around by the nose ring, and the only way to guarantee she would leave him alone was to send her out. I stretched my back, shut off the lights and television, and crawled into bed next to my wife. Despite the unknowns surrounding me, I fell asleep quickly and slept soundly through the night.

Morning came with a knock on the door. I roused quickly and hurried to see who was there.

Chaz. I opened the door and faced him in my shorts. "This can't be good."

"Get dressed and come on. We lost another one."

The only thought that entered my mind was, "We have a serial killer in our group?"

Chaz stared at me. "When you put it that way, it sounds almost palatable."

"*Almost.* Be out in a hot minute."

I threw on a shirt and my shoes without socks. It took all of fifteen seconds. I didn't care what I looked like. There was someone killing our people, and it had to stop.

In the hallway, Chaz let me know. "Marshall Dillon."

"What? What did he do to anybody?"

Chaz didn't answer that. He was an operator. He had killed people, but what had he done to any of the other attendees? That was a completely different question.

In the conference room, Buck waited. Marshall Dillon lay naked on the head table. "He smells of sex," I noted.

"Besides the fact that he's naked."

"Where are his clothes?" I wondered.

Buck pointed at the trash.

I rolled him to one side. The same skull penetration. I let him fall back to the table. I turned to the old cowboy running the Circle B. "I hate to say it, Buck, but there is going to be one more death, and that will be the end of it. But only one more."

"She had to know we'd figure this one out," Chaz said.

"She had to…" My eyes shot wide, and I bolted from the conference room. I sprinted down the hallway. The door to the honeymoon suite stood open. I didn't bother to slow down as I went straight into the room. My feet caught the wire across the door frame, and I went face-first toward the bed, where in that moment, I glimpsed Jenny locked in a life-or-death struggle with Jack.

A snarl on her face as she fought the woman she had grown to hate.

Jack held a spike in her right hand. Jenny's right hand gripped Jack's wrist, arm between the two, holding the spike at bay while she twisted, half sitting up, raised on her left arm, to drive her right elbow into Jack's face.

I rolled to the side to get my feet under me and came to

my knees. Jack snarled and Jenny elbowed her again, this time on the bridge of her nose. The spike fell from the stunned operator's numb fingers. She blinked to recover, and a horrific visage of pure evil formed on her face. Jenny rolled over, getting on top. I dove forward, driving a finger strike into Jack's exposed throat. She gasped for air, gagging and trying to break free with weaker and weaker efforts.

Jenny was much bigger, outweighing Jack by a good thirty pounds. She held her tightly, keeping her from flailing. It was too much for Jack. She grew weaker with each strangled breath. I contorted myself to get to the top of the bed, where I crooked my arm around her head. I twisted, using my legs to leverage off the headboard and my bodyweight to snap her neck.

We tossed her to the floor. I tried to hug Jenny, but she pulled free. She hovered over Jack's body and prepared to spit, but I stopped her.

"You won a fight with a trained killer. You don't need to do anything else to show how much you despised her. You saved your own life and that of anyone else who might have caught her eye wrong." I thought for a moment. "We better check on Dusty."

Chaz appeared in the doorway. I held Jenny's naked body, blocking the view.

"Close the door on your way to get bags and duct tape, if you wouldn't mind." Chaz nodded at my request, slowly backed out, and tried to close the door, but it caught on the wire. He unlooped one end and tossed it on the floor before softly pulling the door shut.

"I told you she was trouble," Jenny declared, chest still heaving from her efforts.

"That she was, my lover." I held Jenny tightly, trying to come to grips with a second attempt on Jenny's life. She vibrated from the exertion and the emotion of the moment, but she didn't crack.

"I told you I could take her." Jenny had trained hard, and it showed.

"I have to admit, you're taking this a lot better than I am."

"When I saw her tying that wire, I don't think I've ever experienced such hatred. I waited for her to come close, and that's when I let her know I had no intention of being her next victim. I hated her with every fiber of my being."

"The effect she had on men was the exact opposite of her effect on women. It was the strangest thing. I wasn't smitten, but she made two of my four hits, and dammit, I accepted her bid on the Gomez contract."

"Just rebid it," Jenny said softly.

"I don't think I'll do that. I'll take care of it myself. I have a drone and a plan." I withdrew to let Jenny see my confident face, but she started to shake. I pulled her close and held her until the tremors left her body.

"I don't ever want to be that angry again," Jenny admitted.

"No more slutty operators at our retreats." I forced a laugh. "She was a psychopath. I wonder how many people she killed outside the contracts besides the two operators."

"Too many, but you take care of your own. If you keep going, you're going to fully deplete the company's ranks."

"I'm going to cull the ranks of those without a moral compass. We kill bad people. Period. She was a bad person who hid among us because she got paid for what she loved to do. And that's the big difference between her and the rest of us. I want to think that we believe in what we're doing."

Jenny hugged me once more fiercely before letting go. "I better get dressed before anyone else sees me naked."

"Hell, no! That treat is for my eyes alone. I'm putting my foot down." I stepped back and stumbled over Jack's body. "I'll put my foot down somewhere else. I don't need Jack to splat."

Jenny snorted and gave the body a wide berth. She dressed quickly. I watched unashamedly to make sure she didn't break down again. The emotions would hit her in waves. When she turned around, I nodded and opened the door. Chaz stood there with Wyatt Earp.

"Your retreats suck," Wyatt said.

"I know what you mean, my man."

"But I wouldn't want to be anywhere else. I've learned a lot already, and the second day hasn't even started yet." He clapped me on the shoulder and headed in.

Jenny and I walked out, leaving the room to the tender mercies of the self-appointed cleanup crew. We stopped by the conference room to find Dillon had already been removed. I sprayed cleanser on the head table and wiped it down one more time. We made our way to the dining room, where the coffee was already brewing.

We embraced our full cups, holding them in both hands and sipping like addicts. Jenny forced herself to breathe deeply.

"I'm sorry for dragging you into such a sordid life, Miss Jenny."

She eyed me curiously. "You forced me into nothing. I'm still trying to find my way in a hard world, but you're right. I won a fight against a trained killer, one who was passionate about killing. I can hold my own, thanks to you. I will never be an operator, but I'm not afraid of those who are. Not in the least."

"That's a big step. I'm proud of you." Her green eyes held me in their grip, but the strain of what had happened weighed heavily on her. "Spa day when we get back."

"You don't like me *au naturale?*" She smiled in a way that warmed my heart.

"That's the way I like you best."

Buck clumped by, through the entry area, and out the door to get the horses. I jumped up and ran after him. Jenny stayed behind.

I caught up with him and matched his stride toward the corral.

"I gotta hand it to you. You throw one hell of a party." Buck snorted.

"Jack was a little less stable than we believed. She was playing tongue games with Dusty. I'm worried about him."

"Don't be. I saw him this morning. He's just fine. He got his and I don't think it was as good as he expected, but she was a looker, wasn't she?"

"It was her secret weapon. I think she hated men."

"She didn't act that way."

"Not like that. They were toys for her amusement. Nothing more. She was like a praying mantis, killing her mates, one by one."

Buck stopped. "Was she that bad? A *real* serial killer?"

"Yes. She was real. We've found at least eighteen murders that we can attribute directly to her." I didn't clarify that sixteen of those were paid work.

"I'll be damned. You take care of your own problems, don't you?"

I shrugged. "Not really. It takes friends that become family, that's all, and then big problems become little problems because we all share the burden."

We shook hands before Buck continued to the stables. I returned to the lodge. Jenny was still in the dining room, flanked by Billy the Kid and Chuck Wagon.

"Jack attacked you? That's some weird crap," Billy said. He blew on his coffee before taking a sip.

Chuck strolled up and waved at me. "Is that real?"

"It is."

"Out of all the operator retreats I've ever been to, this is far and away the wildest. Five stars. Would come again." Chuck softly clapped.

"You are all kinds of wrong, Chuck, but thanks. If they're *all* like this, we'll run out of people."

"I didn't think of that. That would be bad. Don't invite me to those, only ones like this where I'm still standing come the last day. I'm good with that. But I have to admit, no one expects the Spanish Inquisition."

"Maybe we can get Buck to show a Mel Brooks movie. I wonder if he has *Blazing Saddles*, a western for people who wouldn't normally watch a western," I suggested. It was nice to get a vote of confidence, despite Jack's ancillary activities. We spent the morning killing time, talking about internet searches to better develop personal packages. Using the dark web to find passwords and hack into emails. Anything and everything to give the operators an edge.

Only six operators attended the first session. The others were taking care of business.

Jenny stayed near me the entire time.

When the others returned, we talked about it. In the end, we decided to feel sorry for Jack—that she was so broken, she had descended into the abyss. We talked about how to avoid that. What could an operator do for their mental health? We had a hard job, and I was the only one with someone to share the burden.

I counted my blessings. I could see the envy in the eyes of my fellows.

Chaz took center stage at the end of the impromptu session. "I know that all of you are thinking of finding a partner. Understand that it will take someone special to be like Katie Elder here. They have to be willing to throw everything away for you. If they are, then maybe they'll be ready for the truth. Take great care in what you share. We can't get compromised from within, but I won't deny the strength of the team. We saw that yesterday on the laser course."

As I had surmised, once Jack was removed from the group, we came together and learned what we needed to learn, teaching each other and sharing.

No one spent another breath on Jack, but we toasted Marshall Dillon and Audie Murphy. At the end of the day, on our way to the stable for the evening movie, Chaz pulled me aside.

"The man who went by Audie Murphy here. You knew him before, didn't you?"

"He was my first sergeant in the Marines." I didn't know where Chaz was going.

"Your first sergeant was a particularly effective recruiter for talent. He will be missed. His partner, also someone you knew, will have to go it alone."

"My skipper. The captain of my unit. With the first sergeant's demise, it's not an optimal situation."

"None of it ever is," Chaz suggested. "Talking about a situation that isn't optimal, you accepted a bid where the operator can't fulfill the contract. That means you have it for action."

"I know. I'll take care of it."

"That'll be a big payday."

I shrugged. "I'll take it, but we have enough to keep us happy." I chuckled. "Thus, I tell the guy who is responsible for my bonus. Anyway, five mil to complete the contract, but it'll be done right."

"You should never have to worry about money. It

would be nice if you could take some time off, wouldn't it? Maybe a six-month cruise will be your bonus."

"That would be a special bonus. Thank you." Jenny's eyes brightened as she spoke for both of us.

"Just have to take care of a couple things first," I said.

CHAPTER NINETEEN

"If you want a thing done well, do it yourself." Napoleon Bonaparte

The retreat continued through the second and third days without a hitch. Outside of the deaths, it was everything I had hoped it would be. Jenny had a hard time sleeping in the bed when I wasn't there, so I took to working in bed in the morning. It wasn't the best, but it allowed her to get some sleep. I couldn't wait to get home, but we had a little thing that took priority.

Buck kept our car to use as a work beater around the farm. He had the title and could register it if he wanted.

Jack's car was a rental. Roy Rogers volunteered to eliminate the connection of the rental car with the Circle B by returning it. The rental contract said she had picked it up in Albuquerque. He planned on taking it back, dropping it off with the rental company, and walking away. Simple and probably the most effective to get the fewest questions.

Buck got Roy's car, too. He planned on giving it to Dusty as a gift.

I shook hands with Jules aka Jed before finding Buck riding circles around the lodge. He stopped when he saw us, hopped down off his stallion, hanging tightly to the reins, and walked over to us.

"Your group made for an interesting week."

"Just a little. That was never what I intended or expected. I put way too much work into it to let it get derailed by a psychopath."

Buck offered his hand. We shook like old friends.

I looked into his eyes before making the offer. "If you ever need anything, send an email to USMCOldCorps at zippymail dot com. I check that one every now and again. I think you know by now that we have a set of special skills that help keep the world safer from those who seek to detract from good order and discipline. I know you can take care of yourself, but just in case. I'll do anything for you, my brother."

"I know you would. Can't reckon anything that might drag you back here again, but you and the Missus are always welcome if you find yourself in these parts."

"One never knows, Buck."

He climbed back on his horse, tipped his hat, and rode into the morning's rising sun.

"An exceptional exit," I remarked.

Jenny agreed. "I would expect no less. Buck is good people. The world needs more like him."

"I would say the world needs more like you." I tried to catch Jenny's eye. She blushed and looked away. "I don't think words will ever convey how much I love you."

Her hands sought mine, and she pulled me to her. "Ditto."

I chuckled. Her hair smelled different. The lodge

shampoo wasn't what she usually used, but her hair was soft under my lips. I breathed deeply of the new scent.

Chaz leaned against the entrance to the lodge and watched us.

I saw him when I opened my eyes. "We have company," I whispered.

"You two are completely ridiculous," Chaz stated as we approached. "No one would ever suspect what you do for a living."

"We don't even suspect what we do for a living," I replied.

"Good job setting this up, Ian. I think we'll do more of these. Different place every time, of course. I liked the Wild West theme. So, we'll do a different theme, too. Here." Chaz held out a satellite phone. "Untraceable. No record of calls made to or from it. It's a special piece of gear."

He handed me a slip of paper with a phone number.

"Memorize that number and destroy the note."

I looked at it for a moment, determined a mnemonic for it, threes and twos plus multiples. 369-424-1206. I showed it to Jenny. She nodded. I put the small scrap of paper in my mouth and started to chew.

"My fingers were on that," Chaz said.

I ground the paper between my back teeth and swallowed. It sucked. I wouldn't do that again. "Direct calls. That tells me no deposits anymore. I'm good with that."

"I'll call you, and now you can call me. Anytime, day or night. Whether I answer or not, that's a different story." Chaz smiled at his own humor.

"I'm sorry we lost a few operators at this retreat. That couldn't have helped the company."

Chaz shook his head. "I think Elena was our most effective operator. I'm sorry we lost her, but I can't be sure we ever had her complete attention. It's probably best that we parted ways as I think she could have been a real serial killer. If we tracked her, I expect we'd find a wake of devastation and dead men."

"I reckon. But the others…"

"You see that we have quite a few operators. These were all from your region. One or two contracts a year is plenty for an operator to stay sharp and help us retain a healthy talent pool. Some of these good people will now get extra opportunities because you feel more comfortable with them."

I didn't know what to say to that. I'd continue to put out contracts and see who the bidders were. With the time we shared behind us, I had more confidence that they would be able to execute the contracts with less risk to themselves as well as the company. Professional development had been satisfied.

We shook hands with Chaz while I cradled my satellite phone as if holding a newborn.

Jenny and I waited for the others to depart. One by one, we shook hands and hugged them on their way out. I didn't want to know any of their names, but I wanted to find them good work. I would focus my efforts on the potential contracts while trying to shape the perfect hit on Rachel Smith.

Focus. I needed to shake off the multitasking. I'd let the contracts languish for a week while giving one hundred percent of my effort to cleaning up the mess that Jack aka Elena had made. It was worth five million dollars.

I'd take the money, of course, but that didn't motivate me. This was a high-risk operation against a fortified target. In the Marines, we would have bombed them or starved them out, probably a little of both. I didn't have either option available to me.

I fired up our new-to-us car. In the trunk, we had our drone. In the back seat, two backpacks and a suitcase. We needed to do laundry because everything was coated with red dust.

Sometimes the mundane trivialities of everyday life kept me sane.

Jenny drove Audie Murphy's rental car. Her GPS was set to take her to a rental return lot in Phoenix. I let Rush play in the background to help me concentrate while following Jenny. I made it into the third album by the time we reached where we were going.

When she pulled into the rental return lot, I parked outside the gate. She wiped the inside of the car down afresh before climbing out and tossing the key to the return agent. She blew him a kiss and strolled off the lot. The entire process had taken a grand total of thirty seconds before we were on the road and heading east, perpendicular to the interstate.

"What kind of options do we have when it comes to Rachel Smith?" I asked.

"We know she's in a fortress with an army of armed guards. We have no idea if or when she leaves said fortress besides what Antoine has been able to tell us. But she likes to sunbathe."

"Ergo, why the drone is packed with a full can of black powder, courtesy of Buck's muzzle-loading hobby."

"I think it's the easiest way, but how do we egress following delivery?"

"We is I, and I don't. There are a couple surplus stores in Phoenix. We're heading to one now. I'll pick up what I need for a desert ghillie suit and go into the mountains a day prior and stay a couple days after. They won't find me out there, and the weather is cool enough, I won't get roasted to death."

"I don't like this plan." Jenny ground her teeth, but she had already guessed that no direct engagements were possible. The remote option to take out the titular head of the Felipe Gomez drug syndicate appeared to be our only choice. "I don't want you to do this, Ian."

I blew my breath out between my teeth before answering. "You were right about the woman who I was fascinated with for her effectiveness. Now, I'm forced back into the game at the operator level because of her shortcomings. I won't put you at risk on this op. I'll handle it."

"I don't need you to protect me, Mr. Bragg," Jenny said matter-of-factly.

"But I have to anyway, Miss Jenny. Rachel Smith isn't playing games. She owns the cops in her surrounding neighborhoods. This is what I'm protecting you from. Sometimes, the best way to do something is the lowest profile. One person blending with the rocks is better than two. I'll E and E north into the mountains, then head west."

"E and E?"

"Escape and evade. They won't ever know I was up there because I'll infiltrate starting at Pusch Ridge, well on the other side of Mount Kimball. I'll hike through the mountains until I get into a good oversight position. I'll remotely launch the drone from a secondary location and fly it into the sunbather. Boom."

"You've been thinking about this for a while, haven't you?"

"Ever since the cops chased us the first time around, and even before then."

"Do you miss this part of the game?" Jenny was sincere, squeezing my hand while in the background, the GPS issued directions that I followed unquestioningly.

"I do and I don't. It is the ultimate chess match. The

victory is nothing less than absolute. Toppling the king is the end game. The loser doesn't return to play again." Jenny waited patiently as I thought. "And the situation has changed. It's not just me anymore."

"I support whatever you think you need to do, even if I think it's wrong. You should have just bid it again."

"It's an unwritten rule that I couldn't. After kicking it back twice, having an operator fail twice, it's incumbent upon me to carry it out."

"That's garbage. Chaz was right there. You had eight operators in the room. You could have bid it live, right there."

"Crap!" I had been so fixated on the schedule and getting the classes done that I had prepared, I had not allowed for any other possibilities. "I could have done that if I had thought of it. When did you think of it?"

"On the drive down here," Jenny admitted. "Sometimes even two heads aren't better than one. But what you found out is that your dossiers are different and more than what the operators are used to getting. You're doing it *more* right, and I can see Chaz making the other regions follow your lead."

"Those guys are going to hate me."

"Those guys don't know who you are." Jenny smacked her lips and leaned back in the seat, closing her eyes. I caught her smile out the corner of my eye. We pulled into the parking lot of the surplus store. I scanned the area for cameras and didn't see anything. The store came across as run down. I tickled Jenny's exposed stomach. "I'll wait here. I don't like the smell of those places, and you love it."

"The lovely aroma of an old tent, general purpose, one each."

"Stale canvas."

"Exactly. It's what heaven must smell like."

Jenny opened her eyes and raised her sunglasses. "What a sordid life you lead, Mr. Bragg, that your idea of heaven is a smell so revolting that normal people get nauseous."

"I'm normal people," I tried. She waved her hand for me to go away and take care of what I needed to do. I left the car and the air conditioning running and shut the door, and she locked up while I rubbed my hands together in anticipation of going into a Marine's version of an adult toy store.

CHAPTER TWENTY

"The difference between men and boys is the price of their toys."
William B. McDonald

First order of business was to buy a ghillie suit. They had multiple versions of woodlands but only one desert. It wasn't because the woodlands were more popular, but in Arizona, the desert ones sold out quickly. The one for sale was close enough to my size to work. I'd have to roll up the legs since these seemed to be sized for a less fit crowd. I took the two-piece set off the wall display and flopped it on the counter.

An old man with a Vietnam vest and a long beard pulled the suit toward him without looking at me. "If you can hold this for a second, I'm still browsing. This place is like Candyland. I'll be back with more, no doubt."

He grunted confirmation and went back to reading a yellowed paperback. I couldn't see the title.

Displays lined the walls, while bins filled the open areas between them. I picked up three soft canteens with a capacity of two quarts each with their holders and clips to attach to a modular, lightweight, load-bearing equipment rig. The military loves its acronyms, so the pouch system was affectionately called MOLLE. The ghillie suit didn't have the straps and loops because that would reduce how well the suit blended into the background by creating a sharp line instead of breaking up the person's silhouette.

Ghillie suits were used by snipers and other tactical forces, as well as some hunters, to get closer to their prey.

Underneath a table, the store had seabags, the Marine Corps duffel bag that would hold all my gear and then some, making it easier to lug my stuff into the hills. I took one along with a case of Meals, Ready to Eat, or MREs.

They weren't the best, but they were good calories to help me through the grueling part of climbs through the foothills. I intended to go far higher but get closer than we had gone before. I wanted a direct line of sight into the pool area of the Gomez fortress.

Once I hiked in, I had the limitation of thirty minutes of flight and hover time. After that, the drone would need to be recharged. I wouldn't be able to do that. I was only able to buy one extra battery because that was all the store had on hand. That gave me a grand total of one hour of flight time. With the extra weight from the gunpowder, I planned to get half of that.

Which meant I needed to confirm she was there before I launched the drone on its one-way trip. I bought a telescope, too. It was cheesy, with cheap camouflage tape around the barrel, but it would do the job. I only needed it to work this one time, and the distance wasn't too great, no more than two miles.

I stuffed everything into the duffel bag, thanked the man behind the register I assumed was the owner, paid my bill with the gold card, and left.

I threw the duffel bag in the trunk, which was mostly cleared because we had given the laser equipment to Buck for the use of his customers. If families came, they might be able to have fun with the sets. I had covered the drone with a t-shirt.

Buck was a black powder shooter, and his ranch contained a whole workshop of tools. I had drilled small holes into the plastic fuselage and fitted shotgun primers into them. I taped BBs to the tops of the primers. With a high-speed impact, I figured at least one would fire, triggering all the black powder within the drone. I lined the exterior of the unit with razor blades. They provided extra insurance because I couldn't count on the explosion alone to kill her. It was an ugly weapon, and I winced thinking about it. My work preparing it had only taken a half hour.

This would be my crudest hit yet if it went off as planned, but it had to be done. I had determined that the contract was valid. The DEA had pushed hard to make this hit happen, upping their bid twice. I pitied the junkies while hating the dealers who helped the users on their descent to hellish lives.

That had to end. And for this one small part of the world, I could do something about it. It was down to me to make it happen.

On the road to Tucson, I used my new satellite phone to call Antoine Hernandez. He answered on the first ring. "Antoine. It's your favorite fellow researcher. Do you have any updates on the subject of our research?"

"She's out of town right now at a charity event, but I think she'll be back tonight," Antoine remarked.

"Tonight, huh? Interesting. I was looking at stopping by next week and requesting an interview with her. It would be mind-blowingly awesome, don't you think?"

"There's no way she'll give you any time, not if there's any chance you'll reveal that she is Felipe Gomez." I could feel Antoine shaking his head.

"Are you saying she's a dude? I've seen her in a bikini, and I don't think so."

"No, that's not what I'm saying at all." Antoine had missed my jibe but continued with his request. "I have a new line of inquiry that I'm following that might pan out, but I'm going to need some scratch. How about a cool ten grand? That doesn't mean anything to you, and what we'll get from it will be worth its weight in gold!"

I tried not to snort. Antoine was acting like a blackmailer who refused to go away as long as the cash cow was delivering. "Absolutely, but I'm not anywhere near where I can make a transfer. That'll have to be next week, but since that's when I'll be in town, I can do a personal drop off."

"Far out, Daddy-O."

"Have you regressed to the sixties?" I wondered.

"No. I'm working on my approach by coming across as less than tightly-wrapped, you know, to disarm whoever I'm talking with." Antoine sounded proud of himself.

"I don't care who you annoy or why, but don't practice on me. See you in about ten days." I tapped end before he could reply.

I had no intention of giving him any more money. All things being equal, this chapter would be over in a few days, and Jenny and I would be on our way home to Vegas.

"He said that she won't return until tonight. If I can get into place by then, she might lay out tomorrow morning. That means I need to get going. I might have to head into the hills before it gets dark. I'll take the satellite phone and contact you as soon as I can. Stay at the Hilton, the El

Conquistador. Take the gold card and make yourself comfortable."

"Are you sure?"

"Positive. This is one I have to do alone."

"Maybe you can take her on the way home before she gets into her compound," Jenny said hopefully.

I shook my head. "Too dangerous. She'll have police and bodyguards, and I wouldn't doubt her ride is armored. I don't want to get into a gunfight that has a low chance of success. We'll take the remote option. If I miss, they won't find me, so I'll get to regroup and try again."

"Are you sure they won't find you?"

"Marine Corps. I'll be in the hills. I'll stay there for as long as I need to. There are enough gullies and crevasses to hide in. I'll move at night and hunker down during the day. Unless they are flying overhead with an IR scanner, they won't find me, and even then, it'll be doubtful. There are plenty of overhangs to hide under. If I hear anything, I'll disappear. My advantage is that I'm not in a hurry."

"You're telling me that I have to sit and wonder what happened to you while I wait for who knows how long?" Jenny crossed her arms and glared out the front window.

"I'm sorry."

"The game," she snarled. "You're back to playing the game, and I'm on the outside looking in."

"I've been put into the game, and I'm playing it to the best of my ability, so I can get back to our life together. With the training that we provided, I hope that I'll never have to do this again."

"But you like it."

I turned to glance at Jenny, but I wanted to do better than talking to her out the side of my mouth. I took the next exit and pulled into a gas station. I held her hand and we leaned toward each other, resting our foreheads against each other's over the center console. That was how we talked best.

"I don't like it enough to lose you. I am doing everything I can to make this hit with the least amount of risk to me. If that means I sleep on a mountain for three or four days, so be it. We did something that no one else has done: train the operators. I want less wing and a prayer and more expertise. I also see that I'll be completely out of the field soon. Chaz gave me the impression that the company doesn't need me as an operator. They need me, which means they want *us*, to show the rest of the company what is possible. The way it used to be burned out the operators or turned them into psychopaths. I don't want any of that for anyone, definitely not me."

"I know you have to do it, but I'm not okay with it. I'll be holed up in a hotel room, twisted in knots with worry. You are putting me through hell."

I sighed. I could walk away, retire, and be done with the Peace Archive. I didn't think they'd send anyone after me. Having spent time with Chaz, I didn't get the impression the Archive did that. It was a seed that my old captain and the first sergeant had planted, a self-serving seed. If they didn't recruit operators who stayed on board, they would lose credibility.

I did what all men did when their wives were unhappy with their career choices. I made a promise. "This will be the last one."

Jenny kissed me before holding a finger to my lips. "Don't say that. This will be the last one just until next time." Her eyes glistened as tears welled.

My answer was to close my eyes. I didn't have the right words, and I couldn't watch Jenny cry. I couldn't predict what would happen in the future, but I could control my reactions to those events. As long as I worked for the

Archive, I was subject to being an operator first and foremost.

"I'll walk. If I get put into this position again, I'll walk away, and we'll be done with the Archive."

"I don't want that, either." Tears finally escaped and trailed down Jenny's face. "If you don't do it, Ian, how many innocent people might be killed? I'm glad that Jimmy isn't dead. If you had walked away, he would be. I would rather you make the judgment of life or death than anyone else. I see the burden on you. Despite our lives, this is wearing you out. I don't want you to grow old before your time. I also don't want to hold you back. I'm struggling with being selfish. I don't think you manipulated any of this to get this gig. I think you're doing it because you clean up other people's messes. And I don't trust other people for exactly that reason. They make messes. I'm frustrated, Ian, and I want to make love to you under the Arizona stars. But that's not going to happen tonight, is it?"

Sometimes life was hard. Almost too hard.

"Rachel Smith is pissing me off. She had to build a drug empire, and that is making me miss out on some prime time with my wife."

Jenny smiled, but the tears still flowed.

"I know. You'll make the wait worth my while." She sniffled and wiped her face, but our noses continued touching. "I'm getting room service and daily spa treatments."

"Of course. The Archive is willing to pay handsomely for such divine treatment. And if they didn't, I would. I'll call you each day, let you know that I'm okay, but I have to keep the sat phone off. I can't risk it ringing or vibrating at an inopportune time. You can't dial the number from your phone, either. I can call you since it won't register the incoming number."

"Don't call me, I'll call you. Isn't that the worst follow-up line ever from you men?"

"I have never used that line before this very moment. I heartily condemn all men who use it for selfish purposes beyond trying to stay alive to make it home to their families in one piece."

She took my face in her hands and kissed me. "Okay, Ian. I am not holding you to your promise not to do this again, but I will hold you to your promise not to return to being an operator."

"A few nights camping, sleeping under the stars. I'll be okay."

Jenny smirked. "Which means you'll need a spa treatment after you return from sleeping on rocks."

"Indubitably," I replied. I wasn't looking forward to roughing it, but sometimes a man had to reconnect with the world from which he was forged. Or as Marines would say, embrace the suck.

I chuckled lightly, and Jenny leaned back. Her green eyes sparkled from the tears. They were bloodshot, and her face red and puffy.

"It cuts me to my very soul, seeing you like this." I took in every aspect to sear that look into my memory for those times when I felt like I had to do the hard job all by myself. It had to be worth seeing my wife upset.

"Be glad I don't turn on the waterworks just to get my way."

"I wouldn't be with a woman who would try to manipulate me like that."

"Even with how hot I am?"

"You're working me to make me feel guilty about missing out on tonight, aren't you?"

"Maybe just a little."

I moved the car to the pump to top off the tank. Jenny went inside to get something for the road.

When I finished, I looked for her and found her at the counter. She paid and strolled out with a bag full of stuff and two drinks, tall coffees.

I started the car and headed for the highway, curious but unwilling to ask what she had bought, figuring it was something I liked but wouldn't get until after I was finished.

Sometimes, it's good to be wrong.

"I picked up all the beef jerky they had because man cannot live on MREs alone, or so I've heard."

"You are better than I deserve. I count my blessings every day I get to wake up next to you."

"Until tonight. Or nights when Jimmy goes off the rails, and someone has to watch over him."

"He didn't know how to pee between buildings." Sometimes, the little things remained at the forefront of my memory.

"I hope that's not something you expect me to learn, Mr. Bragg. That is where I draw the line."

"Not at psychopaths trying to kill you?" I asked.

"No. I told you I could take that skinny bitch."

"Ouch! Don't cross my wife, or she'll kick your ass. Whereas me, I'm so bad, I kick my own ass."

"I don't understand." Jenny removed a turkey wrap from the bottom of the bag and offered me half.

Who was I to explain a good joke? I'd let her think about it over the next few days. The coffee was hot with Irish Crème, just the way I liked it. The turkey wrap was good with mustard and mayo. All of it was Jenny's peace offering for being upset.

"I won't let you down, Miss Jenny."

"See that you don't. I'd have to waste all that time trying

to break in another man. You don't leave the seat up, which is a valuable commodity in a husband."

"Now you're messing with me. I hope I have other redeeming qualities."

"You've kicked me in the face."

"You've kicked me in the nuts." That wasn't a sparring session I would forget anytime soon.

"True." She took a small bite of her wrap, smiling while I stuffed half of mine into my mouth.

I finished quickly while Rush played in the background. I dialed up *Dreamline* and took Jenny's hand. Our song. Our lives. Together as one.

Next stop, crossing the line of departure on my way to fight a battle.

CHAPTER TWENTY-ONE

"A gem cannot be polished without friction, nor a man perfected without trials." Lucius Annaeus Seneca

"I can't believe the only way to get drinking water at the rest stop was to buy it," I complained as the two of us stood at the trunk, pouring bottled water into my canteens. Once all three were filled, I put on my harness and attached the cases. I put the jerky into my seabag, along with half the MREs and the drone. I disassembled it only as much as I had to. I carried the propellers in a general-purpose pouch on my chest, with the spare props at the bottom of the bag.

I expected to fall because it was going to be rough crossing the area in the dark, especially once I had the ghillie suit on. Moving slowly would be my salvation. I figured as the crow flew, it would be little more than one mile. I also figured it would take me all night to get where I had the optimal vantage point. I hoisted the seabag onto my back. The ghillie suit was bulky and took up space within the bag, but it didn't add weight. I kept my hands free, but Jenny thrust an extra bottle of water at me before hugging me.

Twilight would come soon, but it was still too light out to hike directly toward my desired location. I'd have to go north first before disappearing into an arroyo. That was the extent of my movement plan until darkness concealed me.

I checked myself one last time by patting myself down: water, pistol, sat phone, smartphone to fly the drone, duffel bag with chow, the drone, and the ghillie suit. I gave Jenny the thumbs-up. She climbed into the car and tapped the GPS for directions to the hotel. She looked at me and I at her. Neither wanted to be first, but someone had to. With a sigh, I turned and hiked down a short rocky hillside from the dirt road at the end of a new subdivision. I heard the car slowly accelerate away.

Dirt. Gravel. Garbage. I descended into the shadows that twilight brought. This looked to be a popular place for kids to party. Nearby homeowners wouldn't be surprised to see a vehicle driving around the area. They'd ignore it if it wasn't making any trouble.

Soon enough, traffic noises disappeared. I climbed upward, staying at the bottom of the ravine as it led toward higher elevations. It turned after a few hundred yards, shielding me from the world behind. Fewer people had come this far, but there were still some, judging by candy wrappers and other remnants of a so-called civilized society. I turned east and climbed to the top of a rise.

It was a small hill that rounded before dropping down again. Across an open area, a hiking trail wound its way from right to left, south to north toward the area's highest peak. Beyond the trail, the hills rose sharply to little more than a dagger's edge before dropping into another cut.

Beyond that, it would be like walking across the splayed fingers of a rock giant.

Once the sun was down, I pulled out the ghillie suit. I stuffed my clothes into the seabag to provide a cushion for the drone. When I closed the bag, it was little more than a quarter full. The load-bearing harness and nearly all my gear fit underneath the oversized suit. I did my standard pocket pat before looking the ground over to make sure I hadn't dropped anything or left anything behind.

I tossed the seabag strap over one shoulder, keeping as much of it as possible tucked under my arm and letting the long material that hung from the suit cover it to break up the outline, limit what anyone could see. I moved out, turning back after ten steps for one last look. It wouldn't do to leave evidence that I had been there. I stepped on rocks and away from anything soft to avoid leaving footprints, but it was getting dark, darker than my eyes had grown accustomed to.

That meant doing my best not to leave footprints but not being sure I wouldn't. There were enough people walking the hills thanks to the parties and the hiking trail that a random set of prints wouldn't be unreasonable or out of place. I'd ditch my boots in a place where the police wouldn't look, a used clothing store. They were good boots, newer with a great deal of tread left. I would be doing far more lying and waiting than hiking in them.

Someone would be happy to buy them in short order. I would be happy to return to my staid life of dining in five-star restaurants with my beautiful wife.

I clenched my jaw and put all that out of my mind. I continued, even though my eyes had not fully adjusted to the darkness. That would take another hour or more. I stuck to the military crest, the terrain just below the high point to avoid making a silhouette of myself as I traveled, avoiding the deepest dark, hunched low to avoid the human-like shadow.

When I topped ridges, I looked at the distant city to see if I had gone far enough, but not yet. I needed to climb higher.

I had no idea how far I had gone or had yet to go, but I knew the steepest slopes were ahead. It was better they were shrouded in darkness. Keep moving. One foot in front of the other.

Two hours in, I had more energy than I thought I would. The slow pace I'd maintained wasn't taxing. Up and down, northeast along a ravine and then up the other side. To my left, I kept Mount Kimball in view. It was on its southern slope that I needed to set up. It was there that I could operate away from prying eyes.

With the night came the desert cool. Dry air didn't provide insulation, creating extreme temperature swings from day to night and back again to roasting beneath an unrestrained sun.

The ghillie suit had been warm but was turning out to be perfect for the evening chill.

I trudged onward. A crescent moon lifted away from the horizon. Coyotes yipped nearby, two or maybe three of them. They would leave me alone, or I'd shoot them. Well, I wouldn't have to shoot more than one. The rest would run at the explosion from the hand cannon.

Beef jerky was calling my name. I stopped and helped myself to two packs. I wondered what kind of room service Jenny was enjoying. I allowed those thoughts while I chewed. When I stuffed the wrappers back into the seabag, it was all business. My eyes had adjusted, and the crescent moon had risen enough to cast a few lumens where I needed them. The going was quick after that.

Anyone watching from downhill would see the wisp of

a shadow, but nothing they could focus on. A tumbleweed blown by a night breeze, nothing that looked like a person.

I climbed to the top of a high finger, which I thought might be the right place. I took my telescope from inside my suit top, extended it to its full length and scanned the houses. They didn't look familiar.

One more ridge over. Only one more, but the terrain was rougher here and the climb more extreme. I found myself near the summit of the mountain. The next hill would put it at my back while overlooking the valley below. A trail wound from the suburbs far to my right toward the mountain peak on my left. I waited and watched.

No one was attempting to follow the trail this night. It looked like a prime party location, leading from the houses below. Privacy with a view.

I headed down slowly, doing my best not to dislodge rocks or gravel. Mountain top on my left. Urban sprawl to my right, slowly working its way upward. Desert scrub beneath my feet, going into a valley before rising again. I hit the valley floor, a gap between the mountain's roots. Once again, I waited to see if I had alerted anyone or anything.

Nothing. I continued slowly to the other side, checking the areas between the shadows, looking for the easiest route upward. I turned left and walked toward the summit before finding a level route to the high point of the hillside. From uphill across to the sharp side of a knife's edge. Arrayed like a fish's skeleton, this side of the foothills lacked the steep hillsides of the western approaches. I strolled forward until it turned back toward the mountaintop and next valley over.

Lights dotted the hillside far below me. I sat with my back to a rocky outcropping and looked through my telescope from one house to the next, only looking at those farthest up the slope, like the Gomez fortress.

It was below me and slightly to the western side, or my right. The floodlights showed the interior of the compound. The men with guns walking the perimeter could have no night vision since they were brightly lit during their round. In the back, the pool lights shifted through colors, red to blue to yellow and back to red. The sliding glass door opened, and Rachel Smith walked out. She was dressed as if she had just arrived from an evening out. She carried her phone in one hand, typing with the other, then raised it and made a call before lounging casually on one of the pool chairs.

No way. No one is this lucky, I thought. *But she had returned that evening. If she had any catching up to do, why not do it out by the pool in the cool of a desert evening? No time like the present.*

I pulled the drone out of the seabag and set it up, then wiped it down one last time. I removed the props from the MOLLE pouch and plugged them into place. The view through my telescope confirmed she was there and didn't look like she had any intention of moving from her engaging conversation. I fired up the drone and sent it skimming over the landscape. The view was disconcerting because my screen showed nothing but black. I flew it higher and rotated the nose camera forward until I could see the Gomez fortress. I thumbed the control lever to accelerate the drone, keeping it as close to the ground as I could while still being able to see the floodlights on the walls.

I kept it low and flew fast. Within three minutes, it was there. I could see her on my screen. The drone's whine caught her attention. She jumped up and ran for the sliding glass door. I flew the drone over the wall and straight toward her, jamming the speed to maximum. The image flashed to white noise before she could pull the door open.

I dropped the smartphone, heard the muffled thump, and aimed the telescope downward. A cloud of black smoke obscured the view. The drone had exploded, but where was the woman? My heart thrummed like a Ferrari engine while I waited for the view to clear. I searched the area and found men with shotguns running around the main building to get to the back.

With a breeze that came out of nowhere, the scene suddenly cleared. A servant, the butler from before, appeared from within the house. He pressed a towel against the woman to staunch blood flow from wounds I couldn't see.

Two men arrived from outside the house—the guards on perimeter patrol. The butler pointed up the hill, straight at me, or so I felt. The guards ran for the gate. I waited. I had to know.

I guessed they couldn't reach me in under half an hour. I'd give it fifteen minutes to get confirmation.

Flashlights penetrated the valley far below. The two guards had left the compound and were looking for me. They walked slowly, shining their lights back and forth. The bad news was that they were walking up the hiking path toward me. I found my smartphone, turned it off, and tucked it inside my ghillie blouse. I raised my telescope to resume my verification of Rachel Smith. The butler lifted the towel and quickly refolded it to find a clean spot to press against her.

Wrong thing to do. It was dripping blood. I couldn't see into the shadows beneath the butler, but the water started to show the taint, highlighted as the colored lights continued to change within the pool. Blood ran down an expansion seam of the concrete deck. Another individual appeared from within. He pulled the butler to his feet, and the two men stood next to the body.

The target had been terminated. I packed my telescope and gear, hoisted the seabag to my shoulder, and looked for the guards. The disconcerting sound of an all-terrain vehicle echoed up the cut.

A headlight soon appeared, and it raced past the flashlights.

I headed away from the sound, in the opposite direction from where I wanted to go. I ducked low, my seabag over the shoulder opposite the whine of the rapidly approaching four-wheeler. I moved quicker than I wanted to until the sound came in behind me. He was driving right to the spot from where I'd launched the drone. I should have followed my original plan of setting it up far away from me.

Too late for recriminations. I found a small gap and shoved the bag in, then backed into it and nestled low. I stopped moving and became nothing more than another bundle of dried weeds and sagebrush. I watched from between the rough ghillie material hanging from the hat over my face. The ATV's lights splashed the ground in front of me before swinging widely to the left. The machine stopped and someone got off, shining a flashlight around the area where I had been. A flashlight passed back and forth over the exact spot and then in increasingly wide circles.

They had known where I was and had gone straight there, but confusion gripped him because he couldn't confirm what he knew to be true. He whistled down the cut opposite me.

I moved in slow motion to draw my pistol. Three men searching that area might find me. I had only made it fifty yards before taking cover. They had to know I wouldn't be far. They had to find me. I had brought a surprise if they came too close. The sound of the .45 going off would get their attention. The question was, could I get off three well-aimed rounds before they shot back?

The two men finally reached the ATV driver. They were huffing and puffing, their flashlights bouncing with their labored breathing. They'd just run nearly a mile uphill. The driver waited for a moment before catching them up.

"I think he was right here, but there aren't any tracks. We need to spread out and search this area."

"You search. I'm going back downhill," the bigger of the two runners said.

"Listen here. Felipe put a million dollars on this guy's head. I'll take it all myself, but I can't search this mountain alone. We split three ways, no matter what."

Felipe?

"Fine. Everyone stay where you can see each other. Fifty feet apart."

No one moved.

"Well?" asked the smaller of the two runners, already recovered from the effort of climbing the hill.

"West. There is nothing to the east but more mountains. This guy is trying to escape. The other boys are heading around to wait for him. We'll crush him between us. Come on. It's time to go."

"Is Felipe coming up here?" the bigger man asked.

"Why would he do that? It's our job to find this guy."

They separated and headed over the hillside into the valley east of me. I waited until I could no longer hear them scrabbling and cursing as they searched.

I left my hidey-hole, crouching and stepping carefully. I wasn't going east or west, but south to pay Felipe Gomez a visit. I wasn't second-guessing the hit on Rachel. She was an integral part of the drug business. She had been the face of it, and they were a team, just like Jenny and I. If someone hit one of us, they would have to hit both of us. I know I wouldn't rest until I put Jenny's killer out of my misery. I expected the same from Felipe.

Maybe Felipe wasn't the same way with Rachel. With his wealth, I didn't think a million was a lot of money, but it sent his guards into the hills to earn it. He'd dispatched all of his guards to look for me.

Leaving him home alone to grieve.

I headed down into the valley and hurried toward the house, stopping and blending with the hillside every hundred yards while I peeked back up the hill to see if the others had expanded their search. The ATV sat in the darkness near the rock from which I had launched the drone. Light from the crescent moon reflected off a chrome decoration. Otherwise, it would be lost to the shadows, just like everything else on the mountainside.

No one expected a second engagement. I had not heard any sirens. I wondered what they would do with her body so police wouldn't be crawling around the home of a drug lord.

Less than an hour later, I found myself ready to enter the lit region around the Gomez compound. I dropped to my hands and knees and crawled, moving slowly so as not to trigger anyone watching for movement.

Lights in Tucson had to be yellow-orange to limit light pollution for the observatory located in the city at the university as well as the one at Kitt Peak, some fifty miles to the south. The officials in this area took their stargazing seriously.

To my benefit.

It took fifteen minutes to cover the fifty meters of bleed-over from the lights inside the compound. I stood and leaned against the outer block wall of the compound. The only sound was the pool pump, diligently filtering the water. I jumped and grabbed the top of the wall with my gloved fingers. A rip. A tear and I let go, dropping back to the ground. Cut glass, metal, razors, anything to prevent someone from doing what I had just tried.

I pulled my hands to my chest to stem the flow of blood. Nothing too bad but my fingers tingled, and my blood was on the top of the wall. I applied pressure for a few minutes until the bleeding stopped. I changed my gloves, putting them on backward to keep the cuts on the inside, limiting my skin's exposure to surfaces.

Time was of the essence, I had to keep going. It was not yet midnight, but I needed hours to climb into the mountains and disappear before daylight flooded the area, bringing more searchers.

There were two doors set into the wall on the mountain side of the compound. The men had run through after me. I was counting on them not having secured at least one of the doors behind them.

I was wrong. Both doors were locked, and I didn't have a lock pick kit. I had a .45, but announcing my arrival with a shot from the hand cannon wasn't my first choice. I needed the element of surprise. The compound floods lit the hillside behind where trash was strewn through the area. Cardboard. Bags. Wrappers. But I was carrying my seabag.

It would provide the extra protection I needed to get over the wall. I walked along slowly, looking for a spot with the least number of vertical obstructions. Halfway around the compound, I found what I was looking for—a narrow gap where the builders had embedded glass and less metal. I double-folded my seabag and jumped up to lay it on the top of the wall and dropped back to the ground after confirming the top of the wall was safe.

I jumped and pulled myself up, a challenge with the ghillie suit on. It caught on everything going up and over the wall. I was greeted by the side of the building. The curtains were closed on the two windows facing me. I hit the ground hard but didn't fight it, letting myself roll through the landing. I came back to my feet, ankle tender but okay. My seabag was stuck on the top of the wall. I jumped up, grabbed it, and flipped it up as I came back down, bending at the knees when I hit to soften the landing.

I dropped the bag close to the house and worked my way around back, watching the windows for open blinds. Light escaping around the edges showed me that everything was closed, but the lights were on. I knew one door would be open because I'd blown out the glass. I tiptoed across the pool deck, walking slowly. The ghillie suit created an even bigger shadow, but if anyone saw me, they wouldn't see *me*. If any cameras caught sight of me, a watcher wouldn't be able to pick my face out of a lineup of one.

Rachel had been moved from the deck. The blood splatters had dried brown, but the pools still looked gummy. Bloody footprints marred the surface. A blood trail led through the broken glass and into the house. I stayed to the side, sliding through into a vast living room with scattered couches and a fireplace centered within a sunken area. Heelprints led left into a well-lit kitchen. Someone sobbed within.

Behind me, a hallway led to that wing of the house. Probably bedrooms, an office, a workout room, who knew? I couldn't see the wing on the far side because of the kitchen and dining room jutting into the open social space.

I stayed on the far side of the twelve-person dining table situated close to the floor-to-ceiling patio doors to avoid the shattered glass. I looked over the barrel of my raised pistol as I inched sideways, bringing the kitchen into view. Rachel was on a center island while an older Hispanic man hovered over her.

It wasn't the butler. It had to be him—Felipe Gomez. "Felipe?" I asked.

He blinked once, and I fired. The shock registered on his face for only an instant before the hollow point entered through his left eye, spreading its lead wings on a journey through his brain. It sent most of the gray matter out through a massive hole it created in the back of his head. He was thrown forward by the force of the exodus, and he bounced once off the island and fell to the floor.

"Señor Gomez?" a voice called from behind me. Running feet. I leaned back against the wall. I lashed out, using the pistol like a club to hit the man in the forehead. His feet went out from under him, and he landed on his head. I didn't bother to check if he was still alive. He hadn't seen anything and probably wouldn't remember it if he had. I picked up my shell casing on my way toward the door.

The most important thing for me was to get the hell out of there. But…

A phone on a stand near the kitchen. Old-fashioned. Wired, a landline. I took the receiver off the cradle and let it fall to the carpet. I dialed 911 and walked away, dragging a chair behind me to scuff my footprints out of the carpet. Onto the pool deck and around the house to grab my bag. I hurried to the door to leave the compound. It was self-closing and self-locking. I let it close behind me as I ran through the floodlit area toward the house to the left of me. Once in the darkness, I turned up the trail to the mountain, going in the same direction the ATV had gone earlier, but once I was sure I was out of range of any infrared cameras, I turned again, this time to the east.

I moved across the rise and into the valley where there was no trail, then across the next rise to put even more distance between me and any pursuers. I was on the eastern finger when I heard sirens. Lots of sirens. I dropped prone to watch. Flashing emergency lights, red and blue from the police. Red by itself from an ambulance.

They'd probably need another one and a medical examiner, and then they would bring a forensics team. Now the wait while they looked for clues. Had I left blood on the wall that they would find? Would they be that thorough? This wasn't the movies, where they could take DNA swabs from everywhere and have results in minutes. The Tucson police had a limited budget.

If I was correct, the DEA would dig in and add some horsepower to the investigation, but only for appearances' sake. They had no interest in solving this crime. The opposite, as it could lead back to them. Where did that six million dollars go?

The hit had not been clean. Rachel may have been the face of the organization, but there *was* a Felipe Gomez. They were in it together. I had to convince myself of that, or this hit would haunt me for the rest of my days.

I heard the chop of helicopter blades. I jumped up and hurried into the gap between the fingers to put ground between the helicopter and me. It took up a position over the compound as first responders sped up the long drive. I figured they broke the gate down, happy to have any excuse to get inside the fortress.

I moved down the other side of the hill, which blocked all the lights and most of the noise. I headed toward the bottom and started to climb. By the time I heard the helicopter again, I figured I had gone at least a mile, maybe more. I peered into the shadows, looking for an outcropping. I scrabbled up a short slope and threw myself under a rock, backing into the gap as the helicopter pounded overhead, the spotlight searching the area at the bottom of the cut, the place where someone would have been walking.

The place where I had been walking seconds earlier. The helicopter moved on without hesitating.

I waited. I pulled my sleeve up and checked my watch. It was two-thirty in the morning. I had another two hours to keep moving as long as I didn't get more company. I leaned out from under the rock to see the helicopter had continued north for another mile before moving west. It traveled toward me again. I leaned back and bided my time. After it traveled all the way to the compound, it headed up the next valley over. I stood up and started to move, loping upward, knees bent to fall instead of twisting an already sore ankle.

I was destined to come around the east side of Mount Kimball. The fingers leading from the mountain started turning east. The climb became steeper, and most importantly, trees started to pepper the landscape. Moving in the dark made every one of them look like the police, waiting for me to pass. I carried my pistol in my gloved hand. I knew that my cuts had scabbed over and were one with the material. It would be a painful exercise to remove the gloves, but they needed to get air if they were to heal.

It wouldn't hurt to wash them out, either. I didn't have any kind of medical kit with me. I needed to find water, too, since I had been staying hydrated during the all-night run. Despite the cool, I had sweated. A gallon of water later, I was still danger-low, but that would have to wait until tomorrow if I didn't find it soon because the cool of false dawn was hitting—the time when it became increasingly dark between night and day. The sun was coming, and when it arrived, I would have to stop moving and hide until night shielded me once again.

The landscape became rugged and rocky. I had to slow down while searching for an overhang under which to hide to keep my IR signature from standing out until the heat of the day protected me. But in the light, anyone could see me moving. I would wait. When I looked back toward the city and the mountain below me, I found myself north and east of Mount Kimball, at least two miles from the Gomez compound. Maybe even more since I was well on my way to Mount Lemon.

There was a road that led to the ski resort, but I couldn't have Miss Jenny pick me up. A simple roadblock could stop all traffic going into and out of the area. They wouldn't miss a single woman driving in and coming out with a man. Even if I hid in the trunk. The locals might be irked at the loss of their cash cow and take it out on anyone who looked suspicious.

No. I'd have to walk out to an area that wasn't covered. Tonight I'd head northeast and move slowly away from the mountains and back to the lowlands to a town called Catalina, where my arrival would raise no suspicions. I'd hop in and we'd be gone, heading back toward Las Vegas. Somewhere between where I was and that town, the ghillie suit, the seabag, my boots, the drone parts, and even the .45 had to disappear forever. I'd walk out in tennis shoes, jeans, and a polo shirt, looking like I had taken a casual stroll through the woods.

CHAPTER TWENTY-TWO

"If I possess a conviction that is not firmly grounded in an immovable sense of ethics, morals and values, what I have is a rogue agenda dressed in the finery of a conviction." Craig D. Lounsbrough

I covered myself with my ghillie blouse and thumbed the power-on button of the satellite phone. I pressed the numbers for Jenny's phone. Despite the early morning, she answered on the second ring.

"Ian?" she asked.

I blew out most of my breath and whispered, "Saying my name defeats the purpose of a mostly secure comm system. I'm fine. Contract is complete. It will probably take me two days to get out of here. I'll meet you someplace up around Catalina, maybe as far as Saddlebrook. I have to go, beautiful. I love you." I clicked off before she could answer. I didn't want her to ask any questions because I would want to answer them. There would be plenty of time for that on the drive home.

I tried to make myself comfortable while presenting only the front of my ghillie suit to the exposed side. I curled up in a little hole at the base of the rock, my pistol on safe but in my hand. It didn't take long before I fell into a troubled sleep.

When I awoke, the bright light of day reflected past me into the hole. I slowly started to move my legs back under cover, but the rattle made me freeze. It sounded like it was right in my ear. I had to pee but was hesitant to move. The pistol had fallen from my fingers. I reached for it, moving my hand at a glacial pace.

The rattlesnake was lying on me. The head had to be above me as it rattled its dismay at its moving bed. Snakes struck downward. It could bite me well before I could shake it off. I had to lie still and wait. I tried to go back to sleep, but that didn't happen. I waited, using every bit of my self-discipline not to move. I started getting cramps in my side. My body quivered of its own accord with the pain.

I could feel the snake shift. If it was moving, it would have to recoil to strike. I spun and rolled, catching the pistol up in my hand as the snake's rattle slapped my face. I swung my pistol at it. The head came at me, but I blocked it. I couldn't move, wedged within the opening.

The snake came at me again. I tried to hit it but missed. It lashed toward my leg, digging through the layers of webbing and cloth from the ghillie suit. I felt the burn as at least one fang got through. I dropped the pistol and caught the snake behind the head. I squeezed its neck and drove its face into the rock as its body wrapped around my arm. I worked to my feet until I could get my boot on its head to crush the life from it.

The burning wasn't too bad, but I'd been bitten. Rattlesnake venom was working its way into my veins. My heart raced when I knew it needed to do the opposite. I looked around the area. The trees provided plenty of concealment. They weren't as thick as they would be at a higher elevation, but they would keep me safe.

I took off my gloves, which I had worn while sleeping. They pulled and tore at the wounds. My hands started to bleed anew. I removed my shirt and threw it to the side. I took off my pants to see the bite. It was barely more than a scratch and a puncture. The amount of venom would be minimal, I told myself. Treatment was important, but that wasn't an option. I didn't want to go to the hospital because I was tougher than a rattlesnake.

That's what I told myself.

My body would have to fight it off. I splashed almost the last of my water across it to wash off any residual venom and wiped it down with a dirty strap from my suit. My newest plan, good a few hours earlier, was now out the window. I needed to get off the mountain sooner rather than later.

I had no intention of dying up here.

Two things had to happen. I had to find a place to ditch my gear, and I had to find my way out by the most expeditious route that didn't involve taking an established hiking trail to an area where the Gomez clan waited to collect me and their bounty.

Would it be so bad to take a trail? I wondered. Who knew if they would monitor the roads and trails if they believed the Gomez assassin had headed into the hills? Would it be the Gomez thugs or the police, or would they have their hands full with each other?

I couldn't risk it, even if I started to fade. I drank half a canteen of water and started eating. I adjusted the MOLLE harness with the canteens and extra pouch. I made sure everything that needed to disappear was in the duffel. With my tennis shoes on, I hoisted the bag over my shoulders and headed upward. I moved nowhere near as fast as I wanted.

My ankle hurt, and my other leg felt like it was made of wood.

I pumped my arms to maintain momentum even though my steps were short. I ate jerky to supplement the two thousand calories I had gotten from the MRE and drank more water. I only had had a few sips after the hit, but I was paying for it now. I needed to lubricate my body to keep my blood flowing. I couldn't let the venom take hold.

More water. There were supposed to be a couple creeks running away from the mountain, and by circling around it, I should have crossed them all. But this was Arizona, and a creek on the map didn't mean there was water. I felt like I was dragging my leg more than using it. I cut a branch off a tree to use as a crutch. My hands were tingling as the little venom in my bloodstream worked as it was supposed to.

I drank even more water in the hope that I would find something to drink before I reached the lower elevation. If I had to, I could cut the top off a barrel cactus to get moisture.

Through a stand of trees, I saw the trail.

I waited, forcing myself to take a break. The breeze and a flock of birds suggested I was alone on this part of the mountain. I hurried across and into the trees beyond. Through the opening, I could see I was as high as I was going to get. The rest of the world descended from here.

What was happening back at the Gomez fortress? Were the feds tearing the place apart? There had been two murders. They wouldn't need a warrant. Let the dismantling of the organization commence.

Let the five million dollars flow into my account. That gave us nearly ten million dollars to live out our lives.

Retirement was looking good at the moment.

My leg ached dully through the numbness. My ankle hurt, but less and less. It felt like I was walking on stumps. My fingers tingled, but my heart pumped at a steady rate. I was tired and sore, but I didn't feel like I was dying. Even when I'd been hit with the shrapnel from the explosion back in the Marines, I hadn't felt like I was dying.

I didn't know what it was supposed to feel like. If dying was preceded by a dull ache, it wouldn't be all that it was hyped to be. I expected something more dramatic.

I continued downhill, relaxing with the ease of descending compared to the strain of climbing, but the going wasn't easy. It was rougher on this side of the mountain. I made maybe half a mile over the next hour. The rockfall made for an enticing place to hide my stuff. A gap between boulders with only darkness below. No wrappers or footprints in the area suggested this was not a picnic site. I dropped in the drone's spare propellers. I counted three seconds before they hit. I looked at my smartphone before crushing it with a rock. I tore out the guts and systematically crushed everything that had been within. After carefully wiping off any prints, I tossed them one by one into the hole.

Before throwing anything else in, I limped around the outside to see if there was any way to reach the bottom. I didn't find anything. After working my way back to the top, I drank more water, ate more jerky, and reveled in the beauty of the open air. Temperatures were warm but not hot. It was a nice day for a stroll in the park.

I disassembled the .45. Just like anything used for a hit, it needed to go, as much as I didn't want it to. I wiped my bullets before loading, so I'd never leave a print. With a semi-automatic like the Colt, one could never be sure of recovering all the spent brass. I wrapped my seabag tightly around it and tossed it into the hole.

It was a sentimental piece from Jenny's dad, but I had used it twice now. The attachment didn't matter. I couldn't be caught with that weapon. Period. It would be a life sentence since there was no doubt they had dug the bullets out of the regional director outside Seattle, and there was probably enough of the round remaining from the one that went through Felipe's head to get a match.

It wasn't worth the risk. We could find another pistol.

I left the hillside and continued downward and into an open valley-like area. Halfway across, to my left, I saw what looked like a road. Every step was getting hard. I didn't give myself a choice. I turned left and sought the road. It turned out to be little more than two wheel-ruts, but enough vehicles had taken it to wear down a track.

There was even a falling rocks sign. The going was much easier now that I was unencumbered by anything except a pint or so of water and my satellite phone. A sign pointed to the Cargodera Spring. A foot trail led fifty yards toward a gap. I followed it. Any fresh water would be a godsend. I needed a drink but was shepherding the last of my stock.

The greenery ahead suggested the spring flowed. I increased my pace, leaning heavily on my stick, and limped down a small drop to where a pool of crystal-clear water waited at the bottom. I dipped my face into the water and drank my fill before stripping and climbing in. It was chilly, but not bone-numbingly so.

I let the water clean my wounds, both hands and leg, although the venom had already worked its way into my body. I only spent fifteen minutes soaking. I needed to get going for Jenny to pick me up and despite my desire not to go to a hospital, I thought I would die if I didn't. I needed a doctor to treat me.

The climb out was almost impossible. I had to pull myself up the small hill while lying on my stomach. My legs had numbed to the point they barely worked. At the top, I leaned heavily on my crutch to the point of fearing that I'd break it. No trees in this area told me if I lost my crutch, I'd be stranded. I stumbled a few steps but then got into a rhythm. Walking on the wheel tracks made it possible to keep going.

Fear crept into my soul for the second time that day. It was getting hard to focus. I didn't know where I was to tell Jenny to come get me. I looked for any signs so I could call for a pickup, but there was nothing. I kept going.

One foot in front of the other. Into the flat where I could see mansions but no road signs, nothing that told me where I was. To the bottom where the road and a hiking trail joined to cross a dry riverbed. A sign: the Sutherland Trail.

I dialed Jenny's number one careful button at a time.

It rang and rang. We never set up voice mail. We didn't want that additional record of us, and we didn't want anyone to leave us a message in any case.

Until now. I wanted to leave Jenny a message. I clicked end and dropped to my knees. I closed my eyes, finding it hard to breathe. Everything was becoming a struggle.

Even remaining upright. The phone rang, shocking me back to the present. I clicked the answer button. "Hello," I croaked.

"Ian!" Jenny sounded panicked.

"Rattlesnake. I need you…to pick…me…up. Sutherland Trail. Houses to the north." I paused to catch my breath.

"I'm running to the room now from the spa. I'll pull it up. I'll find you."

"Mansions north of...the trail." With a final heave, I got out the rest of the message. "On the road...in front of mansions."

If Jenny didn't find me, maybe the rich people would take mercy on the lone stranger carrying no identification and a satellite phone with no numbers.

I pushed to my feet. I only needed to follow the riverbed for a couple hundred yards. It looked forever far away. I sat back down, with no energy to push myself back to my feet.

Maybe this is what it feels like to die. My heart pounded. My Jenny was out there, but I was alone while my body was giving out on me. Fear seized me in a rocking convulsion. I could do nothing about it. A tear escaped my eye before the world turned black.

CHAPTER TWENTY-THREE

"Life is not easy for any of us. But what of that? We must have perseverance and above all confidence in ourselves. We must believe that we are gifted for something and that this thing must be attained." Marie Curie

The bed was soft and it was dark, but blinking lights suggested I wasn't waking up in the afterlife. My mouth was as dry as the desert. I cleared my throat with a rough cough. I pulled more air into my lungs for a more robust attempt at clearing the sludge.

"Look who's up," a gentle voice said from nearby. The comfort and warmth of those few words told me that all was right in my world.

"Miss Jenny," I managed to say. "Is that Rush?"

"You have to ask?" she replied. Music played softly from a single Bluetooth speaker sitting on a table near my head. "You said if you were ever in a coma to play Rush to help bring you back. I held your hand, but it got kind of sweaty."

"That's my girl."

"Lights," she said before turning a lamp on. Even though I was ready, it was still too bright.

"Where? How long?"

Jenny handed me a glass of water. My hands were bandaged, but it didn't keep me from holding the glass. I sipped the water before chugging it, managing to dump too much down my chest. Jenny raised the bed until I was sitting. She dabbed at the water with a small towel.

"However did you manage without me?" Her caress sent a tingle through my wracked body. "It's only been a day. You're in the best rattlesnake bite hospital in Tucson."

"They have a hospital just for snakebites? Damn. Why would anyone live here?"

"No. They do other stuff, too. You'd think all the chemicals they pumped into you would have made you superman or something." She leaned close, and her voice took on a desperate tone. "You were much closer to dying than I ever want to see again, do you hear me?"

"Not until we're old and wrinkled," I agreed. My eyes wouldn't focus enough to tell if she'd been crying. I didn't want her to. I stopped fighting it and closed my eyes, but I had to go to the bathroom. "Can you help me?"

"You don't ever need to ask, Ian. I'm here for you."

"What time is it?" She pulled the covers off the bed, and I swung my legs over the side. I had a bandage over the spot where the snake's fang had gotten me. They'd also bandaged my sprained ankle. I snorted. "I must have looked like something."

She offered her shoulder to take much of the weight off my legs. I took hold of the IV stand and rolled it toward the bathroom.

"You can sit down," she offered while trying to steady me.

I tottered over the toilet and smiled at her.

"Men." She shook her head. The nurse picked that moment to enter. She joined us in the small bathroom.

"That's a good sign!" she declared while watching me.

I turned to Jenny. "We wouldn't have gotten our gold star if I'd been sitting down." I finished, shook, washed, and tottered back to bed. "When can I get out of here?"

The nurse looked at my chart and checked my pupils. "Since it's three in the morning, how about we wait until the world starts turning and your primary doctor gives you the hearty heave-ho? You've been a model patient up until now. Don't ruin your perfect streak. I think you should be able to leave today. The antivenin has done its trick. You only need to rest over the next couple weeks, and you should be back to one hundred percent."

She checked the machines and waved on her way out to continue her rounds.

"Have you been here the whole time?" I asked, closing my eyes.

"Where else would I be? Although I do have a massage scheduled for later this morning. I don't think I want to miss that. Antonio is magnificent."

"I'll take you to it. Do you have a nice room?"

"You told me not to scrimp, so I didn't. *We* have a very nice room. It'll be a big bill, I'm afraid, but not as big as this one. They said the antivenin alone was twenty-five grand."

"We don't worry about money, beautiful lady. Everything I do is to make sure you never have to worry about that."

"I'm fine with less money and more of you *not* on your deathbed."

"I would have pulled through. I'm all kinds of hearty."

"Doc said another hour and you wouldn't have." Jenny kissed my forehead. "Move over." The beds weren't made for two, but that didn't matter. There was plenty of room for my better half.

She climbed in on the side opposite the IV.

"You feel funny. I'm not used to you having your clothes on."

"Why, Mr. Bragg, you are incorrigible. And no, I'm not taking my clothes off because you've seen that in this hospital, they'll walk right in."

"But it's okay for the nurse to see my junk?"

"*All* the nurses have seen your *junk*. They even gave me a sympathy card afterward."

"That's my wife in all her glory." She snuggled close. "Thank you for saving my life." I fell fast asleep and didn't remember anything else until I awoke, feeling almost normal with Jenny at my side, breathing slowly and deeply. I closed my eyes but didn't go back to sleep.

I needed confirmation on Gomez and then to look at the other contracts in the queue. There was a great deal of work to do and only me to do it. I was sufficiently not dead to go back to work. Rush continued to play from the speaker near my head. There was no better way to recover.

"Mr. Lawless, you are cleared to go, but take it easy. Don't try to out-man the desert again because you won't win." The doctor offered his hand.

"Thanks, Doc. I have no intention of dying anytime soon. My wife would kill me!"

Hospital rules dictated that I had to ride in a wheelchair on the way out. I wouldn't be under my own power until I was out the door, a place I was happy to be as quickly as possible. They gave me a strap-on ankle brace that provided extra support, and the pain meds were doing their thing. I felt good but not loopy.

Jenny drove. There was no doubt about that.

"We have to go back to the hotel to get our stuff regardless. We might as well stay a couple extra nights. You can work from the room. I can still make my appointments."

"Appoint*ments*, as in plural?"

Jenny smiled and nodded, driving out of the parking lot and to the light to wait at a busy street. She didn't elaborate.

"Of course, my love." There was no reason to argue. She deserved to be pampered for putting up with me. "The authorities didn't know exactly where I was bitten, did they?"

"No. I told them the rolling desert to the west of the interstate. There's no paperwork to link you with anything that happened *elsewhere*."

"Perfect. Onward, trusty steed."

"What happened out there?" Jenny finally asked.

"I made it into position about midnight. When I finally got eyes on the target, there she was: Rachel Smith sitting on a lounger next to the pool, talking on the phone. I sent the drone in right then, and it worked exactly like we hoped. Judging from the state of her body, the razor blades did the trick. Otherwise, she would have survived it. They sent their goons up the hill after me. I hunkered down, points to the ghillie suit.

"One of them mentioned that Felipe had put a million-dollar bounty on my head. Felipe Gomez was a real person. So I went to the last place they were going to look. Into the house. I cut up my hands trying to get over the wall. They had glass and steel embedded as part of the security. They had carried the woman inside, where I found Felipe

Gomez standing over her. I ended him, knocked the butler out, and took off again. Running. Hiding and running some more. When I finally found a place past the summit to lay down, I slept like a champ. I woke up with a rattler lying on me. I almost got clear, but I was wedged under a rock. After that, the rest is kind of a blur."

"It looked like you walked about three miles over rough terrain with a sprained ankle, cut-up hands, and venom coursing through your body."

"Good thing it wasn't four miles." I chose to see the positive side.

"I carried you back to the car from where you'd fallen. Fireman's carry."

"Good thing we worked on that." I had used it as an exercise to build leg strength and endurance, not as a practical measure to carry each other out of danger. I squeezed her hand while she drove.

Once we made it to the interstate, it wasn't a long way to the hotel. Jenny drove to the entrance to drop me off at the door. "I'm not ready to turn in my man card just yet," I said in my deepest voice.

Jenny rolled her head to look at me sideways. "Get. Out."

I argued briefly before we compromised and I got out. I decided it was best to sit on the bench to wait for her to get back. She was right. I wasn't up for walking any farther than I had to. Looking back at the night before, I had walked less than ten miles but felt like I'd done a marathon before getting run over by a truck.

A staff member waited to open the door. A massive overhang shaded the entryway, making it tolerable temperature-wise. It was still early and pleasant. It could get hot during the day, even in November.

Jenny parked and hurried back. I stood to meet her. We

took a slow walk through the door. I tipped my head to the bell. Through reception and to the elevators. "I'm sorry. The suites are a little bit of a walk," Jenny said.

"I'll make it. How is room service?"

"I wouldn't know," Jenny tried. I stared at her until she relented. "It's really good and fairly quick for such a big hotel."

To the top floor and down the hallway. Walking into the king suite was like entering a nice living room: a couch, a dark-wood dining table, and a great view. I saw my computer sitting on the desk. I pointed at it.

"You sounded like you were dying. I didn't have time to lock it up after looking for where you were." She wasn't sorry. I wasn't either.

"Time to get to work. I've been goofing off long enough." I leaned on the desk to sit down, but Jenny held me up.

"What do you think you're doing? Into bed, Mister Man."

"I feel like I lost an argument somewhere." I held my ground for a moment.

"You can come back out here and play while I'm at the spa."

"You know me so well." I took the computer with me to the bed. She propped pillows for me while I stripped. I was heavily bandaged. "You should see the other guy."

"Ian." Jenny was gentle. She fluffed pillows for me to lean against.

"I know." I climbed into bed. It was much more comfortable than the hospital bed. Jenny started taking her clothes off.

"I thought you had an appointment at the spa?"

"You think I'm going to the spa when you're lying up here broken? For better or worse."

"Now I feel like I won." She crawled in next to me.

I opened my computer and accessed the VPN, doing what I had to to avoid leaving a digital footprint. I routed my signal as if it were coming from Mexico City and then searched for Felipe Gomez. The search results were flooded with articles. I started reading. Most were sourced from a single AP article. I searched for that one and read it.

Tucson Police announced the homicide of Felipe Gomez and his wife Rachel Smith. The two were found dead in the Catalina Foothills after a 9-1-1 call was made from inside the home. Four men with illegal firearms were arrested as they attempted to enter the compound after it had been secured for the investigation.

The police remain tight-lipped regarding this investigation, but sources who spoke on the condition of anonymity suggested this was a hit made by a rival drug gang based on allegations that Felipe Gomez was the nominal leader of an illicit drug operation that operated within and well beyond Tucson city limits.

Media helicopters captured these images of the pool and rear deck, showing a massive bloodstain along with shattered sliding glass doors. We believe that one of the victims was thrown through the glass doors, exsanguinating from the resulting lacerations.

Neighbors reported hearing or seeing nothing related to this crime.

Of course, they didn't, I thought. The drone was obvious. The police wouldn't want any copycats. The information regarding a bomb-laden drone with embedded shrapnel would never make it into the news. People would be deathly afraid to leave their homes even though they shouldn't be. Something like that was only going to happen to the drug family, and it had cost six million dollars.

"Hey! I'm the six-million-dollar man," I blurted, but

Jenny was already asleep. I was amazed as well as happy for her. She must have stayed up all night with me. She was warm and smooth, with muscles rippling below her tender surface. I looked forward to getting back into the gym with her. Throw some iron. Run a few miles. Get fit to the point that a rattlesnake fang wouldn't penetrate my skin.

But that wasn't how the world worked. I was fit enough to make it three miles. If I hadn't been in the shape I was, I would have never left that mountain.

I caressed Jenny's back. We had done a job that could have only been done by a team.

We were together solely because I'd had two hours to kill seven months earlier, and she'd been spending time with people who had no interest in her. Fate and karma had been kind to us.

Near-death experiences give one an entirely new perspective on life. It made me appreciate my decisions that much more.

Taking the risk had been worth it. I played with her hair until my computer screen went dark. I put it on the nightstand, shut off the light, and settled in. The blackout curtains kept out most of the light, but I could still see her clearly. I held her tightly as the pain meds ushered me into a deep slumber.

CHAPTER TWENTY-FOUR

"In dwelling, live close to the ground. In thinking, keep to the simple. In conflict, be fair and generous. In governing, don't try to control. In work, do what you enjoy. In family life, be completely present." Lao Tzu

After a day in bed, I felt mostly like myself.

"How about the gym, hot mama?" I asked.

"What is wrong with you?" Jenny jammed her fists into her hips and glared at me. I tried to look innocent. "Five minutes of starting to feel better, and you want to ruin it by working out?"

"No." I shook my head to emphasize my desire not to ruin it. "Easy chest and arm workout."

"Easy. Your organs were starting to crystallize. You see the wound on your leg, and you think leg. I'm telling you, it's not your leg that's recovering."

I scratched my chin. "I didn't hear a 'no.' Get dressed. I'll settle for a little arm work. It will help my state of mind, and you know it."

"I do." She stomped her foot. "Fine."

She never meant that it was fine, only that she would tolerate whatever she said she was fine with. "I can't believe how gorgeous you are."

Jenny stopped and turned toward me. "What would it take to entice you to get back into bed?" My lip started to twitch. "One or the other. Your body can't do both."

"Dammit! What if I *want* to do both? For the greater good of all humanity. We *must* do both."

She put her hands on her hips again for a moment before giving up and returning her attention to getting dressed. She wrinkled her nose at the smell. We'd been on the road for a while. "Fine."

"'You keep using that word,'" I quoted before turning serious. "What do you say we go home today? I'm ready to get out of the desert and go home. You know, to the desert."

She finished dressing. "And clean clothes. A *light* workout. Checkout. And get out."

I took a shirt with me to use on the bar to protect the skin on my hands. They were healing, but it would take more time. The workout room was disappointing despite the boutique nature of the major hotel. I settled for doing curls on the universal machine while Jenny stared at me from the stair stepper. I rotated through a few bench presses at a low weight. I could feel the strain within.

I completed two sets of curls and one set on the bench before calling it quits. We'd been there for four minutes. I sat on the bench while Jenny turned up the speed on the stair stepper for another five minutes.

She hopped off and shooed me out of the way for her to do her own bench presses. She did one light set before going to a maximum weight lift. She put the pin at the bottom of the stack. One hundred and fifty pounds.

"Isn't that what you weigh?" I asked. She held her finger

to her lips. She settled in, crossed her ankles, and pushed. The stack clacked as it tightened against the pin. She powered it up little by little until her arms were straight and the lift complete. She held it for an instant and then let it down a little fast, slamming the stack back to the bottom.

"That would have been inconceivable a year ago," Jenny said as she stood and stretched.

"What a difference a year makes." We hugged. I grabbed her butt. All was right with the world. "Time to go home."

We checked out and Jenny drove, even though I felt fine to drive. She stayed five miles over the speed limit the whole way. By dinner time, we were on the outskirts of Vegas. We had only stopped once for gas. I used Jenny's phone to call for Chinese delivery.

"Ten minute for pickup. Thirty if deliver," the kind and heavily accented voice remarked.

"We'll be there in fifteen. Name is Lawless." Jenny adjusted her course to take us straight to the restaurant. I hopped out and limped inside to pick up our meal. When I came out, the car was gone. I had Jenny's phone on me, along with the satellite phone.

I stood there, dumbfounded. I looked at Jenny's phone, but there was nothing to do with it. I sat on a bench outside the store, waiting for what, I didn't know.

Five minutes became ten became fifteen.

Jenny's phone rang. It was a seven-oh-two number. Vegas. I answered it. "Yes?"

"Cops pulled into the lot, so I bolted. Is this car clean?" Jenny asked.

"I would like to think so. Do not come back here. I'll take a taxi. Damn. Is that it? An unmarked car with two men inside?"

"Yes. When they were backlit by the streetlight, I could see the police lights inside the window."

"Go home, beautiful. I'll be there shortly. Are you calling from a payphone?"

"Quaint, but I didn't know what else to do."

"Get our ducks in a row better. That's what we need to do. It scared me, Miss Jenny. I kind of know how you must have felt. I'll see you at home." I clicked end before searching for the number for a taxi service. When they answered, I gave them the address of a home around the corner from ours. No need to link our favorite restaurant with our house.

My heart pounded and my stomach turned. *Getting weak in your old age,* I told myself.

When the cab arrived, I climbed in, and once I confirmed the address, I didn't bother saying anything else. On the way out of the parking lot, I risked a glance at the police car to find the restaurant's counter clerk dropping off a bag with them. They were there for the same reason we were.

We needed to find a better way to survive by being able to register a vehicle legally. The Peace Archive needed a fake identity department, and we needed to register that car or get a new one.

Until then, we'd enjoy our Chinese food and keep the car in the garage, away from prying eyes.

The taxi dropped me off. I waved and started to stroll up the driveway of the darkened home. Once the taxi drove away, I headed for my house. The lights were on when I arrived.

I had a key in my wallet since I didn't carry a keychain. I let myself in, happy to see Jenny.

"Let's not do that again."

"Don't take my phone." Jenny set out the meals before staring into the empty bag, looking at me, and then checking the empty bag again.

"New phones for us!" I declared. We needed to wire-transfer money to ourselves to reload our cash stockpile. We had spent almost all I had.

"Where's my egg foo young?"

"You were there when I didn't order it," I countered. She was ribbing me.

"Okay," she conceded. Her whimsy faded. "What's next, Ian?"

"I need to vet those contracts that are pending, and we need fake IDs so we can do something as simple as register a car."

"I mean, beyond that. What about next month or next year?"

"With the next cruise ship cycle, we're going to sail around the world. When we get home, we're going to look at what it takes to run this organization from the very top."

Jenny reached over to my plate, took a piece of chicken, and shoved it into her mouth. We had gotten two orders of General Tso's. We were eating the exact same thing.

I continued, "It's time for Chaz and Vinny to retire. I got that feeling when we talked. They didn't want to hand over the organization to someone who wasn't going to do it right. Even though the money is huge, they saw it didn't corrupt me. Chaz also saw *us* in action. I think it rocked his understanding of how things can work. And he saw you battling a psychopath naked."

"That describes every night of my life, sweetie." She casually reached across and snagged another piece of chicken. I took my plate to the table.

I opened my computer and maneuvered through the maze to get to the back end of the bulletin board. Still five pending contracts. On the surface, they looked like scumbags, but I'd dig much deeper into them. I had to know. Even when I dug as deeply as I could go, sometimes I still didn't get the full story. Like with Felipe Gomez.

Anyone who went to that extreme to hide their identity while living in a walled and secured compound warranted more attention, not less.

I pulled up Antoine Fernandez's blog. He had published a new paper regarding Rachel Smith. He was surprised at the appearance of an actual human named Felipe, but it didn't change any of his conclusions. He celebrated the demise of the syndicate and ended with a call to action for anyone looking for a researcher since the hit by a rival gang, according to the AP, had proven him right.

It wasn't going to be me. All ties with Antoine were now cut. Last thing I did before shutting my computer down was check my Cayman bank account. Two deposits recently, one for five million and an additional deposit for a million even.

"Looks like we got our bonus," I said, holding the computer out for Jenny to see. The total in the account was nearly ten and a half million dollars.

"That number doesn't look real to me."

I turned my head to look at it from a different angle. "You're right. It doesn't."

"Honestly, Ian, how much do we need?"

"We don't need any more than what we have."

Jenny took another bite from my dinner. I pushed the plate toward her and moved hers to me. I dumped the extra rice on it before blocking the plate with my arms to eat hunched over like an animal.

"Why are you messing with me?" I grumbled after taking a big bite.

"I'm happy to be home with you. And I always want to see how far I can push you, playfully of course, until we both get naked and take care of business."

"That was foreplay?" I was surprised, but it made me sit up straight. I closed my computer and put my chopsticks down.

"I thought you were hungry?" She pointed at the meal in front of me with one chopstick before taking another bite from my former plate.

"Some things can wait. It's been a while."

"Like, three whole days. I can barely contain myself," she replied, biting her lip. I pushed away from the table and reached for her. She threw her chopsticks down and came at me.

The satellite phone rang. I was already breathing hard, even though we hadn't removed any clothing yet. Jenny smacked her lips and sat down. One chopstick had gone on the floor. She used the other to stab her chicken. She rolled her finger that I needed to pick up the pace. I pressed the phone's green button but didn't say anything.

"Verify who I'm talking with, please."

"Is that you, Vince?"

"In the flesh. Thanks for answering, Ian. I'm sorry to bring you the bad news of Chaz's untimely demise. I know for a fact that I can't run this organization by myself. What do you think about joining me as my new partner?"

I looked at Jenny. She had stopped chewing and was listening.

"Chaz is dead?" I had to say it out loud for me to start processing the news.

"Yes. I have no details beyond his wife relaying the tragic news."

"Chaz was married?"

I stared into space, my mouth hanging slack. It was best that operators didn't know too much about each other. Chaz had lived up to that level of secrecy.

"With two kids. They'll be well taken care of. You and

Chaz were far more alike than you knew. Maybe that's why he liked you so much. The heir apparent, he called you after Seattle."

"What does it mean to join you as a partner?"

"We're going to have to meet in person to discuss that. When can you get on a plane to Chicago?"

The End of A Clean Kill
Ian Bragg will return in The Replacement

While you're waiting for the next story, if you would be so kind as to leave a review for this book, that would be great. I appreciate the feedback and support.

Reviews buoy my spirits and stoke the fires of creativity.

Don't stop now! Keep turning the pages as I talk about my thoughts on this book and the overall project called the *Ian Bragg Thrillers*.

https://geni.us/IanBragg

We can't write without those who support us
On the home front, we thank you for being there for us

We wouldn't be able to do this for a living if it weren't for our readers
We thank you for reading our books

The Ian Bragg Thrillers team Includes
BETA / EDITOR BOOK

Beta Readers and Proofreaders - with my deepest gratitude!

Micky Cocker
James Caplan
Kelly O'Donnell
John Ashmore

AUTHOR NOTES - CRAIG MARTELLE

WRITTEN OCTOBER 2020

I can't thank you enough for reading this story to the very end! I hope you liked it as much as I did.

The response to Ian Bragg has been overwhelmingly positive. I couldn't be more pleased.

A hitman with a conscience *and* a girlfriend.

I bring up True Lies, but the movie is hilarious. Keeping a secret like that from his wife for the entirety of their marriage. I'm married. I can't see how something like that could be done, so Ian came clean. Just like True Lies, his life became better when he included his wife in it.

Jenny and Ian are a team. The whole greater than the sum of the parts. It also adds a level of realism. As a career intelligence officer, I knew what it took to collect information and build out a target profile. I remain skeptical of the stories where a lone actor always seems to know everything. That's a high mountain to climb. Two heads are indeed better than one.

I happen to be in Las Vegas during the short period of time while I'm writing these notes. Jenny and Ian could hide in plain sight here, quite easily. Such a crush of humanity, everyone looking for something or celebrating or distraught. People aren't messing with people who don't wish to be messed with. I'm just here for the food…

It is October and this story doesn't come out for a couple more months. I need to get it through a few more proofreaders just to be sure and then it'll go to the narrator so he (Chris Abernathy) can do his thing.

In a few days, I'll be back in Alaska. It snowed while I was gone, but not much. It has turned cold, however. We have that going for us. I predict it'll be a cold winter this year. Time will tell.

There is more to tell of Ian Bragg. A lot more. The next book is called The Replacement. We do not have a publication date for it yet, but probably late spring or summer of 2021. It is coming, have no doubt. I have a nice cover for it and everything!

While you're waiting, you could check out my space lawyer series. She doesn't put up with much garbage either, righting wrongs where they take place, using the power of the Magistrate. Judge, Jury, & Executioner. It's my most popular series, behind Ian Bragg, of course.

And I'm off to write the next chapter.

Peace, fellow humans.

If you liked this story, you might like some of my other books. You can join my mailing list by dropping by my website **craigmartelle.com** or if you have any comments, shoot me a note at craig@craigmartelle.com. I am always happy to hear from people who've read my work. I try to answer every email I receive.

If you liked the story, please write a short review for me on Amazon. I greatly appreciate any kind words; even one or two sentences go a long way. The number of reviews an ebook receives greatly improves how well it does on Amazon.

Amazon—www.amazon.com/author/craigmartelle

Facebook—www.facebook.com/authorcraigmartelle

BookBub - https://www.bookbub.com/authors/craig-martelle

My web page—https://craigmartelle.com

Thank you for joining me on this incredible journey.

OTHER SERIES BY CRAIG MARTELLE

- AVAILABLE IN AUDIO, TOO

Terry Henry Walton Chronicles (#) (co-written with Michael Anderle)—a post-apocalyptic paranormal adventure

Gateway to the Universe (#) (co-written with Justin Sloan & Michael Anderle)—this book transitions the characters from the Terry Henry Walton Chronicles to The Bad Company

The Bad Company (#) (co-written with Michael Anderle)—a military science fiction space opera

Judge, Jury, & Executioner (#)—a space opera adventure legal thriller

Shadow Vanguard—a Tom Dublin space adventure series

Superdreadnought (#)—an AI military space opera

Metal Legion (#)—a military space opera

The Free Trader (#)—a young adult science fiction action-adventure

Cygnus Space Opera (#)—a young adult space opera (set in the Free Trader universe)

Darklanding (#) (co-written with Scott Moon)—a space western

Mystically Engineered (co-written with Valerie Emerson)
—mystics, dragons, & spaceships

Metamorphosis Alpha—stories from the world's first
science fiction RPG

The Expanding Universe—science fiction anthologies

Krimson Empire (co-written with Julia Huni)—a galactic
race for justice

Xenophobia (#)—a space archaeological adventure

End Times Alaska (#)—a Permuted Press publication—a
post-apocalyptic survivalist adventure

Nightwalker (a Frank Roderus series)—A post-apocalyptic
western adventure

End Days (#) (co-written with E.E. Isherwood)—a post-
apocalyptic adventure

Successful Indie Author (#)—a non-fiction series to help
self-published authors

Monster Case Files (co-written with Kathryn Hearst)—A
Warner twins mystery adventure

Rick Banik (#)—Spy & terrorism action adventure

Ian Bragg Thrillers—a man with a conscience who kills
bad guys for money

Published exclusively by Craig Martelle, Inc

The Dragon's Call by Angelique Anderson & Craig A.
Price, Jr.—an epic fantasy quest

A Couples Travels—a non-fiction travel series

Printed in Great Britain
by Amazon

55058729R00153